"Oh God, Amanda," Beau said, gathering her into his arms. "I've been worried sick about you."

"No need for—"

Before he knew what he was doing, his mouth came down on hers, and his arms tightened around her. Her mouth softened, and her lips parted slightly.

Dear Lord, she tasted sweet. Sweeter than—

Suddenly she stomped his foot—the sore one—and pushed him away. "What do you think you're doing, Mr. Chandler?"

"Ouch, dammit! I was kissing you, that's what."

"Mr. Chandler, I'm a Pinkerton agent, not a strumpet. I don't appreciate being mauled. . . ."

By Jan Hudson
Published by Fawcett Books:

SUGAR ANNE
A HITCH IN HEAVEN

A HITCH IN HEAVEN

Jan Hudson

FAWCETT GOLD MEDAL • NEW YORK

A Fawcett Gold Medal Book
Published by The Ballantine Publishing Group
Copyright © 1999 by Jan Hudson

This book contains an excerpt from *The Silver Wolf* by Alice Borchardt, published by Del Rey® Books. Copyright © 1998 by Alice Borchardt.

www.randomhouse.com/BB/

Library of Congress Catalog Card Number: 98-96875

ISBN 0-449-15027-5

Manufactured in the United States of America

First Edition: April 1999

10 9 8 7 6 5 4 3 2 1

For Hud with love.
One of your very own.

⌒ Acknowledgments ⌒

Several people contributed their assistance to the research for this book. I'm indebted to the staff at the Austin History Center, particularly Margaret Schlankey, photo curator, for help in locating primary sources for everything from newspapers and city directories to cemetery plots. Thanks also to Jennifer Blake, Laura DeVries, Lorraine Heath, and several folks at Painted Rock for a variety of information about the period and its customs.

I used a number of sources in my research, read stacks of books and pamphlets, and paid outrageous library fines to the Ralph Steen Library at Stephen F. Austin University as well as the Nacogdoches Public Library. I learned more about beer and ice making in the 1880s than I ever wanted to know, and I've come to love Austin, Texas. I found these books, now in my personal library, particularly helpful: *The Pinkertons: The Detective Dynasty That Made History,* by James D. Horan; *Austin: An Illustrated History,* by David C. Humphrey; and *History of Travis County and Austin,* by Mary Starr Barkley.

⬿ One ⬾

Austin, Texas
Spring 1886

"Uncle Angus is gone! Beaumont, he's gone!"

Beau Chandler tried to calm his mother and disengage his lapels from her clutching fingers, then he peered over into the open grave. Indeed, the hole was empty. "Are you sure this is where you planted the old fellow?"

"Beaumont, such irreverent talk. Of course I'm sure. We buried him here in this very spot yesterday afternoon, didn't we, Estelle?"

"Yes, Mama," Beau's older sister said.

Frank Banks, Estelle's myopic husband, squinted at the hole, then donned his spectacles and squinted some more as if squinting could make a corpse reappear. "He's gone all right, casket and all. And it was a fine casket. Mahogany with brass fittings. Cost a pretty penny, let me tell you." Frank, who had been Uncle Angus's business manager for twenty years, was always concerned with money. He was so tight that he knew all his nickels by name.

"If you'd been here," Morris said, "you would know where we buried him."

1

"I'm sorry I missed the funeral, Morris, but I got here as soon as I could."

Gravelly voiced Morris Essig, husband of Beau's younger sister Judith, ran the Blessing Brewery for Uncle Angus. Maybe it was smelling fumes all day that gave Morris his sour disposition, but Beau never had liked him worth a damn. He wondered why Judith, who was a beautiful and gracious woman, had ever married him. There were no children—unlike Frank and Estelle, who had six, all girls. Beau didn't have his litter of nieces straight yet.

"Don't know what anybody would want with the old bastard," Aunt Katie said. "He wasn't much good alive. Dead, he's completely useless."

Aunt Katie, eighty-four, was Uncle Angus's baby sister. They had never seen eye to eye on anything.

"Whatever are we to do?" Maud asked, pacing the length of the empty grave and wringing her handkerchief. "I can't believe that Uncle Angus would just—disappear."

"I can," Aunt Katie said. "The old fart always did like to make trouble."

"Aunt Katie!" Estelle said, clearly shocked.

"Oh, Estelle, don't get your bloomers in a knot," Aunt Katie said. "I don't know about the rest of you, but I'm going home. It's starting to sprinkle, and I don't want to ruin my new hat."

Beau bit back a grin as he watched Aunt Katie clomp off with her cane. "She's right, Mama. Let's go home and sort through this thing. Didn't you say that Mr. Mitchell was due at eleven?"

"For the reading of the will," Frank said. "But I suggest we postpone that until we've contacted the police.

This is obviously the work of malicious mischief-makers."

"Oh, merciful heavens," Maud Chandler said. "I may die of shame if this gets out. Perhaps we can keep it out of the newspapers. You don't think it's some of those students from the university, do you? I'd hate to think of poor Uncle Angus—" She burst into tears and clutched Beau's lapels again.

"Shhh, Mama," Beau said. "We'll get to the bottom of this. Come on before bullfrogs pour down from the sky."

The family hurried to the two waiting carriages. His sisters and brothers-in-law took one; Beau and his mother joined Aunt Katie. Actually Aunt Katie and Uncle Angus, neither of whom ever married, were great-aunt and -uncle to Beau and his sisters. Katie and Angus's brother, Beaumont Blessing, had begat Maud who begat Estelle, Beau, and Judith. Like Judith, Beau hadn't done any begatting, though he'd had a close call once with a widow lady in Laredo.

Harve, who had worked as a handyman and driver for Uncle Angus and Aunt Katie ever since they'd come to Texas almost forty years before, helped the old lady into the carriage while Beau got his mother settled.

As soon as the ladies were seated, Beau turned his back to them and spoke to Harve in a low tone. "Somebody's pinched Uncle Angus. Got any idea what might have happened?"

Even though he had a walleye that looked in odd directions, Harve didn't miss much, but this time he looked stunned. Or at least Beau thought that was his stunned expression. With Harve it was hard to tell.

"P-p-pinched?"

"Yep. Guess you don't have any ideas."

"Nope. N-n-not a one." Harve tended to stutter when he was distressed. Otherwise he was sober as a judge. Uncle Angus had always said Harve was an excellent poker player.

During the entire trip back to the Blessing mansion, Maud catastrophized and wrung her lace-trimmed handkerchief. Beau, who adored his mother but recognized her shortcomings, turned a deaf ear to her chatter and tried to figure out why anybody would dig up Uncle Angus and steal his body.

True, the old man had a lot of enemies. He had been an irascible bastard. Even his own sister couldn't stand him, but then Uncle Angus never had much use for Katie either—or for any woman. He was a mean-spirited, sour-faced, sanctimonious son of a bitch. Beau's youth had been miserable, living in the same house with the tyrant, and he'd nearly made a mess of his life trying to get away from the old man's clutches.

Why in the world would anybody steal the man's corpse?

The moment they arrived at the huge limestone mansion on Guadalupe Street, the maid handed him an envelope and his questions were answered.

As soon as he finished reading the letter, Beau let out a string of oaths.

"Beaumont Blessing Chandler! Such language!" his mother said. "What is it?"

"Yes," Estelle said as she and the rest of the party entered the foyer. "Why the colorful comments? Has one of your dance hall floozies run off with a drummer?"

"Estelle!"

"Sorry, Mother."

Beau looked up from the note he held. "Uncle Angus has been kidnapped."

"Kidnapped?" Frank said. "But he's *dead*."

"Even so, according to this, they're demanding a ransom for his return."

"A *ransom*?" Morris said.

Maud put her wrist to her forehead and swooned. Frank grabbed her before she hit the floor and dragged her to a bench at the foot of the stairs. Morris helped him. Even without her twenty-five pounds of clothing and bustles, Maud was a sizable woman. Estelle fanned her while Judith ran for smelling salts.

Having witnessed similar displays countless times, Beau ignored his mother's theatrics and studied the letter. It was a grubby thing with smudges and smears, and half the words were misspelled.

"We must call the police at once," Frank said.

"The note warns against it," Beau told them. "Says if the police are called, they'll toss Uncle Angus in the river, and we'll never see him again. Or words to that effect."

"Let 'em toss the old fart!"

Maud shrieked and popped up. "No!"

Clearly horrified, Estelle said, "Then we mustn't call the police. Besides, think of the scandal. Think of—well, everybody in town would ridicule us. We mustn't let this get out. Frank," she said, clutching her husband's arm, "think of the girls. Think of the humiliation."

"How much do they want?" Frank asked.

"Seventy-five thousand dollars."

Frank swallowed. His face as pale as a redheaded whore's

belly, he glanced at his wife, then swallowed again. He opened his mouth, but nothing came out.

Judith, clutching the smelling salts to her bosom, said, "We've no choice but to pay."

"After all," Maud said, "it *is* Uncle Angus's money. We must pay. We can't allow thugs to keep Angus from his final resting place. It's indecent!"

Aunt Katie snorted and clomped with her cane into the parlor. The others followed.

"I see that we have three choices here," Beau said. "We can call the police, or we can pay the ransom, or we—"

Maud put her wrist to her forehead and moaned again.

"Maud, stop that carrying on and get hold of yourself," Aunt Katie said. "We have another choice." She sat down on a silk settee, placed both hands on the head of her cane, and waited until everyone had turned their attention to her. "We can call the Pinkertons."

When Amanda Swann came off the stage after the second act of the matinee, Sam was waiting for her. He handed her an envelope. "This telegram just came for you, Mrs. Swann."

"Thank you, Sam." Amanda opened the envelope as she hurried to her dressing room to change for the last act.

When she read the wire, she sighed. It looked as if her understudy would have to take over tonight's performance of *A Wife's Peril*. And she'd rather enjoyed playing Lady Ormond too. Well, it couldn't be helped, and anyway, tonight was their last performance in San Antonio. She'd stayed with the company far longer than was necessary, but she dearly loved treading the boards again after so long a hiatus.

Let's see, she could plead a death in the family. A grandmother, perhaps—or had she used that excuse last time? No matter, she would think of something.

Her dresser helped her with the costume change, then Amanda checked her makeup in the mirror and made a hasty exit.

Standing in the wings for a moment, Amanda took a deep breath, shook off her own personality, then allowed the character she played to slowly permeate her form. When she heard her cue, Lady Ormond glided onto the stage.

Later, with thunderous applause resounding through the theater, the cast took their final bows and the curtain closed.

"Wonderful performance, Amanda," said George Hugo, the leading man and director of the production. "You are absolutely divine. I wish that I could persuade you to join our ensemble permanently."

"That would be delightful, Mr. Hugo, but I'm afraid that it's impossible. And—and—" Tears gathered in her eyes. "I've just had a telegram with the most dreadful news. My grandmother—" Her voice broke. "I must leave at once."

"*Leave*? But—"

Huge tears trickled from her eyes. She sniffed. "I loved her so. She was the dearest, sweetest . . . I—I must go."

George gathered her into his arms. "There, there. Of course you must, my dear. How may I help?"

"You're such a lamb to ask." Amanda kissed his cheek. "Could you get me a ticket on the next train to Austin?"

"Of course. Right away."

"Thank you." She gave George a wan smile, wiped her eyes, and went to her dressing room.

Sitting before the brightly lit mirror, she removed the ornate wig and loosened her own dark hair. She rotated her neck and massaged her scalp, sighing with the pleasant sensation. That blasted wig was heavy.

As she creamed away the heavy stage makeup, she pondered the role she would play this time. It was difficult to plan a strategy with the paucity of information in the wire from Chicago.

A cousin perhaps. Wealthy, haughty.

Or a governess. Shy, plain.

A thrill of excitement coursed through her, and she laughed. Whatever her role, it promised to be interesting.

Although she had been lucky enough to find a train traveling to Austin right away and had made the trip in record time, it was still very late when Amanda arrived in the capital city. She considered going to a hotel and calling the following morning.

No, her instructions had said that she was urgently needed and time was of the essence. She hired a cab to take her to the address.

Even with most of it obscured by darkness, the immense residence shouted money and power. She asked the driver to wait and went up the walk to the front door. The brass knocker required some heft to lift. She knocked twice and waited.

A man opened the door. "Yes?"

Since the gentleman seemed to be looking at a spot behind her, Amanda glanced over her shoulder to see who was there. No one was. "Mr. Chandler, please."

"It's late. The family has retired. You want to come back in the morning?"

"No, I do *not*, sir. I'm weary as well, and I've missed my dinner in coming as quickly as possible. Please inform Mr. Chandler that I'm here."

"You one of his dance hall floozies?" a small voice asked. The voice originated near the gentleman's knees.

"I beg your pardon?"

A cherubic child's face, framed with blond sausage curls, peeked from behind the gentleman's legs. "Mama says that Uncle Beau has dance hall floozies. I asked Naomi what a dance hall floozy was, and she said it was a lady who danced and kicked real high. My name is Ellie. What's yours?"

"Kid, you talk too much," the man said. "And why ain't you in bed?"

" 'Cause I'm not sleepy. Aunt Katie said I was a somniact. I asked Naomi what a somniact was and she said it was something to do with church, when you kneel and like that. I don't think that's right. Lady, do you know what a somniact is?"

Amanda smiled. "I believe that you're referring to an insomniac. That's a person who has difficulty sleeping."

Ellie grinned. "That's me."

"Ellie," the man said, "go tell your uncle Beau that he has company. Tell him that it's—" He stared over her shoulder—at least, one of his eyes did—and raised his brows.

"Mrs. Swann. Amanda Swann."

"Swan. That's a bird with a long neck. I saw pictures in a book, and Mama read me a story about a swan. You've got a long neck too. You're real pretty. I'll go tell Uncle

Beau." The little girl lifted her beribboned nightgown and bounded down the hall, then out of Amanda's range of vision.

The odd-eyed man didn't invite her in, nor did he move. He simply watched her in his strange way as she continued to stand outside the door. The bugs flitting around the gaslight became a nuisance. She batted one or two away.

In a few moments, the door widened and the first gentleman was replaced by another, who was considerably more attractive despite the scar along his jaw. He stood well over six feet tall and sported a full mustache and vivid green eyes that bespoke both worldly wisdom and perpetual amusement. Coatless and with his shirt-sleeves rolled up, he was muscular in the manner of one used to hard work or vigorous exercise—unusual in such a prosperous setting unless he was some sort of underling rather than the man she sought.

"Yes?" he prompted.

"I'm Amanda Swann."

His eyes swept over her, then brightened as if to say that he liked what he saw. "Yes?"

"I'm with the Pinkerton Agency."

⸙ Two ⸙

"You?" Beau Chandler asked, shocked by the beauty's announcement.

"I," Amanda replied. "And who are *you*?"

"My apologies," he said with a slight bow. "I'm Beaumont Chandler." He couldn't help staring at her. True, she was a bit blurred, but his senses weren't too dulled to appreciate the woman who stood there. Tall, with rich, dark hair and haunting blue eyes, she was one of the most stunningly beautiful women he'd ever seen. Besides her perfect nose, lush lips, and curvaceous figure, an aura of commanding presence surrounded her, a phenomenon that he couldn't quite describe—but "regal" came close.

Beau felt a slight tug on his pants leg and looked down. The curly haired charmer clutching his britches was Estelle's youngest. Ellie, he believed her name was.

"Is she one of your floozies, Uncle Beau?" she asked in a loud whisper.

"Not by a long shot," he told her. "Shouldn't you be at home in bed?"

"I couldn't sleep, and Mama told me to come over and sit up with Aunt Katie since we're feathered birds."

Beau couldn't help but grin at the little wide-eyed imp.

11

"Birds of a feather. All right, chickadee. Run along to Aunt Katie's room now."

"What's a chicka—"

He cocked one brow and motioned with his eyes.

"Yes, sir," Ellie said and went scampering off.

"Sorry," Beau said to the lady still standing patiently at the door. "Ellie hasn't developed her manners yet."

"I have a hired buggy at the gate, and I must give him instructions. Since your telegram said that time was critical, I came directly from the station instead of going to a hotel with my luggage. Shall I have him wait?"

"No, no. You'll stay here for the night at least." He called instructions over his shoulder for Harve, who had discreetly slunk away earlier.

"Your coat, Mr. Beau." Harve held out the garment for Beau to don. "I'll dismiss the driver and bring the lady's luggage inside. She can stay in the blue bedroom, the one next to your *mother*."

Beau fought a smile. Obviously Harve, too, thought that their visitor was one of his floozies. But this was no floozy. This one was a lady, no doubt about that, and absolutely captivating, but a *Pinkerton agent*?

"I can assure you, sir, that I am as qualified as any male working for the agency—indeed, more so than most."

Amused, he said, "Do you read minds as well?"

The hint of a smile played at one corner of her mouth and touched off a dimple there. "Your thoughts were fairly obvious and of a variety that I'm used to. May I come in?"

Beau felt like a damned fool. "Please." He stepped back and motioned her toward the study. "May I get you tea or something?"

"I would dearly love a glass of milk and a bit of buttered bread if it's convenient. In my haste, I missed my dinner."

"Coming right up. I'll tell Harve. I'm afraid the cook has left and the maid has gone to bed."

As Amanda pulled off her gloves, she walked around the study and took in the information there. One wall was filled with fine leather-bound books, another with a fireplace and large chairs flanking it. The third and fourth walls formed an outside corner and had large windows overlooking the street and a darkened side yard. Between the windows were oil portraits and an intricately carved wooden column that held a bust of an elderly man. These renderings drew Amanda's attention.

She was peering closely at the portrait of a woman and three children, two girls and a boy, when Beaumont Chandler entered. She recognized the beautiful young boy in the portrait as a younger, more innocent version of the man coming toward her. Amanda was struck anew by what a very handsome and—virile man he was. Irritatingly virile and oozing with charm. There was nothing innocent-looking about him now. She wondered how he'd gotten the scar on his face.

"That's my mother, Maud Chandler, my sisters Estelle and Judith, and me. It was painted shortly after we left Virginia and came here to live with my aunt and uncle."

"You don't look very happy."

"I wasn't. I'd had to leave everything I knew and loved. My father was killed in the battle at Bull Run. I was only eleven years old, but I wanted to stay and fight the Yankees. I hated Texas, and I hated my great-uncle

Angus. Later I grew fond of Texas, but I never did learn to like my uncle. My father didn't like him either. Come to think of it, I don't know anybody who did."

Amanda moved to the next portrait of two young men and a young woman in a rose garden. "And this?"

He pointed to the taller of the men. "This was my grandfather, Beaumont McMurtry Blessing. He was the oldest and died before he was fifty. This is Uncle Angus Blessing and Aunt Katie. I can't ever believe they were that young. Aunt Katie is eighty-four now, and she was the baby of the family. Uncle Angus was eighty-eight. My sister Judith did that bust of him a couple of years ago."

Amanda ran her fingers over the bronze patina. "Excellent work. She's very talented."

"Yes. She used to take lessons from a lady around here who was quite celebrated, but Morris put a stop to it."

"Morris is her husband?"

Chandler nodded. "Morris Essig is a yahoo. He runs Blessing Brewery."

Harve knocked then entered, carrying a tray. "Brought your milk and buttered bread, ma'am. Added some chicken left over from dinner and some berry cobbler. Put on an extra bowl of that cobbler for you, Mr. Beau. I know you're right fond of it." He glanced at a decanter on the desk and added in an undertone, "And it might sop up that whiskey you've been a-drinking."

"Thanks, Harve."

After Harve left and Amanda had eaten a few bites to take the edge off her hunger, she said, "The information I received was sketchy. I understand that something valuable has been stolen, and you've received a ransom note. Is that correct?"

Clearing his throat, Beaumont Chandler put down his bowl and said, "Yes, that's about right. That is, if you consider Uncle Angus valuable."

Her brows went up. "Your uncle Angus? I assumed from your conversation that he was deceased. He's been kidnapped? Have the police been notified?"

"We didn't call the police. And he is deceased. Died four days ago."

"And someone kidnapped his *corpse*?"

"That's about it. We found his grave empty early this morning and came home to find a ransom note. Ma'am, you'll excuse me for saying it, but I'm not sure that finding him is a job for a woman. We—that is, Mama and my sisters—didn't want the police involved on account of the publicity and embarrassment to the family, so Aunt Katie suggested the Pinkerton Agency. But we were expecting a man—"

Trying to control her anger, Amanda stood. "Sir, Mr. Allan Pinkerton himself, God rest his soul, hired me and trained me before he retired. I've received numerous commendations for my work in the nine years that I've been employed by the agency. And you can bet your last silver dollar that I'm the best. I can guarantee you that if Uncle Angus can be found, I'll find him!"

Beaumont Chandler had the audacity to grin. *Grin.* It only made her more angry. Why had she ever thought him attractive?

"Yes, ma'am," he drawled. "I believe you will."

"You do?"

"I do. And I think Aunt Katie is going to be crazy about you. Sit down and finish your cobbler. We need to hatch some kind of story."

"A story?"

"Yes, ma'am. I suspect that some folks would find it odd, our having a Pinkerton man—sorry, *woman*—visiting in the house and wonder what's up. And to tell you the truth, I don't think Frank or Morris would cotton to a woman agent. Estelle and Mama might not go for it either."

"Who is Frank?"

"Frank Banks is Estelle's husband. He was my uncle's business manager and handles the money."

"If you're suggesting that I should remain incognito, I quite agree—but for very different reasons, Mr. Chandler. I usually work undercover and find it very effective for ferreting out information. In fact, the fewer people who know my true identity, the better. I've found that even close and trusted relatives or servants are prone to making innocent remarks to outsiders that can damage my investigation. And the truth is, Mr. Chandler, people gossip. And sometimes cases such as this are inside jobs."

"Inside jobs? Surely you don't think that any of my family—"

She held up a hand to halt his question. "I don't have any preconceived notions, sir. At this point everyone is a suspect until that person can be eliminated by the facts. May I see the ransom note?"

He handed her the sorry piece of work, and she studied it for a moment. It told her quite a bit, but she would scrutinize the smudged message more thoroughly later.

While Amanda finished her supper, she listened to the particulars of the crime, and they concocted a cover story. Amanda was to be his fiancée of two months, newly arrived from Houston to meet the family and pay her respects for their loss. She would be a widow, her husband having been killed in a train accident three years before.

"We can discuss this in more detail in the morning," she said, "but I need to know a few personal facts about you, Mr. Chandler, things that a—fiancée would know."

Grinning in a decidedly licentious manner, he moved so close that she could smell the liquor on his breath, took her hand, and brought it to his lips. "You might start by calling me Beau, darlin'." He kissed the back of her wrist. He nipped at the pad of her little finger. "I drink Tennessee sippin' whiskey straight, and I sleep in the raw. I like my coffee hot and my women wild."

Fury ignited a flame inside her, and she silently slid her weapon from its concealed scabbard to her free hand. He tensed when the point pricked his groin. "This stiletto is very sharp. Let go of me, sir, or I'll geld you on the spot."

He chuckled. "Oh, sugar, I don't believe that you'd do a thing like that."

He kissed her wrist again and smiled at her with a way obviously designed to make women swoon. Amanda was sure that the handsome rogue had had a great deal of practice. She, however, was immune to such shenanigans, and the sooner he was clear about the rules of their professional relationship, the better.

"Believe it, you horny bastard," she ground out. "And I'll slit you from asshole to Israel if you ever touch me again without my permission."

Something in her expression or her harsh words must have convinced him, or it may have been the second prick of the blade. He sobered and immediately let go of her hand. "Yes, ma'am."

"It's important that we're very clear on this, Mr. Chandler. You've hired a professional investigator from the finest firm in America. I'm an excellent detective with high moral and ethical standards. I'm neither a whore nor a servant. Is that clear?"

He blew out a silent whistle. "Very. Beg pardon, ma'am. I must have had a few too many this evening and forgot my manners."

"Apology accepted. We'll chalk it up to too much Tennessee sippin' whiskey this time. Now, let's get on with background information. What do you do in the family business?"

"Nothing. That is, I didn't until today. Seems now I own most of it. Before I heard my uncle's will, I owned a saloon in San Augustine—that's in East Texas."

"I'm familiar with San Augustine." Amanda didn't add that it had a reputation as a wild and woolly place. "We can tell people that we met there while I was visiting my sister Susan and her new husband, John Cadenhead, who works for the bank."

"Do you really have a sister Susan?"

"I did. Were you surprised to be your uncle's heir?"

"Shocked is more like it. I thought he cut me out long ago."

"You and your uncle didn't get along?"

His laugh held a hollow bitterness. "Hardly. He threw me out of the house when I wasn't much past sixteen, and when I got in some trouble with the law, he didn't lift a finger to help me."

"Trouble with the law?"

He nodded. "Stupid kid stunt. I fell in with a dumb bunch that decided to hold up a bank over in San Antonio.

I was just minding the horses, but I served seven years in the Huntsville prison. I drifted around East Texas for a few years, and then won half the saloon in a poker game. That was in the spring of eighty-one, and I've been there ever since. I own a ranch outside town and a livery stable inside.

"I haven't been in Austin in quite a while except for a couple of short visits. I always stayed at a hotel then and away from my uncle. My own mother and sisters and aunt had to sneak around to spend a few minutes with me or risk Angus's wrath. My brothers-in-law were my uncle's bootlicks and wouldn't chance being seen with me. I have six nieces that I barely know. Ellie was a baby the last time I saw her, and some of the girls I hadn't laid eyes on until this morning. Mama wrote to me occasionally, but I couldn't write to her or Uncle Angus might find out about it and launch into one of his tirades. I haven't seen any of my family in three years. This is the first time I've set foot in this house in twenty years.

"Turned out I didn't need the old codger. I've done all right on my own. What about you? Anything special I should know about my fiancée?"

"My favorite color is blue, my favorite flowers are lilies, and I like the theater. I belong to the Methodist church and do charity work with children in Houston because I have none of my own. We were planning for you to sell the saloon in San Augustine and take over my late husband's business in Houston."

"And what business is that?"

"He was a . . . mortician," she said, struggling to keep a straight face.

Beau Chandler burst into laughter. "My family will never believe that."

"He manufactured carriages."

"That's more like it." When she discreetly covered a yawn, he added, "Let me escort you to your room. We'll talk more in the morning."

The moment she shut the bedroom door, Amanda slumped back against it, her eyes closed. Staying on this case was pure folly. Staying under the same roof with Beaumont Chandler was madness. She hadn't reacted so viscerally to a man since—well, she didn't like to think of that terrible episode so many years ago.

No, she told herself, lifting her chin. She was not going to run like a scared rabbit just because she found a man appealing. She was older now, and wiser. And a professional Pinkerton agent. As long as she maintained strict boundaries, there wouldn't be a problem.

She had a job to do, and by gum, she planned to do it. No man was going to interfere with her duty to the agency.

A few minutes later as she was climbing into bed, it occurred to her that she had forgotten to ask how he had come by that scar.

⌒ Three ⌒

A blacksmith was using his head for an anvil. Nothing else could explain the fierce pain or the terrible clanging between his ears.

Beau groaned and tried to sit up, but he was paralyzed. Dear God, how much had he drunk last night?

The clanging continued. Louder.

He managed to crack one eye, and he spied two small drummers marching around his bed with tin pots and large spoons. He grabbed the wrists of the nearest one, and roared at the other one to stop. His shout pierced his brain. He groaned louder and flopped back on the pillow, which was surely stuffed with washers and bolts.

"He's awake," a young feminine voice whispered.

Beau rolled to his side, opened his eyes to slits, and found himself nose to nose with a little freckled face.

"Which one are you?" he croaked.

"I'm Naomi, Uncle Beau. Did you forget? I'm seven. This is Ellie. She's only five. Mama and Grandma sent us to wake you up. Aunt Katie said we make enough noise to wake the dead, and that we ought to be able to wake somebody who was only dead drunk."

"I'm not drunk," Beau muttered. "And I remember you

both. You're the fountain of misinformation, and Ellie is the feathered bird."

Ellie giggled and jumped on the bed. Beau clamped his head with both hands.

"Get up, get up," Ellie said, straddling his middle and slapping his cheeks. "The lady you're marrying is already downstairs having breakfast."

Beau's eyes shot wide open. *"Marrying?"*

"Yes," Ellie replied in a patient tone of the sort reserved for extremely dense creatures. "You know, the one who came last night. The lady with the long neck. Mrs. Swann. I like her. She's pretty."

"I like her, too," Naomi said. "She said I was very pre—pre—well, very smart. I have to go now. Harve is driving us to school." She ran from the room.

"Aren't you going to school?" Beau asked the little imp still seated on his belly.

"I don't go to school," Ellie said. "I'm too little. Are you going to get dressed now?" She ran her plump fingers across his jaw. "Your face is scratchy. I can help you shave."

"Thanks, but there are some things a man has to do for himself, sweetheart. Why don't you go downstairs and visit with Mrs. Swann. Tell her I'll be down shortly."

"I'd rather help you shave. I'm a good helper. Aunt Katie says so."

"Tell you what, Ellie, you can help me most by rounding up a cup of coffee for me. I like it hot and black."

When she scampered off on her mission, Beau forced himself out of bed. He had a devil of a hangover, worst one he could remember suffering since he'd celebrated getting out of prison.

Having the whole Blessing fortune thrust upon him had shaken him, shaken him bad. He didn't know the first thing about Uncle Angus's business, and a passel of people were looking to him to take care of things. Beau hadn't been responsible for anybody but himself for his entire adult life—if you didn't count the piano player and the barkeep at the saloon.

The notion of being in charge of the whole shebang had sort of overwhelmed him, and he'd holed up in the study and started thinking and drinking. Pretty soon, he was just drinking—until the Pinkerton lady showed up.

He felt like a damned fool this morning when he thought about the way he'd acted last night—what he could remember of it.

He chuckled. Had she really threatened to castrate him or had he dreamed it?

No, as best he could recall, she'd held a knife to his privates and made a serious threat to unman him. And, as best he could recall, she was a damned good-looking woman who'd got his blood stirring in a hurry.

Amanda. Amanda Swann. A Pinkerton agent. It all came back to him. Until she had shown up, Beau tended to side with Aunt Katie. He didn't really care if they recovered the old coot's body or not. Now, finding Uncle Angus might turn out to be real interesting.

He'd only cut himself twice shaving. Fortified with half a cup of the lukewarm coffee Ellie had delivered, Beau went downstairs to the dining room.

All the women of the family, except Estelle's girls, were seated at the table with Amanda Swann. Every eye turned to watch him as he entered.

"Good morning, everybody," he said, mustering a jolly smile. "I guess you've all met Amanda." He touched her shoulder and turned up his smile a notch. "You look lovely this morning, sweetheart. That dress is the exact shade of your eyes. Is it new?"

Amanda laughed gaily and patted his hand. "You've seen it a half dozen times, dear, and you always say the same thing, but you're very sweet to notice. Sit down and let me serve you breakfast from the sideboard. Cook has made some delicious griddle cakes just for you, and they should still be warm."

"Beaumont," his mother said, "I can't believe that you neglected to tell us about your engagement to Amanda."

"Well, Mama, as I recall, things were kind of hectic around here yesterday. Where are Frank and Morris?"

"Frank had breakfast at his own table nearly two hours ago and left for the office," Estelle said. "He wants to get things in order for you to take over."

"Morris is at work as well," Judith said. "He leaves before sunup for the brewery."

"Have you ladies eaten?" Beau asked.

"Oh, my, yes," his mother said. "We were just lingering over a cup of chocolate and waiting for you. Since the men are early risers, Judith and Estelle and the girls usually have breakfast with Aunt Katie and me every morning."

Estelle and her family lived next door in a great columned and galleried house, and Judith and Morris lived in a handsome cottage flanking the other side of the Blessing mansion. It seemed to Beau that everybody spent more time here than they did in their own homes. Indeed, while he'd shaved, Ellie had informed him, along with a million other bits of trivia, that a covered walkway joined the Banks and Blessing dwellings.

"Don't know about Morris," Aunt Katie added, "but Frank leaves early 'cause he can't stand the noise of seven women jabbering around his table. Amanda, put some of them sausages on Beaumont's plate."

"Oh, Aunt Katie," Estelle said, dabbing her lips, "it's not that. Frank just enjoys reading his paper in the morning and having a few minutes' quiet to plan his day."

"Morris leaves early because he figured Uncle Angus—" Judith cut short her comment and dropped her gaze to her cup.

"Wonder where the old fart is this morning?" Aunt Katie muttered.

"Aunt Katie!" Maud gestured toward Amanda with her eyes. "He's singing with the angels in heaven, I'm sure."

Aunt Katie cackled. "Not likely. Wherever he is, I hope they've got him iced down."

"Aunt Katie!" Estelle exclaimed, glancing toward Amanda as well.

"Thank you, sweetheart," Beau said to Amanda, who had served his plate and was now pouring him a hot cup of coffee. To the others he said, "Isn't she a treasure? Don't be concerned about Amanda. I told her the whole story about Uncle Angus last night. After all, she is practically family."

"I was very sorry to hear of your plight," Amanda said. "It's a terrible thing to—"

A loud crash came from the front of the house, like the sound of shattering glass, accompanied by a shriek.

"Ellie!" shouted Estelle. "Did you break something?"

Ellie came running from the kitchen. "No, ma'am. I'm helping Mrs. Kilgore make a pineapple cake."

Harve lumbered into the dining room with a rock in his hand. "S-somebody heaved this through the pa-parlor window. Lucy was dusting in there and it near 'bout s-scared her to death." He handed the rock to Beau.

"Something is tied to it," Amanda said, peeking over his shoulder.

"A note," he said. "Like the first one—and just as grubby. We have until midnight tonight to collect the money and leave it in the cemetery by Ben Thompson's tombstone. Old Ben was a gunslinger who was marshal around here for a spell," he told Amanda.

"Are you going to leave the money?" Judith asked.

"Not a cent!" Aunt Katie said.

"But you must!" Maud exclaimed.

"You heard from the Pinkertons yet?" Aunt Katie asked.

"I'm expecting contact today," Beau replied. "At the office. We'll see what the detective suggests, but we may have to leave the money to—" Amanda's hand on his shoulder cut short his thoughts about setting a trap. He had to agree with her: the fewer people who knew of such plans, the better. Not that he believed anyone in the family was involved, but women were likely to confide in husbands or friends, and before you knew it, the whole blamed town would be buzzing.

"To—what?" Aunt Katie asked.

"To ensure the recovery of poor Uncle Angus," Amanda said quickly.

"Oh, dear," Estelle said, "I hope nobody gets wind of this. We'll never be able to show our faces in polite society. Not a soul will come to the twins' debut dance." She began dabbing her tears.

"Oh, quit your blubbering, Estelle," Aunt Katie said. "That whole debut notion is too uppity anyhow. I don't aim to worry one minute about ransoms and such. Angus has gone to his reward, wherever it is. If somebody wants his earthly shell, I say let 'em have it."

"What's an earthy shell?" Ellie asked.

"Absolutely not!" Maud said. "Beau—" She turned beseeching eyes to him.

"Ladies, don't worry another second about this. I'll handle the matter. As soon as I finish breakfast, I'm going to the office and getting right on it. Amanda, would you care to accompany me?"

"Oh, dear, I was hoping to visit Judith's studio and see some more of her sculpture."

"But—"

She smiled and patted his shoulder. "Perhaps I can join you later—in an hour or so."

There was nothing for Beau to do but to accept her decision. *Exactly what is she up to?* he wondered.

Amanda hadn't even met Morris Essig yet, and already she disliked him. She'd seen the unmistakable bruises on Judith's arm when her sleeve rode up as she reached for the salt. They were finger marks. After that, Amanda suspected that the other bruise on Judith's cheek, slightly visible under the powder she'd used to cover it, came from a fist rather than an accident with a chisel as she'd claimed.

Bastard.

Nothing made Amanda angry faster than men abusing women. Beatings from her hellfire-and-brimstone-preaching father had driven her from home when she was hardly more than a child. Her years with that sanctimonious hypocrite had left her embittered and wary of obdurate men.

Judith was the quietest of the bunch, her face usually solemn and her eyes downcast, but the moment she led Amanda into the little stone house behind the mansion, her whole countenance changed dramatically. Like a butterfly emerging from its chrysalis and unfurling its wings, she became lighter, airier, more lovely. The edges of her mouth turned up slightly, if not quite in a smile, at least in an expression of serenity.

"This was originally the guest cottage of the big house," Judith said, "but Aunt Katie talked Uncle Angus into allowing me to use it as my studio. She told him that since they never had guests, they 'danged shore' ought to put this wasted space to better use."

Amanda chuckled. "I can just hear her saying that. She's quite a character, isn't she?"

Judith smiled for the first time, transforming her into a beautiful woman. "She is that. She was the only one who would stand up to Uncle Angus after Beau left."

"He must have been a real tyrant."

"Well, yes and no. He was stern, but not really harsh— unless you defied his wishes. I tried to avoid him as much as possible. Beau always butted heads with him."

"What about the other men in the family? Estelle's husband? Yours? Did they get along with him?"

"Better than the women. Still, Frank always jumped when Uncle Angus said frog."

"And your husband?" Amanda asked, running her fingers over a clay bust of a young girl.

"Morris and Uncle Angus were two of a kind." She motioned to the bust. "That's Louise, one of Estelle's middle girls." Judith smiled again. "She's the only one patient enough to sit still for very long. She has wonderful bone structure. As do you, Amanda."

"Why, thank you, Judith. Aren't you a sweetheart? I would be happy to act as model if you need me. Perhaps I could commission a bust. It would be a lovely wedding gift for Beau."

"A commission?" Her eyes brightened momentarily, then the light died abruptly. "Oh—oh, I couldn't take *money*. Uncle Angus would turn over in his grave"—her fingers went to her mouth to hold back a giggle—"if he had one."

Amanda smiled. "I think we can safely say that Uncle Angus won't object. Will you do it?"

Judith sobered. "Morris would— No. But it could be a wedding gift from me. I'm not a professional. This is just a hobby."

Judith escorted Amanda around the studio, showing her projects in various stages. It was obvious that the woman was extremely talented, and her work was far beyond that of a hobbyist. She left after Judith made a few quick sketches, promising to spend an hour posing the following morning.

What would Morris have done if Judith had accepted a commission? Amanda wondered. Beaten her? She'd broach the subject tomorrow at their session.

* * *

When Amanda discovered that the Blessing offices were only three and a half blocks away, she decided to walk. She relished the opportunity to be alone and work out a plan for trapping the grave robbers in the cemetery.

She donned her new hat with the blue bow and yellow flowers, unfurled her yellow parasol, and struck out for Austin's main street—Congress Avenue, the broad thoroughfare that ran from the capitol hill southward down to the Colorado River and over the bridge. Austin was rather an easy town to navigate, laid out in nice blocks, unlike San Antonio, where streets meandered like pig trails. The streets that ran on either side of Congress were named after Texas rivers while the cross streets were named for Texas trees.

She walked down Guadalupe until she reached Pecan and turned eastward. It was a lovely spring day, and even though she was preoccupied, the people she met seemed in good spirits.

In no time, she'd reached Congress Avenue, where construction of the new Capitol had commenced on the hill a few blocks to the north. The old building had burned in eighty-one and was being replaced with a grand red granite structure. Amanda shaded her eyes to watch for a moment. Even though the site was surrounded by a fence, it was easy to see the activity on the rise where the first floor walls were going up. Ten tall derricks for lifting the granite blocks rose up from the building's shell like the masts of a giant sailing ship, and she lingered to see one of the booms swing out to hoist a block from a flatbed railroad car.

"It's something, ain't it?" said a woman leaning on a broom in front of a hardware store.

"That it is." Amanda smiled at the woman and turned right at the corner.

The Blessing office was only a few steps away. A two-story stone building in Venetian Gothic style, it sat regally between a Turkish bath and a department store.

Once inside, the clerk ushered her into Beau Chandler's office. He looked harried—the gentleman with him, more so.

"Ah, Amanda, dear," Beau said, breaking into a relieved smile. "I'm so glad to see you. I don't believe that you've met Estelle's husband."

When Beau made the introductions, Amanda nodded to the balding man, who was not much taller than she was. Clean-shaven and wearing spectacles, Frank Banks was reed-slender, but the beginnings of a paunch strained his waistcoat. And a fine waistcoat it was. All of the dapper gentleman's clothing was of excellent quality and cut, she noted.

"Delighted, Mrs. Swann," Frank said, bowing curtly.

"Am I interrupting something important?" she asked.

Banks looked pained, but Beau hastily said, "No, no. Not at all. Frank is just going over some of the basics of Uncle Angus's business with me. I never realized that his holdings were so extensive. I figured that the brewery was about it."

"Hardly," Banks said. "Shall we continue this later?"

"If you don't mind," Beau told him. "Let this soak in while I visit with Amanda. Do you see any problem in getting together cash for the ransom?"

Frank looked even more pained. "I suspect that there is a quarter of the amount in the safe behind you. We can withdraw the rest from either of two banks. Do you think this is really necessary? I mean—" He swallowed. "Seventy-five thousand dollars is a great deal of money, and we have no assurance that we'll get Angus back. Shouldn't we wait for the Pinkerton detective at least?"

Amanda, who had casually wandered to a spot behind Banks, shook her head and mouthed, "No," to Beau.

"I don't think so," Beau said. "In fact, the detective has been delayed."

Amanda smiled and gave Beau a thumbs-up.

"Oh, dear," Frank said. "When is he to arrive?"

After Amanda shrugged, Beau said, "I'm not sure. Go ahead and gather the money. We'll keep it in the safe here until tonight."

"Who is going to take the money to the cemetery?" Frank asked. "It must be someone absolutely trustworthy. I would volunteer myself except that my catarrh is aggravated by night air." As if to illustrate his point, he whipped out a handkerchief and blew his nose.

When Amanda shrugged again, Beau said, "We haven't decided that yet, Frank." He walked to the door, opened it, and said, "We'll finish going over the list of holdings later this afternoon or in the morning. Meanwhile, let's continue business as usual."

Amanda seated herself in one of the high-backed leather chairs in front of the large desk, and Beau stalked to the one on the other side.

"God, what a mess," he said.

"The kidnapping?"

"That's only part of it. Did you know that there are over sixty saloons in Austin? Seems Uncle Angus owned four of them outright and had shares in another dozen. I have enough trouble running one. He owned the brewery, a barrel factory, and at least fifty pieces of real estate—many that are rented out. And those are just the ones that we've had time to go over. There's more, including bank and railroad stock and God knows what else."

"Sounds like your uncle was an astute businessman."

"I'll have to give the old codger that. He amassed a fortune. I just don't understand why he left it to me."

"From what I've learned about him, I suspect that he didn't believe Katie or your mother or your sisters had sense enough to manage things—being women." She couldn't keep the slight edge from her voice.

"But Frank and Morris could have managed my sisters' interests and Mama's and Aunt Katie's as well."

"Perhaps blood is thicker than a marriage license—or perhaps he didn't trust them."

He frowned. "Didn't trust them? What do you mean?"

"I'm not sure just yet. First, I'd like to meet Morris Essig and do a bit of digging on both of your brothers-in-law. And we have to discuss the trap I intend to set for the kidnappers tonight. I already have a plan."

Before she could go into the particulars, there was a terrible commotion outside the office door.

"Outta my way, you little pissant!" a woman bellowed. "I aim to see the heir."

"But, madam—" the clerk's voice protested.

"Outta my way, I said!" A thud followed.

The office door was flung open with such force that the knob banged a hole in the wall.

Proceeded by a bosom like the prow of a Spanish galleon, a buxom woman strode into the room. Amanda couldn't be sure of her age, but her well-used face sported enough rouge to keep the cast of *The Mikado* supplied for an entire season. Dressed in a garish outfit of blinding orange satin and black lace, she wore a black plumed hat over curls an unnatural hue only a shade or two darker than her dress.

She planted her fists on her ample hips and looked Beau up and down. Her eyes didn't seem to miss much. "You the Blessing heir?"

"Yes, ma'am. I'm Beaumont Chandler. How can I help you?"

"I'll tell you how you can help me. I took that ornery little peckerwood into my bed and put up with his peculiar ways for thirty-five years. Now that he's kicked the bucket, I've come for what's mine!"

⌒ Four ⌒

Amanda had to hand it to Beau Chandler—he kept a straight face although she could see by the flex of his jaw muscles and the slight twitch of his lips that he ached to roar with laughter. Her estimation of him went up another notch when he addressed the tawdry-looking woman courteously.

"Yes, ma'am, I can see that you might have such an interest," he said. "Let's discuss your claim." He dismissed the stricken clerk who had rushed in after the woman and closed the office door, then glanced at Amanda as if measuring her degree of offense.

Amanda smiled brightly. "Good morning, ma'am. I'm Mrs. Amanda Swann, Mr. Chandler's fiancée. Would you like some tea?"

The woman looked at Amanda oddly, then tugged on her corset. "Fanny Campbell. Mrs. Fanny Campbell. And I wouldn't mind a cup of tea."

"Wonderful. Beau, darling, why don't you ask the nice young man outside to bring a tea tray for us."

"A *tea* tray? Uh, right. A tea tray."

While Beau stepped to the door, Amanda seated the woman in one of the matched pair of chairs in front of the desk. She took the other one. "A shame about Mr. Blessing's death. Unfortunately, I never met him. I take it, Mrs. Campbell, that you and he were . . . close."

Beau made a strangling sound and covered it with a cough as he crossed the room to take his place behind the desk. He smiled at Mrs. Campbell, waiting for her response.

"Close?" She held up crossed fingers. "Why, him and me was like that since we met in Fort Worth. It was because of him I pulled up stakes and come to Austin. We're—you might say—partners. I run the Pink Feather Saloon and Fanny Campbell's Boarding House down in Guy Town—been runnin' them a lot of years—and right profitable they are too. Angus always said that when he was gone, they were mine."

"I see," Beau said. "Do you have any documents stating his intentions?"

"Documents? Why, hell no. That old buzzard said he had it all fixed up. Was he lying to me? That sorry son of a bitch! If he wasn't already planted, I'd dig him up and cuss him four ways to Sunday."

Beau made another strangled sound and had a fit of coughing. He'd barely recovered when the clerk entered carrying an impressive silver service and cups.

"Ah, here's our tea," Amanda said. "Sugar, Mrs. Campbell?"

"I'm partial to it."

When tea was dispensed and passed around, Amanda said, "I'm sure that Mr. Chandler intends to conduct an investigation into your claim, Mrs. Campbell. Perhaps Mr. Blessing left directions among his papers."

"Yes, ma'am," Beau said, "I plan to do just that. Guy Town, you say?"

"Yep. Angus owned a right smart of property in Guy Town."

Amanda didn't have to be told where Guy Town was. The notorious district was well-known for its wild saloons, gambling dens, and bawdy houses. And she could tell from Beau's expression that he knew about Guy Town as well.

As Fanny daintily sipped her tea, Amanda chatted about the weather, the building of the new Capitol, the growth of the city, and drew the older woman into polite conversation. After a few minutes, she smiled and said, "Mrs. Campbell, I'll bet not much goes on in this town that you don't know about."

"That's true enough. Sooner or later, me or my girls hear just about everything. Why, some of the stories I've heard would curl your hair. For instance," she said, leaning forward and lowering her voice, "I know where all the bodies are buried in the Blessing family."

Beau had another coughing fit.

Amanda simply raised her eyebrows and said, "You do?"

Fanny set aside her cup and smiled smugly. "I do. But I'm discreet. You can count on that. Unless . . ." She shrugged.

Beau scowled. "Mrs. Campbell, that sounds like—"

"Like you're a very smart businesswoman," Amanda said, interrupting his accusation. "I assume that you mean that you were privy to certain matters about Mr. Blessing."

"Don't know about the privy part, but he pulled a few shady deals in his lifetime, let me tell you, and I know about every one of them. Of course, I plan to take what I know to my grave, unless . . ." She shrugged again.

Beau scowled again, more fiercely this time, and was rising from his chair when Amanda said quickly, "We understand perfectly, don't we, Beau, darling?" She smiled brightly and patted Fanny's hand. "Don't you worry about a thing, my dear. My fiancé will take care of the matter. I'm sure that transfer of titles and such can be handled very easily. I'd love to chat with you further, but I'm afraid we're very busy now. Could I drop by and visit sometime?"

"Drop by?" Beau said. "My God, Amanda, you don't know what—"

"Oh, don't be such an old bear," Amanda said to him. She smiled sweetly at Fanny and rose. When Fanny rose as well, Amanda tucked her arm in the crook of Fanny's and guided her toward the door. "Don't worry about a thing," she whispered. "We women have to stick together."

"Don't I know that?" Fanny chuckled and the wattle under her chin shook. At the door she leaned close and whispered, "You go right on keeping a tight rein on that feller, honey." She gestured toward Beau with a tilt of her plumed hat. "He's a handsome 'un, and them kind is always looking to get into trouble."

"Thank you for the advice."

"Don't mention it, honey. Now, you're a real quality lady, and I'd like to visit some more with you, but your man's right. Guy Town ain't no place for you. I've got a telephone. Call me up sometime and maybe we can meet somewhere. Somewhere we ain't likely to be gossiped about—if you know what I mean."

"I'll look forward to it."

When the door closed behind Fanny Campbell, Amanda turned, expecting Beau Chandler to be furious. Instead, he was grinning like a possum.

"Uncle Angus and *her*? I didn't think that the old boy had it in him." He laughed. "My opinion of the old geezer just went up a notch. Think she knows anything about him being snatched?"

Amanda shook her head. "Not yet, but I imagine that sooner or later she'll get wind of it. It's impossible to keep these things secret very long. But I'll bet that she can find out things that we can't."

"You don't plan on talking to her again, do you? It's true what she says about Guy Town."

"I know about Guy Town. I've had cases in Austin before—and surely will again. And I fully intend to cultivate Fanny Campbell for her excellent contacts."

"But that area is dangerous for a woman."

"Don't concern yourself. I know what I'm doing. Forget that I'm a woman. Just think of me as a Pinkerton agent."

Beau's gaze flicked over her. "It's nigh on to impossible not to think of you as a woman."

Amanda sighed. Sometimes her appearance was more of a hindrance than a help. "Put some effort into it. Now, if you don't mind, I want to meet Judith's husband. Could we drop by the brewery on some pretense?"

"Sure. I'm his new boss. I don't need an excuse. Should I tell him about the latest ransom note?"

Amanda thought for a minute. "Yes. I think you should—and more, I think he would be a good choice to deliver the cash tonight."

"Morris? Why not me?"

"Because I want you to keep your eyes on the rest of the family tonight while I'm otherwise occupied."

"Doing what?" Beau asked.

"I'll be in the cemetery watching for the culprits to pick up the money."

"By *yourself*? No, I don't like that. It's too dangerous."

"Mr. Chandler," Amanda ground out, "I'm a Pinkerton detective. My work by its nature is dangerous. I can assure you that I can handle myself very well. I'm an excellent shot and a fair hand with a blade."

"But no match for a strong man who might want to overpower you." As if to illustrate, he stepped forward and threw his arms around her in bearlike fashion.

She sighed again, then with a few quick maneuvers broke his hold, bounced him against the wall, and threw him on the floor. She was astraddle his back with her arm encircling his neck in a choke hold when the door flew open.

The clerk rushed in with Frank Banks close behind. Pale-faced, the clerk gawked at them, his mouth working like a catfish out of water.

Frank looked as shocked as the clerk. "Dear heavens! What's going on? We heard an awful banging and thumping in here."

Amanda looked up from her perch and smiled brightly. "Beau had one of his spells. His back goes out sometimes, you know, and this technique seems to get it right again. My grandfather learned it on his travels to India." She gave Beau another yank for good measure. "Is it all right now, dear?"

"Perfect. Thank you, sweetheart."

"Delighted." She rose and shook the wrinkles from her skirt. "Do you have back troubles, Mr. Banks? I shall be happy to teach Estelle the technique."

"Er . . . no, Mrs. Swann. My back is right as rain. Excuse me." Banks hurried from the room.

The clerk remained in place, still gawking. "My—my back sometimes pains me when I've stayed bent over my desk too—"

"Out!" Beau roared, pushing himself to his feet.

The clerk ran like a rabbit with an angry farmer on his tail.

Amused, Amanda lifted her brows. "Do you concede that I can take care of myself?"

"You took me by surprise. I concede nothing." Beau crammed his hat on and grabbed her arm. "Let's go see Morris."

Taft Whisenant eased open the door and slipped into a darkened room of the shanty adjoining the rear of the livery stable. Boozer Hemphill, a match at the ready, followed close on his heels.

Boozer shivered. "It's colder'n a well digger's ass in here," he whispered.

"Has to be cold," Taft whispered back. "Our orders was to keep the old feller on ice. Light the lantern, and let's take a gander at him."

"Ain't likely he's gone nowheres since yestiddy." Boozer shivered again, partly from the chill of the room, partly from the thought of sliding the lid off that coffin. His thumbnail flicked across the match. The head flared, then popped off and went flying in a blazing arc. It landed in the straw.

"Oh, shit, Boozer!" Taft shucked off his ragged coat and commenced to beating the flame. He stomped the last glowing ember as his partner lit another match. "Watch what you're doing there." He cuffed Boozer up beside the head. "You could have burned up our fortune."

"I didn't go to do it, Taft," Boozer whined.

"Shut up and light the danged lantern!"

"I don't know why we've gotta look at him anyways," Boozer grumbled as he lit the lantern. The light cast spooky shadows on the unpainted walls.

" 'Cause we're s'posed to, that's why. We might need to add some more ice."

"Lord, I hope not. Clem Estes is bound to suspicion somethin' if'n more comes up missing off his delivery wagon. Why don't we just buy some? The ice factory ain't more'n two blocks away. We could drive the hay-rack over there."

Taft yanked off his dusty hat and whomped Boozer over the head. "Dammit, I've told you a hunnert times. Can't nobody know we need more'n our usual fifty pounds or they might get a notion to ask why."

Boozer threw up his scrawny arms to shield the blows. "Don't hit me again, Taft. Let's see how what we got is holdin' out."

They'd spent most of a day and a night fixing up the shanty where the hay was stored and where they usually slept, blankets thrown over a soft pile for a bed. Now, a thick feed sack was nailed over the window, and a fancy wood casket sat in the middle of the small room. It rested on four hundred-pound blocks of ice. Hastily constructed benches sat along both sides of the casket. Each rickety bench sagged under the weight of another couple of hundred pounds of the Austin Ice Factory's clear blocks. They'd forked big piles of hay all around to hold in the cold.

"Feels like Hiram Helpenstell's meat locker in here," said Boozer. "I don't think we need no more ice. We're gonna dump him tomorrow anyways."

"Maybe."

"What maybe? They're gonna leave the money in the cemetery tonight. What are you gonna do with your cut, Taft?"

Taft leaned on the pitchfork he was using to clear the hay from around the casket. "Gonna hop me a train to New Orleans. And when I get there, I'm gonna buy me some slick new duds, a case of good whiskey, and spend about a week with one of them fancy French whores. Then I'll decide what to do with the rest of it. How about you?"

"Same thing. 'Cept I'm goin' to San Antone and get me a Mexican whore. New Orleans is too far off. Man oh man, five hundred dollars. I ain't never *seed* five hundred dollars at one time. You, Taft?"

"Nope." He started forking hay again. "Let's get to business here before we're missed. Give me a hand."

Boozer laughed and started helping.

"What's funny?"

"I's just thinking. Today will be the last time I ever have to shovel horseshit for old man Jenkins. From now on, I can hire somebody else to do the shoveling." He cackled with laughter.

"Don't go countin' your chickens too fast there, Boozer."

"Meanin' what?"

"Meanin' that something might go wrong tonight."

"What could go wrong?"

Taft shrugged. "They might change their minds and not leave the money. Rich people do crazy things. I think we could use a couple of hunnert more pounds here to be on the safe side. What do you think?"

Boozer leaned close to inspect the ice. "Looks fine to me."

Taft yanked off his hat and whomped Boozer's head. "Hell, you ain't got enough sense to pour piss downwind. You prob'ly won't even know what to do with that Mexican whore when you get her." He crammed his hat back on. "We'll snitch some more ice when Clem comes through the alley to make his next delivery to Fanny's saloon."

"Taft?"

"Yeah?"

"Do we have to lift the lid?"

"S'posed to check on him from time to time."

"Fer what?"

"Don't rightly know. To see if he's still there, I reckon."

"Where would he have gone?"

"Nowhere unless the angels come for him," Taft said. "And knowing the old bastard, I ain't looking for no feathers on the ground. Hell, let's fork the hay back over him."

Boozer let out a relieved sigh. He didn't like messing with corpses and haints in the graveyard at midnight.

"Shore wished we'da picked somewhere better than the cemetery for them to leave that money tonight."

"You know dad-burned well we didn't have nothing to do with pickin' the place. You go muck them two back stalls in the stable, and I'll finish up here."

"How about *you* go muck them stalls, and I'll finish up here?"

Taft yanked off his hat, but Boozer took off before he got whomped again.

Blessing Brewery, an imposing plant built of brick and limestone rubble, occupied an entire block along the north side of the Colorado River. Smoke billowed from two large stacks off a roof that rose three stories at the far end of the complex. A number of wagons filled with bales or barrels were coming and going through an archway connected to the building.

Beau helped Amanda from the buggy, and they climbed a short flight of steps to a foyer. They could see several people working at desks in a large open room to one side. Even in the office areas, a faint odor of hops and yeast and fermentation, slightly reminiscent of stale beer sloshed on a barroom floor, permeated the air. Amanda, who disliked the taste of beer and ale, found the smell offensive.

Mr. Essig was out in the boiler room, they were told by a clerk, who seated them in Morris's opulent office before he went to fetch the boss.

Shortly, Morris Essig rushed in, mopping his ruddy face with a monogrammed handkerchief. His clothes reeked of the pungent brew being processed. "Sorry," he said, "I was checking some new equipment that was just installed this morning. Those dumb bast—" He stopped his harangue when he noticed Amanda by the window.

Amanda could barely be polite as Beau introduced them. She kept remembering Judith's bruises. Morris was a burly man, broad-shouldered and thick-necked. Everything about him seemed square, from square jaw to heavy square hands. He reminded her of a block of the red granite forming the new Capitol, but she suspected that Judith's chisel and mallet would be useless in trying to shape this one into another form.

Morris dismissed Amanda almost at once, turning his attention to Beau. "I imagine that you'll want to inspect the plant and the books. Last year was a very profitable one, and we've doubled our barrel output in the seven years I've been plant manager. Angus was pleased with my handling of the brewery operation. He always told me to treat it as if it were my own." He cleared his throat. "He gave me to believe that I, well, Judith . . ."

"I understand," Beau said quickly. "We'll never know why Angus left things the way he did. But, Morris, I don't know a blasted thing about running a brewery, and I assume that you do. Just keep on as you are, and we'll get things ironed out soon."

Morris gave a curt nod. "Won't you join me in the *bierstube* for a stein of our best?"

Amanda wrinkled her nose at the notion of drinking the nasty brew in the beer room, especially before she'd even had lunch, and Beau quickly said, "Another time. We— I've come about another matter." He related the story of the latest ransom note.

"Tonight, you say? In the cemetery? Wouldn't surprise

me to find this was a gang escaped from the State Lunatic Asylum. What are you going to do?"

"I don't think we have any choice but to pay," Beau told him. "Frank is gathering the cash now."

"Hmmm. Suppose you're right. I know Judith is very upset about Angus being tossed in the river and washing up somewhere downstream or ending up in Galveston Bay."

"And Mama is beside herself. Morris, we need someone absolutely trustworthy to deliver that much cash, and I was wondering if you would consider doing it."

Essig's proud smile sent goose bumps over Amanda's skin. "Certainly. I would be honored. What's the plan?"

While Beau discussed particulars with his brother-in-law, Amanda nonchalantly wandered around the room, reading a plaque here, thumbing a journal there, casually dropping one glove by the big walnut desk.

When she and Beau said their farewells a short time later, Amanda tried to be civil, but the more she looked at the burly brewery boss, the more agitated she became. Ordinarily Amanda was cool as spring water. She didn't allow her emotions to rule her. In her job, she couldn't afford such weakness, but there was one frayed spot in the tight rein she held on her passions, one single area that could arouse her ire and rattle her composure.

Amanda struggled to control herself, clenched her teeth and silently hummed "Rock of Ages," but her usual distractions didn't help. Anger clawed at her stomach and beat on her chest, and her ears roared from the racing of her pulse.

Once they were on the steps, Amanda said, "Oh dear,

I've dropped my glove someplace. It must be in Mr. Essig's office."

"I'll check," Beau said, starting for the door.

"No, you look in the buggy to be sure. I'll return to the office. I know just where I might have lost it." She hurried back inside.

Essig was just picking up her glove when Amanda entered. "This yours?" he asked, holding it out and giving her an oily smile.

"Yes." She took the glove and glared at the man. She knew very well that she never should have returned to his office, knew with a certainty that she should seal her lips, whirl, and leave. But she could have more easily walked into the First Baptist Church stark naked than she could still her tongue. "Mr. Essig, there is something I must tell you," she said quietly.

"Yes?" He continued to smile, a definite lascivious cast to his expression, which only added more fuel to the fire burning inside her.

Lifting her chin and enunciating as clearly as if delivering Joan of Arc's soliloquy, she said, "I find a strong man's using force or violence against a weaker woman or a child the vilest of acts and reprehensible above all things."

His smile soured into a scowl. "What are you getting at, Mrs. Swann?"

"I'm getting at your mistreatment of your wife, Mr. Essig."

His scowl turned venomous and the tendons in his thick neck flexed, as did his fists. "Mistreatment? What the hell has Judith—"

"Judith hasn't said a word, nor does her brother have

any inkling of the matter, but the marks on her face and arms are obvious, so don't bother to deny it." She poked her finger in his chest. "I'm giving you fair warning. If I see another bruise on her body or hear that you've battered her again, I shall tell Beau, and you, sir," she said, with a haughty toss of her head, "will be out on your ass."

⌒ Five ⌒

Beau knew something was wrong the moment Amanda came down the steps. Her color was high and her teeth were clenched tightly enough to snap an ax handle.

"What's happened?" he asked.

She lifted her brows slightly as if puzzled by the question and said, "Why nothing. Mr. Essig found my glove." She pulled on the missing article, then climbed into the buggy with Beau's assistance.

Beau took his place in the seat beside her and snapped the reins, but he wasn't so easily put off. While he didn't know Amanda Swann well—surely not as well as he would like to—he'd spent a great deal of their time together studying her beautifully molded face. How could any sane man not do so? Beau was reasonably sane, and a sharp observer of details. He was well aware of the small mole on her right cheekbone, the single dimple at the corner of her lush mouth that flashed when she smiled, the exact tilt of her head when she was thinking. He could probably estimate closely the number of long, dark lashes that framed her magnificent blue eyes.

Although she'd carefully schooled her features back to

the serene face she usually presented, Amanda had been angry or upset when she left Morris's office.

"Something happened," he said.

"I can't imagine what you're talking about."

"That's peculiar because your cheeks were red as fire, and you look like you could chew a railroad spike and spit out horseshoe nails."

"Mr. Chandler, such crass descriptions aren't endearing to any woman."

"Did Morris say or do anything offensive?" he asked, pressing the issue. "Did he insult you in any way? If he did—"

"No, no. Mr. Essig is simply one of those people whose very presence is irritating to me. There's something about him that I don't like. He and Judith seem ill-matched."

Beau wasn't sure he had the truth, but he decided to let it go for the moment. "I don't like him much either, and I don't know why Judith married him. Maybe, like they say, love is blind. Or maybe Uncle Angus had a hand in it."

"Your uncle? What do you mean?"

He shrugged. "Just a notion I had. I'll ask Mama when we go home for lunch." He checked his pocket watch. "We have time to stop by the office and see how Frank is doing with the money."

"Before we do that, could we drive to the cemetery? I'd like to check the location and speak to the groundskeeper."

"He didn't see a thing," Beau said. "I already asked him."

"Still, I'd like to ask some questions, and I'd like to see the grave."

A few minutes later, they were standing beside the empty hole. "Not much to see," he said.

"Hmmmm." She squatted down and peered about, then walked a few steps around the excavation, examining the mound of dirt, walking a few steps more in various directions.

"What are you looking for?"

"Clues."

"I doubt that you'll find much. Several people have tracked around that grave."

"I've found a great deal," she said, scribbling a few lines on a notebook recovered from her reticule, "and I'll know more when I talk to the groundskeeper and examine his boots."

"His boots?"

"Yes," she said. "I estimate two, perhaps three, men snatched the body and the casket. I would guess that they used a wagon also used to haul hay."

"How did you come up with those ideas?"

"First, at least two men would be needed to do the job. Perhaps one person could have stolen the body, but a solid mahogany coffin is quite heavy. Here, here, and here on top of the excavated earth, I see three sets of boot prints that could belong to the thieves. One or two of them stood in the grave and shoved the casket along here while another pulled upward. And look here at the wagon tracks."

"Couldn't the hearse have made those tracks?"

"No. The tracks are on top of the dirt the robbers dug. And there are several bits of hay about."

Beau nodded. "I'm impressed."

"No need to be. This is very elementary detective work. As I said, I can be more precise when I've seen the groundskeeper's boots and can compare them with the prints here."

"How do you know that some of the prints might not belong to me or to Harve or to my brothers-in-law? We've all walked around here."

The dimple that fascinated him so flashed as she smiled. "Do you have rundown heels or holes in your soles?"

Beau glanced down at the fine boots custom-made for him on his last trip to Galveston. "No. And neither do the others. Good point."

Neither did the groundskeeper, who lived in a small cabin across the road. When they spoke with him, Amanda noted that his boots had thick, sturdy soles of a distinctive type. And he hadn't seen a thing in the cemetery after he'd eaten his supper and gone to bed just after dark.

"Did you hear any disturbance of any sort?" Amanda asked.

"How's that?" the old man asked, his hand cupped behind his ear.

"Did you hear anything unusual night before last?" she shouted.

"Nary a peep. It was quiet as a graveyard." He cackled at his own joke and slapped his knee.

Beau grinned when Amanda merely closed her eyes briefly and gave a slight shake of her head. He thanked the old man and escorted Amanda outside. "Ready for lunch now?"

"Almost. I'd like to take another look at the spot where the cash is to be left. I need to find the best place to hide and watch the exchange."

Beau opened his mouth to argue with her, but he was learning fast that trying to disagree with the lovely agent was a lost cause. Yet, if he put his mind to it, he might come up with a way to get around her. He still didn't take to the notion of her alone and hiding behind a tombstone.

Damn, she was a fine-looking woman. And her fragrance, light as it was, tantalized his senses. It damned near drove him crazy until he figured out that her scent reminded him a little bit of vanilla ice cream and cinnamon cakes and honeysuckle blossoms. He wondered if she tasted as sweet as ice cream and cake. He sure wanted to find out.

"Watch out!" Amanda shouted.

He snapped out of his reverie just in time to dodge a peddler's pushcart.

"Sorry," he muttered. "My mind was on other things."

Estelle and Ellie were missing from the luncheon table, Estelle having gone home to deposit Ellie in her nap bed and dine with Frank.

"Heaven knows, the child needs a nap," Maud Chandler said. "She wanders about half the night."

"She's an insomniac, like me," Aunt Katie said. "And she'd be a right smart more likely to sleep nights if Estelle didn't insist on her taking a nap in the afternoon."

It was impossible for Beau to broach the subject of Judith and Morris with his mother since Judith was at the table. Morris, however, was not.

When Amanda asked, "Isn't your husband joining us?" Judith flushed.

"No. He usually . . . lunches at one of the restaurants

downtown." She kept her eyes on her soup, and her flush deepened. "Business, you know."

Aunt Katie glanced up from her bowl and cut her eyes to Maud, who seemed very occupied with keeping her own gaze downcast and patting her lips with her napkin.

Amanda hadn't missed the exchange. A quick glance at Beau told her that he hadn't missed it either. She wondered exactly what Morris Essig did during his lunch hour. She sincerely doubted that it had anything to do with business—or with anything as innocuous as bird-watching or badminton.

What was Essig's vice? she wondered. Women? Gambling? Liquor? Or some other depravity? He didn't seem the type to visit opium dens or enjoy carnal contact with boys, but she could easily imagine him with a coarse woman. Whatever the distraction, obviously the family, including his wife, suspected. Amanda vowed that as soon as this case was over, she would have a heart-to-heart talk with Judith. It was ridiculous for such a refined and talented lady to waste her life with such a lout.

"What's going on with the ransom plans?" Aunt Katie asked.

"Frank is gathering the money," Beau said. "It should be ready by this afternoon. Morris will make the delivery."

"Morris?" Maud said. "Why not you?"

"Yeah," Aunt Katie said. "I figured you'd want to be right in the thick of things."

Amanda put her hand over Beau's and smiled sweetly. "Actually, he wanted to, but the whole idea made me so nervous that he agreed to let someone else do it. Mr. Banks couldn't volunteer because of his catarrh—"

"Catarrh? Humph. More likely because tonight's the

weekly meeting of his benevolent club," Aunt Katie said. "Don't nothing keep Frank from that benevolent meeting. Beats me what that bunch talks about interesting enough to keep him out for all hours, but he never misses a Thursday night. Sometimes they meet on Mondays too. And then there's the Odd Fellows and the church board and—"

"Well, we all have to have our distractions," Maud said cheerily. "I, myself, would hate to miss my mission society meeting. And speaking of that, Amanda, I would adore having you accompany me next Tuesday morning."

"Thank you," Amanda said, hoping her charade would be ended by then and she would be on another case. "I would be delighted."

"Wonderful. And we must begin to make plans for your wedding. While I know we're in mourning and you're a widow, still, I should think that we'll want to have some parties and such in a few months. Or maybe a few weeks would do for mourning. What do you think, Aunt Katie?"

"I don't plan on mourning past this Sunday for that old fart. I don't cotton to being a hypocrite, and I don't look my best in black."

Judith hid a smile with her napkin.

Beau laughed out loud. "Aunt Katie, you're a treasure. You always say exactly what's on your mind."

"A privilege of age, boy. But then, I've never been one to mealy-mouth around about anything. If I hadn't had a passel of spirit, Angus would have run right over me." Aunt Katie stared pointedly at Judith. "Spirit is good armor."

"You're to be admired, Aunt Katie," Judith said. "Now

if you will excuse me, I have to pick up some supplies that Mr. Sweeney ordered for me."

"But, Judith, you haven't finished your meal," Maud said, "and we're having pineapple cake for dessert."

"I'll have some later," she replied, hurrying from the room.

There was an awkward silence for a moment, then Maud began chattering about some neighbor's new rose bushes.

When she had run down, Beau said, "Mama, why did Morris and Judith get married?"

Maud appeared stunned by the abrupt question. "Why— why for the usual reasons, Beaumont."

Aunt Katie snorted, and Maud glared at her.

"Did Uncle Angus have a hand in it?"

Maud pressed her napkin to her lips, then said, "He encouraged it. He was very fond of Morris. He found him to be an excellent plant manager. He comes from a brewing family, you know. I understand his grandfather was an acclaimed brewmaster in Germany."

"That aside, I can't understand why Judith picked somebody like Morris. They're too different. Did Uncle Angus force the marriage?"

"Certainly not," Maud told her son. "I would have never stood for that. Judith was content to marry Morris. More than content. Delighted. She was delighted."

Amanda knew there was more to the story. Not only was Maud evading the issue, but Aunt Katie looked as if she were about to burst her corset strings.

"Relieved, you mean," mumbled Aunt Katie.

"Aunt Katie!" Maud said, clearly horrified at the revelation. She glanced nervously between Amanda and Beau.

"Relieved?" Beau asked.

"Might as well tell it," Aunt Katie said.

"I've no desire to air the family's dirty laundry." Maud glanced pointedly at Amanda.

"We're family, Mama."

Maud ignored him and began slicing the pineapple cake.

Aunt Katie made an exasperated sound. "Judith took up with some feller who was passing through."

"An *actor*," Maud interjected, then clamped her lips.

"An actor," Aunt Katie amended. "Anyway, after he was long gone, Judith came up in a family way."

Maud's lips stayed clamped as she mangled the cake with angry stabs.

"So Uncle Angus arranged for her to marry Morris," Beau said.

"That's the way of it. So I reckon you could say she was relieved to get a husband."

"And the child?" Beau asked.

"Stillborn. Maud, let me have a piece of that cake before you ruin it completely. Judith ain't the first girl to lose her head over a smooth-talking man, and she won't be the last."

"Of course not," Amanda said. "A similar thing happened to one of my dearest childhood friends, and we're still very close. Mrs. Chandler, you mustn't be distressed. Judith is a lovely and talented young woman. You can be very proud of her."

Maud managed a smile, although her chin trembled and her eyes were moist. As soon as it was polite, she excused herself from the table.

"The old fart!" Aunt Katie said. "He picked a son of a

bitch for a husband while he was picking out a fine brewery manager."

"Meaning?"

"Oh, Judith don't ever say anything—Maud neither—but it's plain them two don't gee-haw a'tall. Gossip is that Morris has a woman set up in some rooms down on Cypress Street."

"On Cypress Street?"

"Yep. In Guy Town. Oh, I know about Guy Town. Though most of them won't admit it, every woman in Austin knows about Guy Town and what goes on down there. Even old Angus did a bit of carrying on, I understand."

"Really?" Beau said, not betraying his knowledge of the matter. "What do you know about such things?"

Aunt Katie gave him a sharp look. "More'n I ever let on. I believe his lady friend's name was Fanny. I 'spect you'll meet up with her sooner or later. She'll come around with her hand out soon as she finds out he didn't mention her in his will."

"Does she deserve anything?" Beau asked.

"Danged right. Not much to the woman, but she put up with his contrary ways for a lot of years. I figure he promised her a cut of some business she runs for him, just like he led Morris to believe that Judith would get a share of his estate—most probably the brewery—which meant that Morris would take it over. Frank figured he'd be running things too. I knew all the time he was just manipulating folks to do his bidding like dangling an apple in front of a jackass. He had sense enough to know that pair of sidewinders your sisters married weren't fit to run things for the womenfolk. And he never did cut you out of his will neither."

"Did he tell you that?"

"Nope. Read his will for myself. There are a few advantages to not being able to sleep nights. I snooped."

Beau grinned. "You didn't."

"Danged sure did. Not much gets by me. Angus always intended for you to be his heir. You might have rubbed together like a pair of porcupines, but you were the only blood-kin male in the family. Knew you'd turned out to have a head on your shoulders. He kept up with you, you know."

"No, I didn't know. How?"

"Oh," the old woman said, "he had his ways. Not much got by Angus either. Have you heard from the Pinkerton agent yet, Beaumont?" she asked, looking pointedly at Amanda.

Beau cleared his throat. "I'll let you know when I do."

Aunt Katie glanced back and forth between Amanda and her nephew. "You two may have fooled the others, but don't think you've pulled the wool over these old eyes. If you need another hand, let me know." She rose and took her cane.

"Aunt Katie, you called Morris and Frank sidewinders. What did you mean by that? Didn't Uncle Angus trust them?"

"Oh, he trusted them well enough—especially when he had the upper hand. They ain't crooks or nothing—leastwise, not that I know of. Now, I've flapped my jaws too much as usual, and I ain't saying another word. Maud will give me old Billy-Rip as it is."

She clomped from the room.

When she was gone, Beau looked at Amanda. "Do you think she knows you're the agent?"

"I think she suspects. She's an astute old lady. I want to talk with her more later." Amanda rose. "If you'll excuse me, I need to make a few arrangements and prepare my wardrobe for tonight."

"Your *wardrobe*?"

"Yes. Surely you didn't think I would stake out the cemetery wearing a flowered hat and a bustle?"

☙ Six ☙

Although Amanda was enjoying herself immensely, as soon as she'd finished her dessert, she pleaded a headache and retired to her room with a remedy that Maud had foisted upon her. She was still smiling when she went upstairs. It wasn't often that she dined with such a large and spirited family. She rather liked the Blessing bunch, except for Morris, who looked daggers at her during the entire meal.

Angus had always insisted on the entire family, from little Ellie to Aunt Katie, dining together on weeknights and at Sunday noon. The tradition had continued after his death, but Amanda doubted that it was quite as lively when the old curmudgeon sat at the head of the table instead of Beau.

Amanda rarely allowed herself to think of family. Dinners when she was growing up were far from the sumptuous production she'd just experienced. And certainly no one ever laughed. After a long, harsh prayer pronounced by her father, meals were meager and quick with her father and the boys eating first and her mother and the girls getting the leftovers. Amanda had always counted herself lucky if she got a wing from the fried chicken.

They were all gone now. They'd perished in a house fire two years after Amanda fled. Except Susan. She'd been told that her sister had also run away from home. California, someone said, but she'd never been able to locate her.

Amanda had long ago put her past aside. She'd become independent, focused on other things; she had learned to do without a family. But occasionally, just occasionally, a poignant moment made her regret . . .

She shook off the feeling and began unbuttoning her dress.

In a half hour, Amanda was completely transformed. Gone was the lace and bustle and dinner dress. In their stead she wore slightly ragged trousers and a loose shirt. Scuffed boots replaced her slippers. Her intricate hairdo had been brushed out, braided into a coil around her head, and topped with a curly red wig and a boy's cap.

A few deft strokes of pencils and paints from her makeup box altered her hands and face and gave her a healthy crop of freckles along with an unwashed effect. A set of upper front teeth, carved from ivory and made crooked and slightly protruding, fit perfectly over her own and changed the shape of her mouth. She pulled on a well-worn coat and transferred her weapons into the pockets especially made for them.

When she examined her reflection in the cheval glass, she smiled, then schooled her features into a vacuous expression. Her best friend wouldn't have recognized her. She looked the part of a scruffy, slow-witted boy of fourteen or so. And, if required to speak, she could sound the part as well.

Checking the time on an old pocket watch she carried,

she decided to give the family a few more minutes to disperse before she slipped from the house.

True to his word, Beau tried to keep an eye on everyone. Aunt Katie, Judith, and his mother went into the parlor to play a game of Black Lady Hearts with Maud grumbling that Katie always cheated.

"No such thing, Maud," Katie said. "I'm just lucky. And a derned sight better at playing cards than you are. Pay attention to what you're doing if you want to win."

"Perhaps we could play a word game instead," Judith suggested. "The Minister's Cat is a good one."

Maud sighed. "I'm worse at word games than cards."

"That's the truth," Aunt Katie said. "Judith, get the cards. Beaumont, you want to play?"

"Thank you, but not tonight, Aunt Katie."

After a whispered exchange with Beau about meeting in the alley in an hour, Morris went home to do some reading. Estelle, Frank, and their brood left as well.

Feeling like a damned voyeur, Beau peeked through the hedges and saw Frank leave, walking at a fast clip. Beau followed him until he turned on Pecan Street and disappeared. He casually walked along Pecan himself and noticed a sign that announced the Austin Benevolent Society and had an arrow that pointed upstairs. Obviously this was where Frank had his meeting. Beau turned and hurried back home.

Aunt Katie, Judith, and his mother were still playing their card game. The cook and her helper had finished, and the kitchen and scullery were empty. Beau helped himself to another piece of pecan pie from the safe and peered out the window toward Estelle's parlor as he ate with his fingers. He could see his sister sitting between two of her girls on the piano bench and could hear the faint notes of a song on the evening air. He felt a tug at his heart, then a warm fullness that made him smile.

Strange, he hadn't realized how much he'd missed his family over the years, until he came home. Maybe it was because he was getting older and sentimental or because he'd sewn his wild oats and was ready to settle down, but he liked being a part of a family again. He'd been restless the last couple of years, but he hadn't known why. Maybe it was because he'd discovered that being a loner wasn't all it was cracked up to be.

In some ways he liked the feeling that his relatives needed him, looked up to him. It made him feel—if not important, at least useful. He just wasn't sure that he was up to running everything. That much responsibility made him as skittish as a fresh-broke stallion.

A shadowy movement near the stable caught his eye, but by the time Beau went outside to investigate, he saw nothing, heard nothing but Estelle's piano. But when he checked the back stall, he noticed that the mare he'd chosen for Amanda was missing.

Damn. She was on her way to the cemetery alone. She might be a Pinkerton agent, but she was also a woman, and he still didn't like the idea of her being hunkered down behind a tombstone with crooks skulking about. As soon as he handed over the bag of money to Morris, Beau planned to hightail it over to the cemetery and keep an eye on her.

Amanda had plenty of time to get to the city cemetery, so she decided to make a brief trip through Guy Town to

study the lay of the land. It wasn't an area that a re-
spectable woman would ordinarily visit at night, but she
felt no apprehension wearing her boy's garb. Anticipating
her jaunt, she'd brought along a dented growler, a small
tin pail used to transport beer home from the saloon, and
hung it over the saddle horn—not that she planned to
drink any of the nasty stuff even if she might purchase it.
The growler simply provided her with an excuse to be in
the bawdy district.

"My pa sent me to fetch a pail of beer," she would say
if need be.

While the rest of the town was relatively quiet and
dimly lit, Guy Town was rollicking. Laughter and shouting and music spilled out of the saloons. Men, young and
old and in high spirits, reeled down the streets or slipped
into the parlor houses interspersed among the saloons
and gambling halls. Now and then she saw gaudily dressed
women leaning out windows or against doorjambs, calling to passersby.

As a fiddle played a lively ditty in the background, one
brassy blonde who stood near the Pink Feather Saloon
shouted, "Hey, kid! You wanna have some fun?"

Amanda stilled the mare and glanced over her shoulder.

The blonde laughed. "You, Red. I'm talking to you.
You got two dollars?"

Amanda stared at the woman, who on closer inspection
didn't look much more than sixteen. She shook her head
and nudged the mare's sides just as a fight broke out two
doors down. A ball of arms and legs rolled into the street,
cursing and crunching and smacking fists on flesh and
bone. Half a dozen men followed, shouting and cheering.

Deciding that this wasn't the best time to check out

Guy Town, Amanda turned her horse and beat a hasty retreat. She didn't dare risk getting involved in something that would interfere with the business to be conducted that night.

She backtracked and cut over to San Jacinto Street, which took her past the Capitol site, then turned toward the cemetery that lay east of the university. The area was poorly lighted, but with the illumination from the waxing moon, she easily found her way to the grounds.

She tethered the mare out of sight in a stand of cedar elms, then walked back to the cemetery, careful to stay in the shadows in case the robbers had the same idea. In a short time she found the large tombstone that she'd chosen earlier, one fashioned of gray marble and decorated with a pair of lambs at the base and a dove on top. She could easily blend in with the lambs, peering over them as needed to keep an eye on Ben Thompson's grave.

Long accustomed to spending hours waiting and watching, she'd brought along a small canteen of water and a bit of food wrapped in a napkin—not that she was likely to need it that night, with less than two hours to tarry until the appointed time. Still, it paid to be prudent. The robbers might bide their time before they picked up the ransom.

It was around eleven by the time Beau reached the cemetery. He left his horse in a gully a quarter of a mile from the entrance and made his way quietly to the rear of the groundskeeper's house. Since he was deaf as a doorpost, the old man wasn't likely to hear Beau's approach, but he didn't want to alert either Amanda or the robbers in case they had arrived early.

Wearing dark-colored trail clothes and with his six-shooter strapped to his side, Beau crept closer, keeping to the bushes and making his way slowly. Beau hadn't survived as a gambler or running a saloon in San Augustine, one of the most dangerous towns in Texas, without being tough. He was no stranger to trouble—or to guns. He could hold his own with any man. And he meant to keep Amanda safe.

When he heard the whinny of a horse, he froze. The robbers? Amanda's mare? Someone else? It was too early for Morris to arrive. Listening with every fiber of his senses, he waited, breath held, movements bridled.

Was that the creak of a wagon on the road? He dared not move. Slowly Beau sank to his knees behind the bush that hid him and waited. The wagon rumbled past.

Late for a wagon to be about. Could it be the culprits, surveying the meeting place? Deciding that he'd best not move lest he reveal himself, Beau hunkered down to wait. Though he was some distance away, he had a clear view of Ben Thompson's monument as well as the one where Amanda was supposed to be hiding. He didn't see any movement from either place.

Everything was quiet. There was only an occasional hoot from a distant owl and the maddening chirr of crickets. Not even a breeze stirred.

After half an hour, he had to relieve himself. Why in hell hadn't he thought of that before he got there? Still as the place was, he didn't dare take care of things there for fear that Amanda—or anyone else around—would hear him. Not only might he offend her sensibilities, he was sure to make her madder than a stirred hornet by just being there. And he couldn't risk scaring off the robbers.

The more he tried to ignore his condition, the more serious it became. After what seemed like an hour but was probably no more than ten minutes, he was sure that he was going to bust. Deciding it was better to sneak out then than wait, he eased off his boots lest he scrape leather against a rock. He left his boots, with his hat atop them, behind the bush and started to steal away, keeping low and quiet.

Beau hadn't counted on his foot being asleep. He lost his balance and went sprawling, rocks crunching and scattering. He hissed a curse before he could stop himself, then lay there with his face in the dirt, madder than hell for pulling such a damned dumb-fool stunt.

He waited for what seemed an eternity. Nothing moved. Nothing made a sound but those damned crickets. He wiggled his foot and scrunched his toes until the feeling came back, then he crawled, then duck-walked to the road. After pausing in the cover of a cedar, he bent low and made a quick dash for the back of the grounds-keeper's cabin.

Everything would have been fine if he hadn't stepped on that blasted cactus.

Amanda had heard him arrive about three-quarters of an hour before. Sure that it was one of the crooks staking out the place to be sure there were no traps, she'd stayed stone still and waited. She'd heard him leave, noisily and with muffled curses. Drunk probably. She'd found that culprits of the sort she suspected were often ignorant, inept, and given to vices such as drunkenness.

It wouldn't be long now.

In a few minutes, she heard hoofbeats. She peered

around a lamb's flank just in time to see Morris Essig
alight from his mount at the cemetery entrance. He untied
a bag from the saddle and strode toward Ben Thompson's grave. He stopped for a minute and looked around,
then set the bag in front of the monument, turned, and
walked away.

Expecting Morris to mount and ride off, she was
shocked when she saw him slap the horse's rump, then
scurry back inside the area and duck behind another
monument.

Damnation! That fool was going to ruin everything.
She wanted to yell at him; she wanted to march over to
where he hid and slap him silly. If there was one thing she
couldn't abide, it was amateurs meddling in her cases and
mucking things up.

Furious, but powerless to do anything lest she reveal
her presence, Amanda seethed silently and turned her attention to the money-filled bag.

She didn't have long to wait. A faint crunch of gravel
set her heart to hammering.

An arm snaked out from behind Thompson's monument and a hand felt along the base for the bag. No sooner
had the fingers clasped the handle when Morris came
rushing from his hiding place, obviously determined to
capture the crooks when they retrieved the ransom.

"Damnation!" Amanda ground out as she watched the
scuffling. Looked like two men were wrestling Morris for
the money bag. She was going to laugh while she staked
that Essig idiot over an anthill!

One fellow was astride Essig's back and another was
attacking from the front. With shouts and moans and fists

flying, there was nothing for her to do but wade into the fray.

"You bit my goddamned ear!" she heard Morris roar.

"Ow, ow, ow," a high-pitched voice whined. "Git 'im, boy. Git 'im."

She was almost to the monument when someone tackled her from behind. She kicked free, raised the sap filled with bird-shot, and brought it down hard on the back of her assailant's head.

By the time she scrambled to her feet, Morris was on one knee, dazed and moaning, blood running down one side of his face. The bag was gone.

"Fool," she yelled at him.

He roared, staggered to his feet, and lunged for her. She sidestepped. He turned and lumbered toward her again, growling like a wounded bear. She danced around, then sidestepped. This time his momentum carried him on toward Uncle Angus's open grave. Morris braked at the edge, flailing his arms like a weathercock, trying to get his balance and keep from falling into the hole.

Amanda couldn't resist. She put her boot to his rump and shoved.

She ran back to her attacker and lifted his head by the hair to see his face. Double damn! It was Beau Chandler— out cold.

She didn't have time to do more than make a hurried evaluation of him. She heard men cursing and crashing through the underbrush of a wooded area to the north. She left Beau on his own and dashed for where her horse was hidden.

By the time she mounted, Amanda saw a pair of riders top a hill a fair distance away. She kicked the mare into a gallop and, bending low over the horse's neck, took out after them. She didn't gain much on the two who rode as hell-bent as she did, but she kept them in sight as they raced through the deserted town.

Boozer glanced over his shoulder. "He's a-gainin' on us, Taft."

"Let's cut through here."

They flew past the depot, crossed Congress, and rounded Colorado Street, riding flat out. When they reached the alley behind the livery stable, they pulled up and walked their mounts into the shadows. The rider following them sped on by.

"Hurry," Taft said. "We gotta get these nags put up 'fore he doubles back."

They high-tailed it to the front of the livery stable. Boozer slid off his horse and opened the wide doors that had been closed for the night. Soon as men and mounts were inside, he closed the doors again and dropped the bar.

Boozer fell back against the door. "Man, I ain't never been so skeered in my life. I thought a haint had us for sure."

Taft snorted. " 'Tweren't no haint. 'Twas some fereign-talkin' bastard. Mean devil—and strong. Had fists like ham hocks. He danged near broke my nose, and he knocked out one of my front teeth." He spat a mouthful of blood.

"Oh, they's about all rotten anyhow. Probably saved you six bits to keep from havin' it yanked out. Bet you're glad I got a-hold of his ear so you could conk him with that rock."

"I must not a-conked him hard enough, 'cause he took

out after us awful quick. We was lucky to get away from that double-crosser, and that's the God's truth."

"Did you get it?" a voice whispered from the shadows.

"Yes, ma'am, we shore did," Taft said. "I got the satchel right here."

⸜ Seven ⸝

"Help! Help!" came a muffled shout.

Beau roused. His thoughts were confused and his head throbbed something awful. He heard the shouting again, then a string of angry foreign words.

German, maybe. Morris? Oh, hell, it was Morris. He'd fouled up everything. He was going to kill that beer-making son of a bitch.

As he moved to push himself up, Beau groaned and grabbed the back of his head. He felt a knot as big as a musk melon.

"Help! Help!"

"Keep your shirt on, you stupid bastard!" Beau roared as he stood unsteadily and started toward the sound. "Dammit!" he yelped as his foot came down on the cactus spines embedded in his sole. Cursing every step of the way, he hobbled in the direction of the shouting.

Amanda. Oh, God, where was Amanda? "Amanda!"

She didn't answer.

He cupped his hands around his mouth and shouted louder. "Amanda!"

She was probably chasing dangerous armed crooks while he was limping around barefoot and with his britches unbuttoned. A hell of a lot of help he was. He couldn't even hold on to that kid he'd grabbed. He felt like a damn fool.

"Help! Help!" Morris let out another muffled string in German that Beau figured would have blistered his ears if he could have understood a word of it.

Following the sound, Beau hobbled to the edge of Uncle Angus's grave. He struck a match and looked in. Morris lay in the bottom of the hole moaning and swearing. The side of his head was bloody, and his eyes were wild.

"Oh, Beau, thank God. Thank God."

"Don't thank him yet. I may shoot you and kick dirt over you, you stupid son of a bitch. Come out of there."

Morris groaned louder. "I can't. My ankle. I think it's broken."

Beau spat out another colorful oath. "Here, give me your hands, and I'll drag you out."

With his head still throbbing and his foot on fire, Beau wasn't too careful about how he hoisted the bastard out of the grave. A heavy bugger, that Morris, and practically dead weight. Beau wasn't sure the idiot didn't have a stump tied around his middle. Grunting and straining for all he was worth, Beau finally managed to drag his brother-in-law clear of the hole.

Breathing hard and sweating, Beau dropped to his knees. "What in God's name came over you, Morris? Why the hell did you attack those men?"

"I intended to capture them and save the money."

"Well, you did a piss-poor job of it. They're gone and so's the ransom."

"I didn't realize that the entire gang would come," Morris said indignantly. "One man I could handle, two even, but I was no match for three. Still, you can be assured that the money is safe."

"Safe? How can you say that? The bag is gone. And Amanda. Where the hell is Amanda?"

"Amanda? Are you daft, man? She's at home in her bed. And, yes, the money is safe in my office at the brewery. I switched the bills for useless bundles of paper before I came tonight." He sounded very proud of himself.

"You *what*? You stupid ass!" It took everything Beau had to keep from shoving Morris back in that grave and filling him full of lead. And if anything had happened to Amanda because of that dumb peckerwood, he might just do it anyway.

He tarried long enough to pull the worst of the cactus spines from his foot and yank on his boots before he limped the quarter of a mile to his horse and rode back to the cemetery for Morris. If it hadn't been for Judith, he would have left him there to rot.

Still wearing his nightshirt and with a pair of pants hastily pulled on under it, Dr. Taylor examined Morris, cleaned the blood from his face, and stitched his ear. The ankle, he said, was twisted, not broken, and he wrapped it in bandages as he rattled off directions for soaking it in salts water and keeping off it for a few days. He also gave Morris a bottle of medicine for pain.

Morris attended to, the doctor turned to inspecting Beau's injuries. He didn't get anything for his pain. Instead, the doc recommended cold compresses for his head and a hot bath for his foot. "Then you can work the spines out with a needle or some small tweezers if you have them. Rub this salve on the area when that's done. That'll be five dollars."

"*Five* dollars?" Beau exclaimed.

"Five dollars," Dr. Taylor replied. "It's the middle of the night."

"Pay the man," Beau told Morris. He pulled on his boot and hobbled out the door.

It was almost dawn, and Beau was worried sick. He'd looked everywhere for Amanda. She wasn't in her room; her mare's stall was still empty. He'd gone back to the cemetery twice and traced various routes home. He'd looked everywhere he could think of. No sign of her.

He sat on a crate in the stable, his head in his hands, trying to contain the throbbing and the terrible thoughts that tumbled in his mind. What if she'd been captured by the crooks? What if she was tied up somewhere? The robbers were bound to be mad enough to blow fire when they discovered they had paper instead of cash. What if they took their temper out on Amanda?

The thought of her being harmed had him frantic. He was ready to go to the police chief and spill the whole business when he heard the faint creak of the stable door.

Amanda!

He jumped to his feet and struck a match to the lantern as a figure led a horse inside.

He was about to call her name when he saw that it wasn't Amanda coming into the stable, but a scruffy, bucktoothed boy leading her mare.

Beau's gun cleared leather. "Hold it right there, kid. Where's the lady who was riding that horse?"

The boy only stared at him for a minute. Then he

reached up and yanked out his teeth. "You and Morris Essig ruined everything. You turned the night into a fiasco! Who appointed you two as the cavalry? I cannot do my job if you keep interfering."

"Amanda?"

"Of course it's me."

"You look like—"

"I'm in disguise. And I'm angry." She tore off her cap and threw it on the ground. "I could have had them if you two hadn't made such a botch of things. As it was, I was able to follow them to Guy Town, then I lost them. I've been combing—"

"Oh God, Amanda," Beau said, gathering her into his arms. "I've been worried sick about you."

"No need for—"

Before he knew what he was doing, his mouth came down on hers, and his arms tightened around her. She went rigid for a moment, then as his tongue teased her lips, he felt her sag against him. Her mouth softened, and her lips parted slightly.

Dear Lord, she tasted sweet. Sweeter than—

Suddenly she stomped his foot—the sore one—and pushed him away. "What do you think you're doing, Mr. Chandler?"

"Ouch, dammit! I don't think, I know. I was kissing you, that's what. Why did you stomp on my foot? It's already smarting something fierce."

"Mr. Chandler, I'm a Pinkerton agent, not a strumpet. I don't appreciate being mauled."

"Mauled? I was kissing you. And you were kissing me back."

"I was not!"

"Felt that way to me."

"You were mistaken." She turned and began unsaddling the horse.

"Here, let me do that." He reached for the cinch, but she slapped away his hand.

"I'm perfectly capable of taking care of this horse. Remember, I'm a detective, not a woman."

Beau grinned. "I'll admit it's hard to think of you as a woman in that getup. I wouldn't have recognized you if we'd passed on the street."

"That's the idea. I would have been rather conspicuous wearing skirts and carrying a parasol. These clothes give me much more freedom of movement."

Beau leaned back on a rail and watched her as she competently tended the horse. "I'm sorry that Morris took matters into his own hands and—"

She stilled and gave him a piercing look. "He wasn't the only one who interfered tonight."

"Yes. Well, I'm sorry." Danged if she couldn't make him feel lower than a gopher hole. "I can't help it if I'm concerned about a woman—even if she's the world's finest Pinkerton agent—taking on three ruffians."

"Two."

"Two what?"

Amanda sighed. "There were two ruffians."

"I saw three with my own eyes. The two Morris was tussling with and the one I tackled."

"You tackled *me*."

"*You?*" Beau's hand went to the tender swelling on the back of his head. "Why did you *hit* me? And what in the devil did you hit me with?"

"I didn't know it was you. You were supposed to be

here—keeping an eye on things, remember? And I hit you with a sap."

"A *sap*?"

"Yes. It's a small leather bludgeon filled—"

"I know what a sap is. I'm just surprised that you know how to use one."

"You shouldn't be. I told you that I can take care of myself. In any case, I didn't realize that it was you until later, after I'd disposed of Mr. Essig."

"Are you the tall, burly fellow he described to me? The one who tossed him into Uncle Angus's grave and wrenched his ankle?" Beau couldn't keep the amusement from his voice.

"A slight exaggeration, but I was angry at having to stop to defend myself. If you two hadn't mucked up the operation, I could have followed the men back to their base and retrieved Mr. Blessing's body. As it is, they have both the money and the corpse."

"Uhhhhh, not exactly," Beau said. He told her about Morris's switch.

"Morris is a fool! You'd do well to fire him and kick him out of the family. Judith deserves better." She turned and strode from the stable.

Beau hurried after her, wincing and hobbling and muttering curses.

"Shhhh. You'll wake up the whole household," she whispered. "What's wrong with your foot?"

"I stepped in a cactus bed."

"And the needles went through your boot?"

"Uh, not exactly. It's a long story, and I know that you're tired. Let's try to get some sleep."

"You need to attend to your injury. I would recommend a hot soak."

"That's what the doctor said."

Amanda left Beau in the kitchen, an ice pack on his head and his foot soaking in a tub of hot water, and she sneaked up to her room by the back stairs. Once the door was closed behind her, she yanked off the red wig and slammed it down on the bed. Still angry, she struggled with the feelings.

Becoming emotional wasn't productive, she told herself. She knew that. These weren't the first clients to meddle in an investigation and make her work more complicated. Allowing herself to become flustered was irrational. She sighed in resignation, then stood still for a moment and took five deep breaths.

As she sucked in each deep breath through her nose and blew it out her mouth, she cleared her mind and dissolved her irritation. The exercise never failed to restore calmness to her spirit.

But she discovered that she was still agitated as she hurriedly exchanged her costume for a dressing gown. When she sat down at the vanity table to take off her makeup, she was surprised to find that her hands were trembling.

How odd, she thought.

What had affected her so? She'd been in a dozen situations more dangerous than tonight's operation without becoming overwrought. She was well-known in the agency for her cool head and steel nerves.

Of course she'd been concerned about Beau's welfare

after she'd hit him—more than concerned, she admitted—but she'd felt his pulse and found it strong. She'd known that his condition was only temporary.

No, something else had made her jittery. What?

She unpinned her braids, then stopped to study her reflection. Her fingers went to her lips. The kiss? Was that what—?

No, of course not. How silly.

Her restoration complete, she stuck a needle into the bodice of her robe, took a pair of tweezers from her box of instruments, gathered a towel and some soft linens for bandages, then went downstairs.

When she reached the kitchen, she set a bright lamp near the spot where she would work, dragged up a stool, and sat down. "Is your foot feeling better?"

He nodded. "Some."

"Your head?"

"The ice helped."

She spread a towel over her lap, then patted her thigh.

Beau raised his brows in question. "Put your foot up here so I can pull out the spines."

"You don't have to do that."

"I know that I don't. But I can do it much more efficiently than you can." She patted her lap again. Why was he so hesitant? Though it was many years ago, this was a task she'd performed countless times for her brothers and sister. Especially in the summertime when everyone went barefoot, there were always splinters or stickers of one kind or another. "I used to be something of an expert," she said, smiling.

He shrugged, lifted his foot from the water, then rested his ankle on her thigh. The leg of his trousers was rolled up to his knee, and his muscular calf was exposed. She dragged her attention from the tantalizing curve of his leg to the afflicted area.

His foot was big. Big and . . . manly.

She took in a deep breath through her nose, blew it out through her mouth, and proceeded to blot his foot dry with the towel. She took in another deep breath, pulled the lamp closer, and took the needle from her bodice.

"Some of these are very deep," she said, bending close to his sole and probing for a spine.

"I know."

"I'll try to be gentle." She glanced up over his toes, and her heart stumbled when she saw the look in his eyes. His gaze captivated her, disarmed her, and bound her as surely as if he had used a rope.

At first she couldn't put a name to the expression. Penetrating, inquisitive, scrutinizing came to mind initially, but as she stared, another word struck her: Hungry. Exceedingly hungry.

She went warm all over.

"Ouch!" His foot jerked.

"Sorry," she said, ducking her head. She took another deep breath and directed her attention to the stickers.

As she coaxed each bit of a barb from his skin, then removed it with her delicate tweezers, she became more and more familiar with the shape and feel of his heel, his arch, his toes. The feet were very private parts of one's anatomy. She'd never realized how intimate handling a foot could be. How very intimate and . . . revealing and . . . sensuous.

His were long and angular and sinewy. They were strong and callused, but at the same time soft and pale and . . . vulnerable. His second toe was longer than the big one, reminding her of feet on marble statues of Greek gods. Such a configuration was said to signify wisdom. And passion.

The notion of Greek statues brought her attention to his bare, sturdy calf, again similar to photographs she'd seen and exhibits she'd viewed in museums. Her musings strayed higher, wondering at other similarities between this flesh-and-blood man and those scantily draped marble ones.

Tiny beads of perspiration popped out above her upper lip, and she felt a trickle between her breasts. A vague hum quivered in her belly, and she felt a strange tightening—

"Ouch!" His foot jerked again.

Her heart racing wildly, she abruptly pushed his foot from her lap and stood. "I think you need to soak some more. I'll boil another kettle of water."

He stopped her with a hand to her wrist. "Amanda?"

"Yes?"

"Do you feel it too?"

"Feel what?"

He smiled. "This powerful thing building between us."

She lifted her brows and gave the best performance of her life. "Mr. Chandler, I don't have any idea what you're talking about."

⌒ Eight ⌒

Amanda felt as if she'd barely closed her eyes when a tapping woke her. She ached to put a pillow over her head and sleep until noon. Instead she roused enough to mumble, "Yes?"

The door opened a crack and a small blonde head poked through. "Miss Amanda?" Ellie said in a loud whisper.

"Yes?"

She scurried into the room and stood by the bed. "Uncle Beau sent me to see if you're awake. He said he needs you something awful. He said there's another gollderned letter and an infernal nosy reporter is waiting in the parlor."

"I think your uncle Beau shouldn't use such language around children."

Ellie grinned. "That's what Gramma said."

"Please tell your uncle that I'll be down shortly."

"I will. Want me to bring you some coffee? I brought Uncle Beau some coffee yesterday, and he said it hit the spot. Naomi said that meant it went into his inside belly. That's where chicken and cake and coffee go—to your inside belly." She patted the area to demonstrate. "Inside where you can't see."

Amanda smiled. "Some coffee would be lovely. Thank you."

"I'll be right back." Ellie ran from the room.

All Amanda's years on the stage had trained her for speedy dressing. Before Ellie returned with the coffee, she had donned a rose-colored day dress and twisted her hair into a simple style. On the stairs she met Ellie, who was carefully carrying a tray with a cup and saucer.

"You didn't wait," Ellie said, a pained expression on her face. "I have to go slow or it sloshes."

A great deal of the coffee was in the saucer or on the tray. "I'm sorry. Your uncle's message sounded so urgent that I didn't want to tarry. Let's sit down right here, and I'll have a bit of coffee."

"Sit down on the stairs?" Ellie looked incredulous.

Amanda nodded and sat down. She took the tray, then said, "Won't you join me?"

Ellie sat on the stair next to Amanda and peered over at the tray. "I tried to be very careful, but I spilled some. I think the napkin got a little wet."

"It's just fine, Ellie. You're a very thoughtful little girl."

Ellie beamed. "I'm glad Uncle Beau is marrying you. When he does, I can call you Aunt Amanda. Naomi said so." She scooted very close, leaned her head against Amanda, and sighed. "I wish I could call you Aunt Amanda now."

Amanda's throat caught, and tears gathered briefly in her eyes. She put her arm around Ellie and kissed the top of her head. "That's the nicest thing anyone has said to me in a long time." She drained the few sips of coffee that remained in the cup. "Ahhh. Wonderful. That hits the spot." She winked.

Ellie giggled. "I'll take the cup back to Mrs. Kilgore. Uncle Beau is in the study. Lucy put some more coffee and stuff in there if you want some more. Mrs. Kilgore made cinnamon buns. They're my favorite. I had two. Did you know Uncle Beau hurt his foot? He's limping. It was a duty line hurt. I'm going to ask Naomi what that means."

Amanda was still smiling when Ellie scurried off, the china rattling on the small tray.

Harve stood in the foyer as stoic as a guard at Buckingham Palace. When she approached and greeted him, he merely nodded and opened the door to the study. She suspected that he kept silent to avoid stuttering. All the commotion in the household seemed to be affecting him deeply. From what she'd learned of Harve, she surmised that the man had been very devoted to his deceased employer. She also suspected that Harve might know a great deal more about things than anyone else.

Amanda found Beau drinking coffee and with his feet propped on Angus Blessing's ornate desk. He had changed into fresh clothing, but he looked as though he hadn't slept at all. He rose slowly and rubbed a hand over his face.

"Sorry to roust you, but we've got problems," he said, pouring her a cup of coffee from a large silver pot on the tray.

"So I understand from Ellie. Something about a gollderned letter and an infernal reporter." She chuckled as she accepted the cup. "I also understand that the cinnamon buns are very good." She selected one of the fragrant rolls and took a few nibbles as she scanned the letter spread out on the desk.

"That was stuck under the front door—sometime early this morning I imagine. Harve found it."

This note was as grubby as the others. The paper was folded in quarters and B CHANLER was printed on the outside. Inside, in what looked to be the same hand as the previous communications, was a demand for delivery of the ransom at eleven o'clock that night. The bag was to be left in a barrel that stood near the corner of Brazos and Pecan where the new Driskill Hotel was being built. The note concluded: *No mor funee bidnes. This is yor last chanst.*

"This time I'll deliver the cash myself," Beau said. "I wouldn't trust Morris again, even if he could walk. Judith isn't too happy with him being laid up. I think he's rather demanding. She said that your plans for the morning will have to be postponed. What were you two up to?"

"I was going to be her model. Tell me about the reporter."

"Tarnation! I forgot about the reporter. Harve has him cooling his heels in the parlor. He showed up not two minutes after I got the note. Harve said he was yammering about some tip he got. Mama and my sisters will croak if he's gotten wind of the kidnapping. I guess we'd better talk to him. What in the devil are we going to tell him?"

"Simple," Amanda said. "Tell him that the grave diggers made a mistake and you're having to move him."

Beau went to the door and spoke to Harve. Amanda was about to select another bun when a young man with a great mop of curly brown hair and a considerably less dense mustache came rushing in. His features and bearing reminded her a bit of a small bulldog. She immediately sensed that he could be trouble.

"Mr. Chandler," he said as he strode directly to Beau, "I'm Edwin P. Brown of the *Dispatch*. I received an anonymous tip early this morning, and I've just come from the city cemetery. What I saw there was most peculiar, most peculiar. Mr. Angus Blessing's grave—"

"Mr. Brown," Amanda said, turning on her brightest smile and offering her hand, "I'm Mrs. Swann, Mr. Chandler's fiancée. I declare. A member of the press? How exciting. Isn't it exciting, Beau? Come in and sit down right here." She patted the arm of a wing chair.

When the reporter merely looked dazed, she sashayed over to him, fluttered her eyelashes, took his arm, and led him to the seat. "We're having our morning coffee, Mr. Brown. Beau, dear, pour a cup for the gentleman."

"But I—"

"Oh, but you must join us," she said, turning up her smile another notch. She handed him the cup that Beau had filled. "And we were having some of these cinnamon buns. They're absolutely scrumptious." She plunked one on a plate with a fork and handed it to him.

Mr. Brown didn't seem to have had much practice balancing plates and saucers on his knees. Looking dismayed, he awkwardly juggled the dishes.

Beau bit back a grin as he watched Amanda work. God, she was fantastic. In two minutes, she'd blunted the reporter's spear and put him on the defensive.

"Oh, here's a napkin, Mr. Brown." She flicked open the cloth and spread it across his lap. "We wouldn't want you to get crumbs on your suit. And a very handsome suit it is, sir. I've always been fond of stripes. Haven't you, Beau?"

"Always."

"Oh, my, I almost forgot. Did you want cream, Mr. Brown?"

"Er, uh, no," Brown replied, looking from the delicate cup and saucer on one knee to the plate on the other. The cup clattered in the saucer if he tried to move, so he held on to both of them for dear life. "Mr. Chandler, Mr. Blessing's grave is—"

"Sugar?" she asked breathily.

"Pardon?"

"Would you like sugar in your coffee, Mr. Brown?" She moved close, bent over, and paused with spoon and bowl ready.

"No." He cleared his throat. "No, thank you, Mrs. Swann. Mr. Chandler, Angus Blessing's grave is . . . well, it's empty. I received a tip intimating that something strange might—"

Her eyes wide, Amanda gasped and slapped her hand against her chest. "Empty?" She clutched a handful of Beau's coat sleeve and glanced back and forth between the two men. "*Empty?* Does this mean he has . . . ascended?"

Mr. Brown gaped at her as if she were a lunatic. Beau made a strangled sound trying to keep from laughing. "Uncle Angus? Not likely, dear." He patted her hand, then glanced at the reporter and winked in a gesture of male camaraderie. "I had hoped to keep this from the rest of the family, Mr. Brown, especially the fair ladies, but it seems that the grave diggers made a mistake and dug in the wrong plot. He was to be quietly moved yesterday."

"Oh, Beau, you can't mean it," Amanda said. "How dreadful. Your poor Aunt Katie will be devastated. And your mother. Oh, dear. I'm afraid this may throw her into one of her spells. The grave is open and empty, you say, Mr. Brown? Oh, my, whatever could have happened? Beau, I feel faint." She pressed the back of her hand to her forehead, leaned heavily against him, and made a swooning sound.

Mr. Brown leapt from his chair. He rescued the coffee cup and saucer, but the plate, fork, and cinnamon bun hit the floor. The plate was saved by the thick rug, but the bun bounced and rolled under a green settee. Totally flustered, the reporter set his coffee on the desk and scrambled on his hands and knees to retrieve the other items. He couldn't quite reach the bun, especially with Amanda's skirts in the way after Beau lowered her to that particular settee.

From his kneeling position, the reporter said, "You mustn't be distressed, ma'am. I'm sure that the men simply haven't finished their work."

"You mean—"

"I'm sure that they moved Uncle Angus to his new resting place," Beau said, "but perhaps it grew dark before they could fill in the old spot."

"I'm sure that's what it was," Brown said.

Amanda clutched the reporter's shoulder. "No one must know of this terrible mistake. Aunt Katie might never recover if she heard of it. She's eighty-four, you know. And frail."

"Oh, ma'am," Brown said earnestly, "no one will ever hear of it from me. There's certainly nothing newsworthy here. A mistake. A simple mistake."

"Thank you, Mr. Brown," Beau said. He helped the man to his feet and pumped his hand. "You've done my family a great service by bringing this to our attention. I'll have someone go to the cemetery right away and cover the old grave." He walked the reporter to the front door, handed him his hat, and thanked him profusely again.

When he returned to the study, Amanda was eating another cinnamon bun and studying the note. "You're amazing," he said.

She smiled. "I told you that I was very good at my job."

Shortly before noon, Beau pulled the buggy to a stop on East Pecan, a half block from the hotel construction site. He helped Amanda from her seat, and they strolled along the walk, acting like sightseers, but there to scout the area where the bag was to be left.

After a turn up and down both sides of the street, they went into a decent-looking restaurant across from where Mr. Driskill was building his extravagant new hotel. Beau requested a table by the window.

While they were studying the menu, Beau leaned across and said, "That trash barrel must be the one they're talking about. The one on the corner."

"Mmmm. I'm sure it is. I think the chicken pie sounds tasty. What are you having?"

"A steak, I guess. Where are we going to hide out to watch for them?"

Her eyebrows lifted, and she glanced up from her reading. "We? I thought that we'd already had this discussion and had come to an agreement. You make the drop and go home. I'll be hiding and watching. Alone."

"Where are you going to hide?"

"I'm not sure. I have several possibilities in mind. Yes, I think I'll definitely have the chicken pie. And carrots."

"Amanda, there are half a dozen saloons around here. It will be late, and the men will be getting rowdy. I can't allow—"

"Ah, here comes our waiter. What will you have with your steak?"

As soon as they had ordered and the waiter had left, Beau again tried to broach the subject of Amanda keeping watch alone. When her color rose and her eyes flashed, he knew he'd gone too far.

"Mr. Chandler," she said in that clipped tone that he was beginning to recognize, "for the last time, I don't need your assistance. I should think that last night taught you a lesson. Either you let me handle this case my way, or I shall resign and leave Austin immediately."

For some reason, the thought of her leaving Austin was much worse than the threat of danger from drunken men or the fear of Uncle Angus being tossed in the river.

"I won't say another word on the subject. I'll get the money from the safe at the brewery, leave it, and go home."

"Good."

"That new hotel is really going to be something, isn't it? Supposed to be the finest in the state when it's done."

"Really?" she said absently. He could tell that her mind was already back on the coming night's plans.

Their lunch was soon served, and while they ate, he watched Amanda study the area through the window. Beau could almost see wheels and gears turning in her beautiful head as she devised strategy.

And she was beautiful. Bright as a new penny and unbelievably beautiful. The most beautiful woman he'd ever met.

And the most cunning. She could lie with all the facility of a drummer for a medicine show. He pitied the poor fool who might fall in love with a woman like Amanda Swann. How would he ever know when she was telling the truth and when she was only putting on an act?

And stubborn. She was the most stubborn woman he'd ever encountered. And independent didn't begin to describe her.

Yes, he pitied the poor fool.

And envied him.

Life around Amanda would never be dull.

Their meal finished, he said, "What now?"

"I would like to take a last walk around the area, then I need to make a purchase at the hardware store."

Beau yawned. "I wouldn't mind a nap myself. Aren't you tired?"

"Not at all."

And damned if she didn't look as fresh as spring clover when she pushed back her chair and strode from the restaurant.

Beau's butt was dragging by the time they'd spent a half hour walking up and down the street. And his foot didn't feel any too great either, but he'd sooner have eaten ground glass than admitted to Amanda how bad it smarted. She'd already taken him two falls out of two and was bouncing around like a ball of boundless energy. Hell, he had *some* pride.

He leaned against a counter while she carried on a spirited exchange with the owner of the hardware store. He couldn't imagine what she planned to do with that brace and bit she bought—or with the wooden crate she told the proprietor that she would have picked up later that evening.

He tucked her wrapped parcel under one arm and offered the other to Amanda. When she smiled up at him and took it, his chest swelled. He hadn't missed the covetous looks of the other men in the store, and he felt like the cock of the walk having her beside him—even if it was play-acting.

Going home, he took the long route around, walking the horse slowly, enjoying the warm, clear day and the feel of her skirts against his thigh. A man could get used to this, used to sweet feminine smells and a soft form pressing against him. He felt her head on his shoulder and glanced down.

She was sound asleep.

Something stirred deep inside him, and an odd feeling tightened in his throat.

Yes, a man could get used to this.

⌐ Nine ⌐

"Is Mr. Essig feeling better?" Amanda asked Judith at dinner that night.

"Much better, thank you. The doctor says that he'll be able to move about without crutches by Monday."

A tray had been sent to Morris so that Judith could join the family—a relief, Amanda knew. The poor woman had dark circles under her eyes and seemed jumpy as a cricket on a griddle. Little wonder. Being cooped up with an injured and grouchy Morris Essig must be akin to spending time in Hades.

"Is Uncle Morris sick?" Naomi asked.

"Does he have chicken pops?" Ellie asked.

Judith smiled. "No, he had . . . an accident. He hurt his ankle."

"Poor Uncle Morris," Ellie said.

No one else voiced sympathy or seemed very concerned. The conversation turned to a piano recital where the sixteen-year-old twins would be performing the following week. Amanda still had difficulty telling Barbara from Bonnie. Barbara seemed a bit more animated than Bonnie, but they were both shy girls who giggled a lot. Amanda couldn't believe that she had been their age when she'd struck out on her own. She'd considered herself more mature, but perhaps the difference in their backgrounds had made her grow up faster.

In many ways Helen Banks, at thirteen, was much more mature than her twin sisters, who seemed wrapped up in each other and in frivolities. The only dark-haired one among the six girls, Helen seemed to be the level-headed leader. Although Naomi and Ellie, the youngest of the brood, were charmers, Amanda felt a special kinship with Helen, just as Judith did with the quiet Louise, who often posed for her.

"How I envy your opportunities for excellent schools and piano lessons," Amanda said. "I've always wanted to play the piano."

"Not me," Helen said. "I'll be happy to let you have my afternoon with Miss Blodgett. I hate to practice. I wish I'd been Daddy's boy. Then I could go fishing and climb trees."

Amanda started to mention that she'd fished and climbed trees when she was a girl, but since Estelle was already glaring at her daughter, she kept quiet.

"I've never needed a boy," Frank said. "I couldn't be happier with my girls." He smiled at them, and Amanda warmed to him considerably.

After dinner, Frank had another of his meetings, the twins were off to a party, and Estelle pleaded a touch of dyspepsia. Judith, of course, had to tend to the cantankerous Morris. She seemed loath to leave. A shame that his stupidity had caused his wife additional grief.

Amanda took Judith's arm as she was leaving. "Perhaps you could slip Mr. Essig a double dose of his pain medicine when he gets too difficult."

Judith looked stunned by the suggestion.

"Just a thought," Amanda said, shrugging. "See you tomorrow."

Judith smiled wanly. "Enjoy the play."

Hesitating to plead another headache, Amanda and Beau had informed the family that they were going to a performance at the Millet Opera House. Since changing into her disguise would be a problem, earlier she had tossed a satchel out the window to Beau, then had come downstairs in her burgundy silk gown. After the others left, she retrieved a matching cape from her room.

Beau was dressed in his best dinner coat and tucked shirt, and as Amanda took his arm at the foot of the stairs, Maud sighed and dabbed away a tear. "You two are such a perfect couple, and you look so handsome tonight. I'm reminded of Beaumont's father and myself when we were young and in love, before the—" A pained expression passed over her face, and she made a dismissive gesture. "Before."

Beau kissed his mother's cheek. "Don't wait up for us. We may be late."

"I'll be up," Aunt Katie said, glancing up meaningfully over her spectacles.

"Beaumont," Maud said softly, "I haven't had a moment alone with you to ask, but what is happening with Uncle Angus? And don't you dare pat me on the head and tell me not to worry about it. I'm worried sick. It's almost a week now since he died and—" She glanced at Aunt Katie, who was busy stitching beads on a purse.

"And he'll be getting dicey," Aunt Katie said, not missing a stitch.

Maud looked as if she might faint, so Beau quickly

said, "Amanda and I are dropping off the ransom on our way to the play, and since Morris is stove up and can't mess up things, we should have him back tomorrow."

"Oh, thank Heavens. I've lived in mortal fear that the whole episode would be splashed across the pages of the *Statesman* or the *Dispatch*."

"Beau would never let that happen," Amanda said. "Would you, dear?"

"Absolutely not. I predict that Uncle Angus will be replanted by tomorrow night. Good evening, ladies." Beau offered his arm to Amanda.

They took the buggy, with the mare tied behind it, to a small hotel where Beau had secured a room earlier. He told her that he'd picked the Chicago House because it was clean, discreet, and only two and a half blocks from their rendezvous site. He wanted to escort Amanda to her door, but she was emphatic in her refusal.

"That would draw twice as much attention as my entering alone would," she said. "While I change, you can get the money from the safe at the brewery. If I'm gone when you return, don't be concerned. I have some preparations to make. Just follow through with the plans. I'll be watching."

He scowled. "Amanda, I don't like—"

She stiffened. "There is nothing more to discuss."

She was surprised that his molars weren't ground to nubbins, but he finally agreed. He tied the mare to the hotel's hitching post and left in the buggy.

Amanda managed to slip inside and find room twelve without being seen. Quickly she changed into the boy's costume she'd worn the night before. She didn't think the robbers had seen her at the cemetery—and she didn't plan on them seeing her that night either—so she wasn't concerned about being recognized by them.

When her makeup was finished, she familiarized herself with the brace and bit she'd bought that afternoon, closing her eyes and getting the feel of the tool, then placed it and the other items she'd need in a gunnysack. She checked her weapons, stuck her room key in her pocket, and sneaked out of the hotel with her sack.

She rode the mare slowly around the block where the construction site was, noting with a smile as she passed that her wooden crate had been left outside the hardware store, which was closed for the evening. As it grew darker, the streets quieted, and there was little activity in the center of town, save for several saloons on Congress Avenue and Pecan Street, but they were not the rowdy sort that Guy Town sported.

Satisfied that it was dark and quiet enough, she dismounted in front of a small saloon on East Pecan, a half block away from the hardware store. She tied the mare to the post and casually sauntered down the street with her gunnysack. When she reached the crate, which had been left in the shadows next to the building, she looked around carefully.

Finding the coast clear, she dragged the crate near the edge of the sidewalk, but still in the shadows away from the street lamp, positioned it just so, then opened the top and climbed in.

It was blacker than a bear's mouth inside, but Amanda dared not strike a match or light the stub of a candle in her sack unless it was absolutely necessary. Passersby would wonder at light coming through the cracks of a crate. Instead, she took five deep breaths and blew them out slowly. Then she removed the brace and bit from the sack.

She'd used such tools before and knew exactly what to do. She carefully felt for the proper angle, then steadied the bit against the side planks and began cranking. In a short time, several holes punctured the crate all around. She had an excellent view of the barrel where the ransom was to be left, as well as up and down the street and the sidewalk behind her. Though the area wasn't well lit, between moonlight and a gas street lamp nearby, she'd be able to spot the robbers when they came for the money.

Amanda stepped out of her hiding place briefly to scatter the shavings made by the bit and check her handiwork. Knowing that she had quite a while to wait, Amanda considered stretching her legs some, but she decided against it. She deliberated too about taking a short nap, but she dared not. Even though she had gotten a few hours' sleep that afternoon, she was still behind her quota. No, she would stay where she was and remain alert.

She settled inside the crate, leaned her head against the rough boards, and, as she had found it doing frequently these past two days, her mind soon wandered to a certain tall, handsome gentleman. Where, she wondered, was Beau? What was he doing just then?

Beau was snoring.

Bone weary from lack of sleep the night before, his tail feathers had been drooping badly by the time he returned to the Chicago House with the bag of money. Amanda was already gone.

She was out there somewhere alone. Dressed as a boy and totally vulnerable. He didn't like it. He didn't like it a damned bit, but there wasn't anything he could do about it—short of firing her, and he didn't aim to do that.

He'd checked his pocket watch and saw that he had nearly two hours before it would be time for him to leave the money. He tried pacing for a while, but his foot hurt like hell, so he gave that up and sat down on the bed.

She'd left her dress spread over one side of the mattress. He ran his fingers over the fabric. It was as soft as her lips, as smooth as her skin. He leaned back against the headboard, pulled the garment closer to him, and rubbed his cheek against the silk.

It carried her scent.

He could almost imagine her there on the bed beside him, almost feel the warmth of her body next to his. He closed his eyes and took a deep breath and savored that tantalizing fragrance that was hers alone.

Closing his eyes had been a serious mistake.

Things had been quiet for several minutes when the two riders passed by. Amanda roused from resting to full alert. She wondered what time it was, but she could only estimate that it was nearing eleven. Beau hadn't arrived to leave the bag yet.

She watched the two men stop in front of the saloon where her horse was tied. They dismounted, but they didn't go inside. Instead they strolled back her way, walking in the dusty street instead of on the board sidewalk.

When they drew about even with her, they stopped and one of them trotted across the street to the barrel. Amanda's heart stumbled, then began beating furiously. *Dear Lord, these were the robbers after the ransom, and Beau hadn't delivered it yet!*

Where was he?

The one standing near her whispered loudly, "Hurry up, Boozer."

Boozer pulled his head out of the barrel and whispered back, "It ain't here, Taft."

"It's gotta be there."

"Well, it ain't. You wanna come take a gander fer yourself?"

Suddenly there came the sound of hoofbeats and the clatter of a speeding buggy.

"Hurry, Boozer. Somebody's coming. Git back over here. Quick. Let's git outta sight behind this crate."

Blood drained from Amanda's face as the two scrambled behind her hiding place. She dared not shift to look, lest they discover her. Where the devil was Beau? Where the devil was the money?

The buggy that she'd heard pulled to a stop at the corner construction site. Beau. Thank heavens. As she watched him step down with the bag, she allowed herself a deep, silent breath. As she breathed in relief, she also took in a whiff of foul odor. It smelled as if she were sitting on a dung heap and holding a full spittoon.

"That's the money, Taft," came a bare whisper behind her.

"Shhhh."

The stench grew stronger, permeated the crate, and filled her nostrils. It was more than the odor of ripe manure and old tobacco, though that was a big part of it. Those two reeked of horse and stale sweat and of rank bodies unwashed in years. Her eyes crossed. She pinched her nose and tried to breathe quietly through her mouth, struggling to keep herself from gagging.

Hurry, Beau, hurry, she pleaded silently.

As if he heard her thoughts, Beau climbed back into the buggy and snapped the reins. As soon as he'd rounded the corner, boots shuffled behind the crate.

"Hold yer horses. Wait till he's good gone. Remember last night. Let's jist stay still behind this here crate fer a spell."

He's gone! He's gone! Move! Amanda wanted to shout, but she stayed still as well, forcing herself to endure the stench.

An eon passed.

"Boy, oh boy, it won't be long now till I've got me that senoriter," one whispered.

"Hush up. I'll git the money, and you go git the horses."

"Why don't I git the money, and you git the horses?" the first one whined.

"Dammit, Boozer."

There was a *whop, whop*, and a cloud of fetid dust billowed through the crate's holes and cracks. It tickled Amanda's nose, and she clamped her teeth together and held her nose to keep from sneezing.

"I'm a-goin', Taft. I'm a-goin'."

Amanda watched one man run across the street while the other hurried to the horses. She dared not move yet.

Excitement coursed through her. Before the clock struck twelve this night, she would have captured the robbers and recovered the corpse. The police would have the crooks in jail, and another of her cases would come to a speedy and satisfactory conclusion.

She worked her joints, stirring the circulation and making ready to spring from the crate and follow as soon as they were on their way.

Boozer returned with the horses, and the men mounted. They moved slowly toward Congress Avenue, turning in their saddles to look behind them.

Amanda considered following on foot, but decided against it. As soon as they were out of sight, she ran for her mare. Figuring they were headed for Guy Town again, instead of choosing the same route, she took out fast in the opposite direction, then turned south and circled around by the depot, hoping to draw up ahead of them.

A good move. They came down the avenue slowly, still looking over their shoulders, then turned east toward Guy Town. She gave them a few yards, then nudged her mare into a walk and started whistling "Camptown Races" as she fell in behind them.

The pair stopped in front of a livery stable and turned to watch her. She rode on by and continued whistling. She pulled up at a saloon a few doors away and climbed down. As she unhooked the tin growler from her saddlehorn, she watched them open the stable door.

By the time their horses were through the opening, she'd slipped in as well, hugging a wall and fading into the shadows. Before they could drop the bar, she had her gun out and pointed at them.

"Hold it right there, boys," she said, moving into the dim lantern light. "I'm a Pinkerton agent, and if you move, I'll drop you where you stand."

"Why, he's jist a kid," the taller one drawled, going for his gun.

Amanda pulled the trigger, taking a chunk out of his arm.

The other one threw up his hands. "I give up. I give up. I ain't got no gun." She recognized Boozer's voice.

"On the ground, facedown, both of you. Now."

Boozer dropped down immediately. Taft held his arm. "But I'm bleedin' somethin' awful."

"I just creased you, but the next one will be through your heart. On the ground. Hands behind you."

He dropped to the ground.

Amanda quickly manacled their wrists, then bound their feet with rope she found in the stable. "Where's the corpse?" she asked as she made the last knot.

"I don't know nothin' about no corpse," Taft said.

Amanda stuck the muzzle of her gun against Boozer's ear. "Where's the body?"

"It's in the shed out back," he said quickly.

"Who else is here?"

"Nobody," Boozer said, his voice cracking. "Nobody. Swear to God."

She lit another lantern and looked around. Satisfied that he'd told the truth, she picked up the bag of money and went to the back.

⌐ Ten ⌐

To hell with his sore foot, Beau thought. He paced. He'd been waiting in the stable for over an hour, impatient for Amanda to make it home and cursing himself for every kind of lop-eared mule he could think of. He may have ruined everything by falling asleep in that hotel, clutching Amanda's dress like some cow-eyed boy.

He couldn't believe that he'd pulled such a dumb-fool stunt. If that door hadn't slammed down the hall in the hotel, he'd probably still be asleep. As it was, he'd been fifteen minutes late with the money. What had gotten into him lately? Seemed like he'd stepped into every pile in the corral since Amanda arrived.

She probably thought he was a bumbling fool who didn't have sense enough to track a wagon through a mud puddle. And it was more than stung male pride talking. He wanted her to think well of him. More than that, he wanted her to look up to him. A woman couldn't be attracted to a man she didn't respect.

He should be out there taking care of her instead of waiting here and wearing a rut in the floor.

God almighty, what a predicament. He slammed his fist into his palm. Ten minutes. He'd wait another ten minutes, and if she wasn't back, he was going to start scouring Austin for her.

He was about to saddle a horse when he heard the door creak open. "Amanda?" he whispered.

"Yes."

Relief broke out all over him, and he grabbed her around the waist. He was about to kiss her, buck teeth and all, when she pushed away.

"We don't have time for this. I captured the robbers and found the corpse. Here's the money bag."

"You captured them? Dear God, were you hurt? Where are they?"

"Of course I'm not hurt. They're tied up in Jenkins's Livery Stable down in Guy Town. It's on Live Oak Street, a few doors down from the Pink Feather Saloon."

"*Guy Town?* You've been in *Guy Town* alone? My God, Amanda, don't you know—"

"Beau, button your lip for a minute. I'm perfectly all right, but one of the robbers got nicked."

"*Nicked?* Like shot? My God—"

"Hush! It's nothing serious. I started to get the police and have them thrown in jail, then I realized that as soon as I did, the news would be out, and you can bet your last dollar that some nosy reporter like Edwin P. Brown will get wind of it. I figured that I'd better check with you before I did anything about them. Too, we need to get your Uncle Angus in the ground before morning, and for that, we'll need some help."

"Right. Did you get anything out of the robbers? Was anyone else involved?"

"We'll discuss that later. Who can help us bury the body?"

"Morris is out, but I'll roust Harve and Frank. They can help."

"Good. Bring shovels and a lantern. I'll go back and hitch up the hay wagon to carry the coffin to the cemetery. And Beau, don't tell the men who I am. Just call me Pete."

"Amanda—" he started, but she was gone before he got the words out. That woman was going to have him gray before his time.

He went next door to Estelle and Frank's house first. Everybody seemed to be asleep but Ellie. She was sitting on the back porch, her nightgown tucked under her toes, eating an apple.

"Ellie, it's after midnight. Why aren't you in bed?"

"I'm a somniact, remember? I'm not sleepy. Want an apple?"

"No, thanks, honey. I need to talk to your daddy. Would you go get him for me?"

"I think he's still meeting."

"Meeting?"

"Uh-huh. He went to a meeting, and I don't think he's back yet." She took another big chomp of her apple.

"Would you check for me? It's important."

"Okay." Ellie jumped up and ran inside.

In a few minutes Estelle came out, blurry-eyed and clutching a robe around her. "Frank's not home. He went to some kind of meeting. The Odd Fellows, maybe? Or was it the tax committee? I forget. Is something wrong?"

"No. We just needed him to man a shovel."

"A shovel?" She shook her head, as if to clear it. "Do you mean—"

"We have some work to do before morning," Beau

said, glancing meaningfully at Ellie, who stood beside her mother. "Tell Frank we're sorry to have missed him, but we found everything just fine."

"Found everything?" Estelle asked. "You found Uncle—"

"Everything. We'll discuss details later. I have to hurry."

"Mama, was something lost?" Ellie said.

"No, dear, go inside."

Beau hurried home to wake Harve. He met Aunt Katie just inside the door and explained briefly what had happened before he rapped on Harve's door.

Harve offered to bring along two men to help. "They're big fellows, and they can be trusted to keep their yaps shut for a fiver."

While Harve was dressing, Beau went upstairs and changed into work clothes. Aunt Katie caught him on the way down.

"Where's Amanda?" she asked.

"Why, she's asleep in her room," Beau replied, winking.

Aunt Katie nodded. "I figured as much."

As soon as Amanda had hitched the team of mules to the hay wagon, she went to where the pair of malodorous robbers still lay tied and manacled. Knowing that Boozer was more likely to spill what he knew than Taft, she removed the gag from Boozer's mouth.

"You have one last chance to talk. The police will be here shortly to take you to jail, and I doubt that you'll ever get out. Who put you up to kidnapping Angus Blessing?"

"Kid, please don't send us to jail. I'd go crazy locked up." He was wild-eyed and weepy. "I've told you and told you what I know. We don't know nothin' else. I'll swear on my mama's sainted head that we don't know her name and never did see her good. She always stuck to the shadders and had one of them thangs on her hat that covered up her face."

"But it was a woman?"

Boozer nodded, and she stuffed the gag back in his mouth. A woman? The first person that popped into Amanda's mind was Fanny Campbell, Angus's mistress, or one of Fanny's girls. But she knew better than to jump to conclusions. It could be anybody using a woman as a go-between to preserve anonymity. One thing she was certain of, the two men trussed up on the floor hadn't masterminded the operation. She'd never encountered two dumber, dirtier pieces of scum than that pair.

A few minutes later there was a rapping at the door. Amanda lifted the bar and opened the big doors for four men on horseback. Beau, Harve, and two burly men she didn't recognize dismounted.

"Pete," Beau said, nodding to her. "Where is it?"

"Back through there." She thumbed over her shoulder.

Harve nodded to her as well. Neither he nor the two men with them gave Boozer and Taft more than a disinterested glance. They followed her to the back shed.

After the rest of the hay was forked away, the four men lifted the casket from its icy nest and carried it to the hay wagon. Nobody said a word as it was secured on the bed.

When Amanda climbed onto the seat, Beau climbed up as well. He took the reins from her. "I'll drive, Pete. Why don't you stay here?"

"Nope. I'm going."

Beau muttered a curse. "Harve, get the doors."

With the three riders bringing up the rear, the rickety hayrack bumped along the Guy Town street, taking Angus Blessing to his second burial.

When the last shovelful of dirt was tossed on the mound, Beau leaned on his handle and mopped his face with his handkerchief.

"Seems fittin' we should say something," Harve said.

"Have at it," Beau told him.

They finally decided on saying the Lord's Prayer in unison. Hats off and heads bowed, they stood in the lantern light around the fresh grave. When they had finished, one of Harve's friends began singing "Auld Lang Syne."

The crickets and tree frogs quieted as the rich tenor strains lilted across the grounds and among the gravestones. What might have been amusing, wasn't. Chill bumps raced over Amanda's body, and tears stung her eyes from the poignant beauty of the song and the gifted, emotion-laden voice of the singer.

When the last echo died, Harve said, "Th-thank you, Boyle."

Boyle nodded and crammed his hat on. Beau handed each man a half eagle. Harve tied the lantern and the shovels on his horse, and the three helpers left.

Beau helped Amanda into the wagon and took the reins. If he was tired before, he was half dead then. "I could use some sleep. How about you?"

"About two weeks' worth ought to do it." She stretched, then pulled out her teeth and stuck them in her pocket.

He grinned. "Lord, those things are ugly. You're the

only woman I know who looks better without her false teeth."

She laughed. "Thank you—I think."

"Tell me what you found out from those two back at the livery stable."

"Not much really. The night before your Uncle Angus was buried, a woman showed up at the livery stable very late one night. She wore a veil and kept to the shadows so that they couldn't see her well, and she spoke in whispers to disguise her voice. They couldn't even tell if she was young or old. She offered them five hundred dollars each for their part in the kidnapping, which was basically following her orders. She was supposed to show up after they picked up the money tonight, but she didn't. I'm afraid that she might have heard the shot I fired, and it scared her off. I regret that I didn't apprehend her as well."

"I'm glad that you weren't hurt."

"There wasn't much chance of that," Amanda said. "I'm a crack shot and certainly more than a match for those reeking bumblers. I don't know how they stand each other. We have to decide now whether to hand them over to the police or not."

"I've been thinking about that," Beau said. "The best thing to do might be to put the fear of God into them and run them out of town."

"If you don't want anyone to know what happened to your uncle, I agree."

As the wagon bumped and creaked along the lonely road, an owl hooted somewhere in the distance and the tree frogs were back to their shrill song. The moonlight cast silvery pools on the hills, and the air held the sweet scents of spring.

It was a perfect night to be courting a beautiful woman. Perfect. And the beautiful woman was sitting beside him. The only thing was, every time he looked her way he saw a freckle-faced boy, and worse, he was so damned tired he couldn't think of anything except falling into bed—alone.

He snapped the reins again, but the mules only seemed to go one speed. Slow.

When they finally reached the livery stable, Amanda hopped down and opened the doors for the wagon to pass through, then closed them.

She heard Beau curse, and her eyes went immediately to the spot where they'd left Boozer and Taft. "They're gone!"

"I know," Beau said. "Worse, they took my horse. And yours."

❦ Eleven ❧

It was Amanda's turn to curse, and Beau's brows went up when he heard the colorful phrases she uttered. She hurled a broken manacle against a wall, and the loud crack set the horses to snorting and shifting in their stalls. She muttered some more and stomped around as if she were killing a nest of stinging scorpions.

"I can't believe that I did something so stupid," she said, still fuming. "Look at this, just look at this." She held up a handful of cut rope, shook it under his nose, then threw it down. "I'm an idiot!"

"Whoa," Beau said, putting his arms around her. "Don't be so hard on yourself. So they got away, so what? We were going to let them go anyhow."

She pushed away. "Not with our horses, we weren't! And they didn't get loose by themselves. Don't you see? They had help. While we were gone, someone cut these ropes and broke open the manacles. That someone is probably the mastermind behind the kidnapping. And I missed capturing the boss." She slapped the heel of her hand against her forehead. "What a fool I am! I've bungled the whole case. I'm acting like an amateur. You

smile in that way you do and get me so flustered that I—"
She clamped her mouth shut.

He couldn't help the grin that stole over his face. "I get
you so flustered that—what?"

"Never mind. If you want me off the case, I understand. Of course, there will be no charge for my services
thus far, and I'll repay the cost of the horses and saddles."

He leaned back against a rail, crossed his arms, and let
the grin go full out. "Forget the horses. I don't give a
damn about a couple of nags. I want to hear some more
about my smile making you flustered."

"No. I mean, I don't know what I meant by that. It's
nothing. I'm tired, and I know that you're exhausted too.
I'll drive you home in the hay wagon."

"What do you mean you'll drive *me* home?" Beau said.
"Aren't you coming?"

"Yes, later. I'll pick up another horse and deliver the
wagon back here. I'd like to poke around here a bit to see
if there are any clues, and I still have to change my
clothes at the hotel."

Beau shook his head. He was worn out, and he could
tell, even with the makeup Amanda wore, that she was
pale and almost past going. "Forget about all that stuff for
tonight. We're going home. Now."

He was tempted to take one of the horses stabled there,
but Texans were funny about folks taking horses without
asking first, and he didn't know which ones were for hire
and which were being boarded for customers. Figuring
the mules were a safe bet, he unhitched the pair and
slipped a halter on one of them. He'd get Harve to return
the animal early and soothe Mr. Jenkins with a gold piece.

He climbed on and held out his hand to her. Amanda swung up behind him.

And so it was that the new heir of the Blessing fortune rode home to the mansion on a bareback mule—a slow bareback mule. Amanda, still in her britches and cap, clung to his waist.

He liked the feeling of her arms around him, of her body pressed to his back—even if she did sit stiff as a preacher's collar. They hadn't gone two blocks when she sighed and he felt her sag against him. He could tell from her position and the warm breath through his shirt that she was asleep.

A strange catch sprang to his throat, his heart filled with tenderness, and he felt a new surge of vigor as the mule plodded along. Amanda would've been incensed to know it—incensed, hell, she would've been spitting barbed wire—but he suddenly felt very protective of her, very . . . proprietary. He'd discovered that the lovely lady agent wasn't always as tough and confident as she led folks to believe. And knowing that she had a chink or two in that armadillo shell around her made him feel like a man again.

Thinking about her getting flustered around him, he grinned. He was glad to know that he wasn't the only one affected and acting peculiar.

Heavy breathing woke her. Amanda cracked one eye and saw Ellie, her elbows propped on the mattress, her chin in her hands, staring at her.

"Are you awake?" Ellie whispered loudly.

"I think so," Amanda mumbled.

"Good. Uncle Beau said he'd tan my hide if I woke you

up. I woke him up, but he didn't tan my hide. He was grouchy. He told me to go soak my head, but Mama said I shouldn't get my hair wet on account of her having one of her awful sick spells and not feeling like putting it in curlers. You have funny freckles. I've never seen your freckles before. Naomi has freckles, but I don't."

Freckles? Amanda frowned. She didn't have—

She swiped the side of her nose with her finger, then squinted at it. Makeup. Oh, dear, she'd gone to bed without cleaning her face. And, come to think of it, she didn't remember going to bed. Or did she? She had a vague memory of Beau carrying her—

Her eyes popped open, and she felt around under the covers. She was alone. But instead of her nightgown, she still wore her boy's shirt and pants. She wiggled her toes. Somebody had removed her boots.

"Are you gonna get up now?" Ellie asked. "You missed breakfast. It was a looooong time ago. We didn't have buns today. We had eggs. And ham. And biscuits. With butter and honey. Naomi had blackberry jelly, but I don't like blackberry jelly. I like honey."

Amanda's stomach grumbled. She was starving. "Me too. Think there might be one biscuit left?"

"I'll go see. Want me to bring you some coffee? I asked Uncle Beau if he wanted some coffee, and he said he liked hot coffee and wild women and go away."

"I would love some coffee, Ellie."

She beamed. "I'll try to hurry, but I'll be very careful."

As soon as the door closed behind the little girl, Amanda threw back the covers and got up. Her hair was still braided, but it had been loosed of its pins, and her wig and cap were on the chest with her jacket covering them. Her boots were under the bed.

She quickly stripped and stashed her boy's clothing in her trunk, donned a robe, and sat down at the dressing table. Her makeup—what there was left of it—was a mess. She washed away all the traces of her disguise, then unbraided her hair and massaged her scalp.

She was brushing her hair when a knock came at the door. "Come in," she called.

The door opened and Ellie poked her head in. "It's me. I was quick because Lucy helped carry it upstairs. She didn't slosh hardly a bit. Here's a tray with some coffee and a biscuit with butter and honey. And ham. Mrs. Kilgore said to ask if you wanted anything else, but it's only an hour until lunch. We're having chicken and dumplings. Grandma said I could stay and eat some. It's my favorite thing besides chocolate cake. I helped roll out the dough. Do you like chicken and dumplings?"

"I adore chicken and dumplings." Amanda put down her brush to take the small tray from Ellie and set it on the dressing table. After she sipped from the cup, she smiled and said, "Perfect. Thank you."

"You're welcome. Your hair is so pretty." Ellie's small hand stroked the dark length that was crinkled from braiding. "Can I brush it? Mama lets me brush her hair sometimes. I'll be very careful."

Amanda smiled and handed her the brush. "I know you will."

While Ellie brushed, Amanda ate her late breakfast. "Is your uncle up yet?" she asked the child.

"I don't think so. Aunt Katie said he was grouchy because he was out very late and didn't get much sleep so he's sleeping a long time today. Are you gonna yell at him?"

"I hadn't planned to."

"Sometimes Mama yells at Daddy when he stays out very late. She yelled last night something awful, and she cried. She said how could she ever hold up her head in public if people knew—"

"Ellie, dear, conversations between Mama and Daddy are private. I don't think you should repeat what they said."

"That's what Aunt Katie said too, but I forgot. She said families have secrets sometimes and I shouldn't go blabbing stuff to everybody I meet. What happened to your freckles?"

"Oh, those weren't freckles. That was a special cream to make my complexion soft and pretty. Did it work, do you think?" Amanda examined her face in the mirror.

Ellie stroked her cheek gently, then said seriously, "It worked. Want me to take your tray downstairs?"

"That would be lovely, thank you." Amanda held open the door while Ellie left walking very slowly, the empty cup rattling in its saucer.

Hmmm, she couldn't help but wonder why Estelle had been yelling at Frank. What had he been doing to all hours that would cause her public shame? It sounded as if his meetings might be more than sincere civic concern. Did he, like Morris, have a lady friend?

This family was an interesting one, and it certainly had its share of secrets. Her inquisitive nature made her itch to uncover every one of them. She'd been sorely tempted to let Ellie tell all, but she had too many scruples against such methods of obtaining information. Too, she needed to talk to Beau before she proceeded. Her unprofessional behavior last night may have cost her the case.

Beau yawned and stretched, savoring the last vestiges of a very erotic dream of Amanda. He was still hard from the images undulating through his head.

Every moment he spent with the lovely Amanda convinced him that he wanted to keep her around for a long time. She fascinated him; she excited him; she made him think about the future. And he'd never been one to give the future much thought.

His blood had run cold last night when she'd talked about quitting the case. He didn't want her to quit. Not that he really gave a damn about who was behind the kidnapping. Uncle Angus was replanted; his mother and sisters were saved from embarrassment. As far as he was concerned, that was it, but Amanda seemed to think that discovering the mastermind was important. If she was game to dig around and try to find out, he'd be more than happy to foot the bill.

He crossed his arms behind his head and smiled as he stared at the ceiling. Yep, he was all in favor of finding the mastermind. He didn't figure she had a snowball's chance in hell of uncovering the culprit, especially after those two hightailed it from the livery stable, but the investigation ought to keep her around a while.

One thing he'd have to insist on: they'd have to keep up their pretense of being engaged. They'd have to do all the things that engaged couples did. They'd have to go picnicking and dancing and walking in the park . . . romantic things. And fiancés were expected to steal a kiss or two.

His smile widened. Yes, he was beginning to like the notion of being engaged to Amanda.

There was a knock at the door. "Beaumont?"

"Yes, Aunt Katie?" he called.

"Come quick. There's a policeman downstairs, and Harve is about to faint."

⌒ Twelve ⌒

Beau threw on some clothes and took the stairs two at a time. He saw a policeman standing in the foyer with Harve, who looked as if he might pass out at any minute. His mother, Aunt Katie, and Ellie stood there as well. He wouldn't have been surprised to find Lucy and Mrs. Kilgore with an ear pressed to the door.

The policeman, dressed in a uniform with sergeant's stripes on his sleeve, looked stern. Aunt Katie stood beside Harve and scowled while Maud wrung her lace-trimmed handkerchief and looked as if she might burst into tears if anyone so much as coughed. Little Ellie was mute for once as she glanced from one person to the other.

Since the trouble in his younger days, Beau had shied away from the law whenever possible. Just seeing this policeman in the hall tied a knot in his belly, but a faint heart never filled a flush, so he slowed his pace, put on his best face, and ambled to the group.

"Good morning, Sergeant. I'm Beaumont Chandler. What's going on here?"

The officer and Harve both started to talk at the same time, but Harve was stammering so badly that he couldn't string two words together that made any sense.

"Harve's no thief!" Aunt Katie shouted, banging her cane.

Maud looked as if she might keel over in a swoon. Ellie was bug-eyed.

"Sergeant," Beau said, "let's step into my study and see if we can't get this mess straightened out. Ladies, if you'll excuse us?" He escorted the men into the study and closed the door. He poured a shot of bourbon and offered it to Harve. "Drink this and sit down over there." To the policeman, who quickly identified himself as Sergeant Keethley, he said, "Tell me what the problem is."

As the story unraveled, it seemed that Mr. Jenkins, the owner of the livery stable, had arrived that morning to find the place unlocked, a mule and his two employees missing along with a cash box he kept hidden behind a board in the wall. A bunch of sliced-up rope littered the floor. There was also a lot of wet hay and ice in the shed behind the stable. It all seemed mighty peculiar, and he sent for the police.

The sergeant was trying to figure out what happened when Harve showed up with the mule. "We questioned him about his part in whatever went on at the stable, but we couldn't get anything out of him that made a lick of sense, Mr. Chandler. And he was stuttering and stammering something awful."

"Ah," Beau said, smiling. "I think I can shed some light on things. Is this the livery stable down from the Pink Feather Saloon?"

"Yes, sir, that's the one."

The deference in the officer's tone tickled Beau, and made him stand a bit taller. This was one of the benefits of being Uncle Angus's heir and living in a mansion. A pile of money would command respect every time.

"Last night," Beau told him, "my friend and I left our horses with two men at the livery stable while we"—he winked—"tended to some business. When we returned, the men and our horses were gone."

"They stole 'em, you mean?"

Beau shrugged. "That I couldn't say for sure, but that's what we figured. My friend and I borrowed one of the mules to get home. Harve, who is employed here, went to return the mule and see if the men turned up with our mounts. They were valuable animals."

"Looks like them two skedaddled with your horses and the cash box—though I can't quite figure how the ropes come to be cut up like that."

"Beats me." Beau shrugged. "Sounds very strange." And he was truthful when he said that. The whole tale would've sounded even more peculiar if Amanda hadn't thought to stick the busted manacles in her pocket before they left the livery stable.

"Could you describe them, sir?"

Beau described the horses, the gear, and the men. "I think I heard one of the men call the other one Taft."

"That's them, all right," Sergeant Keethley said, "a mangier pair you'll never want to meet, but Jenkins is tight-fisted, and they worked cheap. I guess he learned his lesson all right. Looks like now he owes you for two horses."

Beau smiled. "Seems a shame to hold him responsible. Tell Mr. Jenkins that I'll stop by later today, and maybe we can work something out."

"That's right neighborly of you, Mr. Chandler." The

policeman tucked the notebook into his pocket. "And my condolences on the loss of your uncle. He made a fine brew. I'm right partial to Blessing beer, and I've hoisted a few at the Pink Feather myself. And at the Wild Ox—I believe that was one of Mr. Blessing's saloons too."

"Glad to hear that, Sergeant." Beau clapped him on the back. "Next time you're in, tell the barkeep I said to give you a couple on the house. My compliments."

"Thank you, sir."

Beau escorted the officer to the door. When the policeman had gone, Aunt Katie and Maud were eager for an explanation. Amanda came downstairs before he launched into a modified version of the truth.

"Ah, good morning, dear," he said, kissing her cheek. "Sleep well?"

"Very well, thank you," Amanda said. "Sorry I was such a lazybones this morning. Was that a policeman I saw just leaving?"

"Yes. Seems that a pair of thieves working for a livery stable here in town stole two horses that Harve and I left there. They ran off with the owner's cash box and the horses in the middle of the night. Harve was real upset about it."

Maud perked up. "All that was about stolen horses? I thought—"

"No. The police don't suspect a thing." Beau glanced down at Ellie, then added, "You might want to put some flowers on Uncle Angus's grave later today."

Maud perked up even more. "You mean—?"

"I mean everything is back in its rightful place—except for the horses." He winked and offered his arm to

Amanda. "I understand that we're having chicken and dumplings. They're my favorite."

"Mine, too," said Ellie.

"Mine, too," said Amanda gaily as she slipped her arm through Beau's.

As soon as they could gracefully escape the luncheon table, Beau and Amanda left to "take care of a bit of business," he told the other ladies. They took the buggy first to the office to stash the unused ransom.

"I get edgy carrying around this much cash," Beau said as he placed stacks of bills in the big safe. "Frank can put it back in the bank on Monday."

"Where is Frank today?"

"He had business in San Antonio—something about a land deal. He should be back late this evening or tomorrow morning."

"Frank certainly is gone a lot," Amanda said. "He's hardly ever home. Not only does he keep long hours at the office, but he stays out very late at all sorts of meetings, and I don't think your sister is very happy about that."

"Really?"

"It seems so, but I hate to pry into their lives unless it seems relevant to the case. Which brings up another point. Since we've recovered your uncle's body, are you interested in pursuing the case?"

"Absolutely," Beau said quickly. "We can keep up our 'engagement' while you poke around for clues. I think it might take a spell to flush out the boss of the scheme, don't you?" He struggled to keep a smile off his face.

"Not necessarily. As I've said, I'm quite a competent

detective. Though I'll admit that with no more information than the pair from the stable gave me, it might take a bit longer than usual. I'll get on it right away. There are several people I want to interview, and I need to go through Mr. Blessing's papers."

Beau's smile faded. "Oh, I don't think there's any hurry. You deserve a couple days' rest. I was thinking that after we pick up your things from the hotel, we might have a dish of ice cream and then go for a drive in the country—or maybe a boat ride on the river. Do you like strawberry? I'm right partial to it myself."

"Oh, the hotel. That reminds me. I'd like to make arrangements to keep the room there. If I'm to continue the case, I'll need another base of operations, especially if I want to use disguises or interview unsavory sorts." She smiled. "Somehow I can't picture your mother appreciating a visit from Fanny Campbell or one of her girls."

Beau laughed. "That does strain the imagination. Keeping the room sounds like a good idea. We can stop by, and I'll tend to it. Told them last time it was for my sister."

"And we need to drop by the livery stable as well. I'd like to ask Mr. Jenkins a few questions."

"And then we'll get some ice cream."

She smiled. "And then we'll get some ice cream."

Amanda closed her eyes, let the creamy coldness bathe her tongue, and savored the sweet vanilla scent and taste. "Heaven," she sighed. "Absolute heaven. I haven't had ice cream in ages. And I've always loved it. This is especially delicious."

"The strawberry is better."

"This vanilla is excellent." She spooned another bite

into her mouth and let it melt slowly to relish the wonder-ful sensation.

Except for a family of four in the corner, they were the only patrons in the parlor on Congress Avenue. They sat at a small marble table by the window surrounded by cool, confectionery aromas that mingled into a distinctive blend, a scent that stirred old memories. Memories, years old, of a naive girl sampling the wonders of an entire new world flashed through her mind. Had she ever been truly that young and naive?

"Where are you?" Beau asked.

She startled. "I beg your pardon?"

"You seemed a million miles away."

Amanda smiled. "I suppose I was. I was remembering the first time I had real ice cream—not snow flavored with honey or cane syrup, but real ice cream."

"And when was that?"

"When I was sixteen."

"You didn't have ice cream until you were *sixteen*?"

She shook her head. "My family lived on an isolated farm, and we were poor. When we did go into town, there wasn't money for such frivolous things as candy or ice cream. My father almost had a fit when the grocer gave my little sister and me a lemon drop. He made us put them back and go sit in the wagon. Called them the devil's en-ticements. When my sister cried about it, he beat her. And when I tried to shield her, he beat us both."

"My God!"

Amanda startled. "I'm sorry. I didn't mean to drag up ancient unpleasantries." She smiled. "I've always adored lemon drops. And ice cream. After my first dish of vanilla, I fell in love. I ate ice cream at least twice a week for months."

"Your father sounds like a real bast— Sorry."

"Actually, in the true sense of the word, I believe that his parents were married. In the other sense, you're right. He was a harsh and uncompromising man, a preacher, if you can believe it. He sermonized frequently about God's rules and retribution. He never recognized God's love."

"And your mother?"

"Spiritless. Submissive. Resigned, I suppose."

"Do you ever see them?" Beau asked.

She swallowed the lump that came at the odd times when she allowed herself to dwell on the past. "No. They're all gone now. Where are Estelle and the girls today?"

"There was some program at the school, I believe. Here, try a bite of my strawberry and then tell me that your vanilla is better." Grinning, he held the filled spoon to her lips.

She tried to decline, but he insisted, teasing her lips apart.

Finally she relented and opened her mouth. He slipped the spoon inside, then pulled it out slowly when he was satisfied that she had the sample on her tongue.

"Well?" he asked.

"It's quite good."

"Better than your vanilla?"

"Well, I wouldn't go so far as to say that."

He scooped another spoonful and held it to her lips. "Try again."

"Really, Beau—"

In went the bite of strawberry. Out came the empty

spoon. He scooped another from his dish and held it to her mouth.

"Beau—"

In went the spoon. He winked, and she got tickled as she tried to swallow. She put her fingers over her lips and waved him off with the other hand.

"I'm going to keep feeding you strawberry until you admit that it's better."

"Never!"

He touched a dab to her nose. "On your nose, on your chin, or in your mouth?"

"Beau!" She wiped the spot away.

He shrugged and grinned like a mischievous boy. Laughing, she said, "The strawberry is excellent. Try my vanilla." She offered him a spoonful in the same way he'd coaxed her.

Instead of taking it into his mouth, his tongue flicked out and licked across the small, sweet mound, took it inside to savor, then flicked out again. She watched his tongue, entranced for a moment, then she made the mistake of glancing up to his eyes.

His eyes were a glorious shade of fiery emerald touched with lighter hues like the color of spring willow trees reflected in water. They captured hers and held her as surely as if she'd been manacled to him.

Something passed between them, something old and mysterious and exciting. She tried to look away, but this thing she felt was too potent, too tantalizing.

So tight was the constriction in her chest that she could barely breathe. She felt a rippling sensation rush through her breasts and a throbbing ache begin lower in her body. Dear Lord, what was happening to her?

"Don't say you don't feel it this time too," Beau whispered.

Knowing that she was treading on dangerous ground, she opened her mouth to deny her feelings, but the words stuck in her throat.

"You folks want another dish of ice cream?" the proprietor said.

The spell was broken, and Amanda looked away. "No, thank you, but that was delicious." She stood quickly and gathered her things. "We need to get on with our errands." Feeling flustered and a bit panicked, she hurried to the door, leaving Beau behind to pay their bill.

Amanda stood on the sidewalk and sucked in five deep breaths. It didn't help.

She climbed in the buggy and took in another five, closing her eyes and letting the air out slowly, trying to control her emotions and calm down.

She only succeeded in making herself dizzy.

Oh, drat, what was she to do? There was no way to deny it. She was totally smitten—and with a client, of all things. Very unprofessional. Very. Mr. Pinkerton would have a fit if he knew how she was carrying on in Texas. Worse, he'd have her job.

She was simply going to have to get hold of herself and the situation. She could handle this. She could. Stiffen her backbone, and stiffen her resolve: that's what she'd have to do.

Beau climbed into the buggy. He cocked an eyebrow and looked amused. "Armor back in place?"

"Armor? I don't know what you mean?"

He chuckled. "Amanda, Amanda, Amanda. What am I going to have to do to get you to admit it?"

She bit her tongue and stared straight ahead. He snapped the reins, but he only drove a block before he stopped again.

"Wait," he said. "I'll be right back."

He hurried into a confectioner's. Why, she hardly gave a thought. Her mind was a muddle of other concerns. She tried deep breathing again. Ten breaths this time.

She stopped at eight when she began to see spots.

Beau came out of Lamm's carrying a paper-wrapped parcel. He handed the heavy item to her and climbed into the buggy.

"What is this?" she asked.

"A present for you."

"A present for me? What's the occasion?"

"It's Saturday." He chuckled, then leaned over and kissed her nose. When she drew back, he merely looked very innocent. "You still had a speck of ice cream there. Open it." He motioned to the package.

She couldn't recall the last time anyone had given her a gift, especially for no reason. She tore off the wrappings and found a large jar. Inside were—

"Lemon drops," he said, grinning. "I bought all they had."

Her heart melted. It simply melted.

Thirteen

On Sunday morning, the entire Blessing clan took up two pews at the First Presbyterian Church. Everyone was there, even Morris, who hobbled in on crutches, and Frank, who sat with the choir and did a brief solo during the offering collection.

"I didn't realize that Frank was such an excellent singer," Amanda said to Estelle as they were leaving the church behind the rest of the crowd.

"Oh, yes, he has a fine voice. He sings around the house all the time. I suspect that's where Louise and Helen get their talent. Certainly not from me. I sound like a cat with a mashed tail. You sing a lovely alto yourself, Amanda. I noticed during the hymn."

"Thanks," Amanda said as she stepped into the carriage that Beau was driving. "We'll see you at the picnic."

With Judith beside him, Morris was already seated in the rear, his foot propped on a plump tasseled pillow. Aunt Katie rode with them as well. The rest of the family was apportioned into another carriage and a buggy.

They stopped by home only long enough for the ladies to change their frocks and shoes for clothing more suitable for an outing and to pick up the picnic baskets. This was the formal spring opening of Blessing Gardens, a park near the Blessing Brewery and the river that boasted a bandstand, picnic tables, a small zoo, areas for games, and swings for the children.

As soon as they arrived, the children began to scatter, with Estelle calling after Helen to watch Ellie. Harve started setting up a croquet course, and Beau and Frank, shirtsleeves rolled up and ties loosened, launched into a game of horseshoes.

The day couldn't have been more perfect. The sky was cloudless and a dazzling blue, and the temperature was moderate beneath the canopy of large live oak trees. A slight breeze stirred the corners of the tablecloth that Judith and Amanda spread over a long picnic table; it carried the hum and bustle from other families setting up nearby and was punctuated by shrieks of children's laughter and shouted greetings.

All the women helped unpack the platters of fried chicken and pork chops, potato salad, pickled cucumbers and beets, corn relish, and onions. Then there were biscuits and rolls and cakes and pies.

"I've never seen so much food," Amanda said as she set a stack of plates on one end of the table.

Estelle said, "Oh this is nothing. Later in the summer we'll have fish fries and cook mounds of fish and potatoes in iron washpots, and there will be barbecues when whole sides of beef are roasted over coals. We'll boil huge pots of corn on the cob and new potatoes."

"Yes," Judith added gaily. "And there will be shaved ice and watermelon and an organ grinder for the children. I've always loved special Saturdays or Sundays in the gardens."

"Blessing Gardens is an unnecessary expense," Morris said gruffly. He sat on a bench like a great warty toad, scowling, with his foot propped on the same tasseled pillow. "I never could understand why Angus persisted in sponsoring it."

Amanda glanced up at Judith, who opened her mouth, then quickly closed it, her shoulders sagging.

"I'll tell you why, Morris," Aunt Katie announced. "He did it because it was good advertising for the Blessing name—and because I threatened to pitch a hissy fit if he closed it down." She banged a spoon sharply on the side of a lemonade jar. "Beaumont, round up the children. It's time for victuals."

Amanda and Beau, their plates filled, strolled down to the river. Beau spread out a blanket he'd brought along. He helped Amanda sit down, then handed her a plate and sat beside her.

"This is wonderful," Amanda said. "If I stay in Austin very much longer, I'll be able to hire on as the fat lady at the circus."

"If you'll stay, I'd chance that."

She laughed. "But I wouldn't. Why is it that food always tastes better outside?"

"I'm not sure. Maybe it's something in the air. I know that no coffee is ever as good as the kind made over a campfire."

"Have you done that often? Had coffee from a camp-fire, I mean."

He nodded. "There was a stretch of time after I got out of prison that I knocked around a lot. I even signed on for a hitch to drive a herd of longhorns north. I soon discovered that I wasn't cut out to be a cowboy. Eating trail dust and nursemaiding a thousand ornery head of cattle from a saddle is a hard way to make a living."

"I agree. What else did you do before you became a saloon owner?"

"I tried my luck prospecting for a time, and I worked on a steamboat on the Sabine River. Didn't like that much, either. I found out that I was likelier to find gold and silver at the poker table than in the ground, and I preferred being a passenger on the steamboats to shoveling coal for them, especially when I was danged near killed when one of them blew up with me."

"Were you injured?" Amanda asked.

"I got a scrape or two, but I was lucky. Real lucky. The other men down there died. To this day, I'm not sure how I got out alive."

"Is that where your scar came from?"

His fingers traced the line on his face. "Nope. I got that in a knife fight in New Orleans. A couple of fellows decided to relieve me of my night's winnings on my way back to my hotel. It really wasn't all that much, but I was determined that they weren't going to have it." He rubbed at the scar. "Ugly thing, isn't it? I'd of been better off giving them the money."

"Ugly?" She smiled. "Oh, I don't know. I've always thought scars were . . . intriguing."

He grinned. "A lady once told me she thought it was sensual."

Her brows went up, and she almost choked on a bite of chicken.

"You don't agree?"

"I—I didn't say that. It's not . . . unattractive." She felt her face heat, and she busied herself spreading apple butter on a piece of biscuit.

Beau leaned forward and opened his mouth. Without a thought she popped the bite of biscuit into his mouth. Unsettled by her impulsive and intimate gesture, she drew back, but he captured her hand and licked a dab of butter from her fingers.

"Mmmmm. Delicious." He smiled in that charming way he had.

She set her plate aside and leaned back against the trunk of a tree. She plucked an Indian paintbrush growing at the edge of the blanket and began toying with the orange flower. Beau stretched out and rested his head in her lap as if it were the most natural thing in the world.

She didn't object. In fact, she rather welcomed the intimacy, which seemed perfectly natural for some unfathomable reason.

He laced his fingers over his middle and closed his eyes. Amanda didn't say a word, but there was a definite flutter in her stomach as she looked down at him.

His lashes were long and thick and curly. They were darker than his hair, as was his mustache. She touched the flower lightly to the scar on his jaw and traced its path. Her gaze trailed over the curve of his lips, and the flower moved to follow as she remembered how those lips felt on hers. Soft and hot and—

They suddenly curled up at the corners, and she was aghast to find his eyes open and him grinning at her.

"You thinking about what I'm thinking about?" he asked.

"Certainly not!"

He chuckled. "How'd you know what I was thinking about?"

She felt embarrassment heat her throat and travel upward. "What *were* you thinking about?"

"Dessert." He licked his lips as if deliberately taunting her. "Want some?"

She was positive that he didn't have food on his mind, but she chose to ignore him, and said innocently, "I can't eat another bite."

"Are you sure? Not even ice cream?"

"What ice cream?"

He sat up and glanced toward the picnic area. "The ice cream that Harve is cranking now. He's signaling that it's my turn to give it a few spins. Want to help? If you crank for a while, I'll let you lick the dasher." He grinned. "It's vanilla."

"I'll help."

Laughing, he pulled her to her feet, and they joined Harve, who was chipping ice from a block to add to the wooden tub.

Amanda insisted on cranking for a while, then Beau took over the task when it needed more muscle.

"Feels like it's done," Beau said a few minutes later. "Call the kids."

Aunt Katie banged on the empty lemonade jar with a serving spoon. "Ice cream!"

All the girls turned up except Ellie.

"Where's your baby sister?" Estelle asked Helen.

"I don't know," Helen said. "Louise was watching her."

"I was not," Louise said. "Mama told you to watch her."

"I'll find her," Amanda said. "Have your ice cream."

Beau left the dishing up to Harve and joined Amanda in the search for Ellie. They tried the swings first, then the area by the zoo. Actually, it wasn't much of a zoo. There were three monkeys in a large cage and a young camel in a pen. Ellie wasn't around.

At the river, they split up, with Beau going north and Amanda going south. Amanda found the little girl sitting under a tree with a bouquet of wildflowers in her lap and staring out at the water.

"Ah, there you are," Amanda said, kneeling beside her. "We're having ice cream. Want some?"

Ellie shook her head and kept staring out at the water.

"Honey, is something wrong? I've noticed that you've been very quiet today. Do you have a tummy ache?"

The child shook her head again, but a big tear rolled down her cheek. Then another. And another. Amanda pulled Ellie into her lap and hugged her close.

The dam broke and Ellie began sobbing against Amanda's breast. "Helen said I was a damn liar, and Naomi said to keep my silly baby mouth shut. But I'm not a liar. I'm not. I'm not."

Amanda rocked her and made soothing noises and kissed her crown of blonde curls. "Of course you're not."

Beau appeared, looking alarmed. Amanda made a shushing gesture and continued crooning words of comfort to Ellie.

"I don't tell lies," Ellie sobbed, "and I'm not a baby either."

"I know, sweetheart. Why would your sisters say such a thing?"

"Because I told them that Daddy wore rouge and perfume. But I heard Mama say it. He got home awful late last night, and I heard Mama yell about him wearing rouge and reeking of lily of the valley perfume—which was something *she* never wore. And she said she could never hold up her head in public again, and Miss Blodgett had reminded her that the bill for piano lessons was overdue. Naomi said men didn't wear rouge and perfume, and Helen said everyone knows we're rich and I was making up stuff, but I'm not a damn liar," Ellie wailed. "I'm not."

Amanda's eyes met Beau's over the top of Ellie's head. "Of course you're not a liar." She plucked a handkerchief from her pocket. "Dry your tears, sweetheart, and go have some ice cream. Don't mention this to your sisters or anyone else again, and Uncle Beau will talk to your mama and daddy. I'm sure that it was just a silly misunderstanding, and nothing for you to worry about."

"But Mama was awfully upset. I think she had one of her headaches. She sat downstairs in the dark for a long, long time and had to take a lot of her medicine. I picked her some flowers," Ellie said, drawing away, "to make her feel better." She looked down at her lap. "They got squashed."

"Maybe not too bad," Amanda said, helping gather the orange and pink blossoms. "We'll pick some more. Uncle Beau will help, won't you, Uncle Beau?"

"Sure will." He pulled a handful from a nearby clump and offered it to Ellie.

Ellie laughed. "You're not supposed to pull up the roots, silly."

"Oops. My mistake." He grinned. "Show me how to do it."

In a couple of minutes Ellie had a fresh bouquet and

ran off to give the flowers to her mother and have some ice cream.

"You heard?" Amanda asked.

Beau nodded. "Sounds like Frank may have a lady friend on the side too."

"Sounds like it. And why wouldn't Frank be paying his bills? I should think that he has a good salary."

"An oversight, maybe?"

Amanda shrugged. "Perhaps. But Frank doesn't strike me as the sort who makes that kind of mistake, especially a second time. I wonder just how serious his cash shortage is."

Beau's brows went up. "You mean—?"

"I only mean that this bears investigation."

"Surely you can't believe that Frank would be behind Uncle Angus's kidnapping? *Frank?*"

"I've learned through the years that you can't rule out anyone in a case like this."

"But Taft and Boozer said they talked to a woman."

"Maybe it was his lady friend."

Beau shook his head. "Somehow I can't picture Frank with a mistress. He seems too . . . prim."

"I've also learned not to let appearances fool you. You might be shocked. Perfectly ordinary looking people do some very strange things. First, I think we should very quietly look into Frank's finances."

"Shouldn't we just talk to him first?"

"No. If he's guilty of something, alerting him will only give him time to cover his tracks. If he's not, he'll be insulted, and it will cause a family rift. Trust me on this. If things are okay, he'll never know that we suspected him."

"When should we begin?" Beau asked.

"The office is closed today, and Frank is otherwise engaged." Amanda brushed leaves and clinging blossoms from her shirt. "I think now is a perfect time for me to do a bit of snooping."

"For *us*," he said. "I'm going with you."

She sighed. Beaumont Chandler was making this a very difficult case.

⌒ Fourteen ⌒

"I feel like a thief," Beau whispered as he locked the front door of the Blessing offices behind him.

"I can't imagine why," Amanda said. "This is your building, and though I wouldn't invite a band, there's no need to whisper. No one is here." She strode straight for Frank Banks's office, which was locked as well. "Let's see if your master key will fit his door."

It didn't.

"Hmmmm. Very curious," she said. "You might keep watch, just in case."

"In case of what? And how do you propose to get into his office?"

"Let me worry about that." She studied the lock for a moment, then opened the small leather folder she'd brought along and extracted one of the skeleton keys from the tools there. These were precision instruments confiscated from a jewel thief she'd nabbed in St. Louis— not traditional issue from the Pinkerton Agency, which frowned on such practices. It took less than a minute for her to open the lock.

"You're good at that," Beau said, obviously astonished at the speed and ease with which she gained entry.

"Yes, I am." She crossed to the front door, peeked out the shade, then wedged a chair under the knobs. "I don't like to be surprised. This will buy us time in case we have a visitor."

"What are we looking for?" Beau asked as he followed her into Frank's office.

"A ledger with Frank's personal accounts. I doubt that he would keep it at home, though it's possible. We'll keep our fingers crossed that it's here."

She sat down at Frank's large desk with its ornately carved legs and drawers. It was cleared except for a neat stack of papers on one corner, a leather-bound appointment book to one side, and a rather fine silver desk set and blotter—Fabergé, if her eye didn't deceive her—and a handsome collection of crystal inkwells.

Amanda sat in the leather chair for a moment, eyes closed, getting a feel for Frank and his habits. Then she made a quick survey of the desk drawers, opening and closing them quickly, offering only a cursory glance as she headed for the last drawer—the lower left one.

It was locked.

She wasn't surprised. Frank's bearing fairly shouted his predictability. "I think we've found it." She opened her small folder once more.

In less time than the door had taken, the bottom drawer slid open. Inside were several large envelopes and a ledger. She went straight for the ledger and for the most recent entries.

"Hmmm," she said after she'd read for a while.

"Hmmm, what?"

"No wonder the piano teacher hasn't been paid."

"He's in debt?"

"Yes. Up to his eyebrows."

"Hell," Beau said, "that doesn't mean anything. I'm in debt *past* my eyebrows half the time myself. And with six kids to feed and clothe, I'm not surprised that it costs a pretty penny to run his household. Especially with a wife and all those girls to buy geegaws for."

"Geegaws?" Amanda rolled her eyes. "This is a serious amount of debt. Odd, since according to this record, Frank makes an excellent salary, and until about two years ago had nice savings as well. The savings are totally depleted." Amanda flipped back through several pages. "And here's the reason things have changed. Here, here, here." She tapped her finger against several entries as she leafed through the account.

"What?"

"In the past two years there have been several large payments to a 'B.P.' "

"His lady friend, you think?" Beau asked.

"Possibly, but she's certainly expensive if the payments are to her. I need to copy several of these pages so I can study them more carefully when I'm not rushed. Keep an eye out front while I do it."

"If Frank's broke and behind the kidnapping, Estelle is going to be mighty upset if it comes out."

Amanda glanced up. "Do you want to continue the investigation? I can stop now."

Beau studied the ceiling for a moment, then heaved a sigh. "Might as well flush out the fox in the henhouse. I can decide who to tell what later."

Amanda took the ledger into Beau's office and wrote fast and furiously for almost two hours, copying selected sections. When she was finished, her hand felt cramped and her fingers were stained with ink. She blotted the last page and closed the account book.

"I'm finished," she said as she pushed back the desk chair.

"Good. Let's get out of here."

She chuckled. "You'd make a terrible detective. I have to wash my hands and relock everything."

"You're right about me being a lousy detective. Funny, I can raise a hundred-dollar bet holding nothing but a pair of queens and never break a sweat. I can stare down a drunk sailor with a ten-inch blade and me armed with nothing but a stick of stove wood, but this kind of stuff makes me jumpy as a frog in a hot skillet."

Amanda smiled. "I didn't mean to impugn your courage or your masculinity. It's simply that being a detective takes a special kind of disposition. It helps if one has not only steel nerves, but also a curious nature and a dogged determination. I've always found that most agents enjoy encountering a bit of danger now and then. And, of course, it's often rather like acting on the stage."

After depositing the copied pages in a portfolio, she cleaned her hands and returned the ledger to Frank's desk. She itched to go through the other things there, but she was pushing her time limit, and she knew it. Still, she took a moment and fanned quickly through the papers in some of the envelopes. Mostly receipts. She made a couple of mental notes about interesting items that caught her eye, then locked the drawer. She was just pulling the door to Frank's office closed when she heard the unmistakable sound of a buggy, then footsteps on the sidewalk outside.

Beau peeked out the shade. "My God!" he whispered loudly. "It's Frank!"

There wasn't time to relock the door to Frank's office. She quickly pulled it to and ran to the front door where a key was rattling. She shoved the wedged chair aside and threw herself into Beau's arms.

"Kiss me!" she demanded, pulling his head down and grinding herself against him.

Beau didn't hesitate. He wrapped his arms around Amanda and kissed the devil out of her.

Her heart began pounding like a hammer driving rail spikes. The kiss went on and on, stealing her breath, her senses, the strength from her knees. She was only vaguely aware of a stammered apology behind her.

Beau drew his lips away. He glanced over her shoulder and said, "Frank, what can I help you with?"

"I—I just wanted to pick up some papers in my office."

"Pick them up another time," Beau said sharply. "We're busy here."

"Yes, fine. I can see—I mean, excuse me. I'll be running along."

Amanda didn't turn around, but she was sure that Frank was bowing, tipping his hat, and backing out. She bit her lip and rested her forehead against Beau's lapel. As soon as the door closed, her shoulders began to shake, and when she heard footsteps in retreat, she burst into laughter.

"Bravo!" she told Beau as she clapped. "You were magnificent!"

He grinned in a cocky way. "Maybe magnificent is too strong a word, but I wasn't half bad if I do say so myself."

"No, your performance was definitely magnificent."

She gave him a quick kiss on the scar that marked his jaw. "I have to lock Frank's door."

When she turned from her task, she bumped into Beau. His arms went around her. "How about we take up where we left off?" he asked, lowering his face to hers.

How tempting his suggestion was. How very tempting. But she refused to allow herself to give in. She pushed him away, laughed, and said lightly, "Don't confuse acting with something else. We were simply playing a role for Frank's benefit. I think we need to get home. Your mother and aunt will be waiting dinner for us."

"Amanda, dinner isn't for two hours yet."

"Really?" Butterflies filled her stomach, and she began pulling on her gloves hurriedly. "That's good. I'm a bit tired. I'll have a chance to rest a few minutes before I change. And I need to—"

"Amanda."

She glanced up. "Yes?"

Beau was grinning again—and his expression had a definite smugness to it. "You're putting your glove on backward."

"Oh, bother!" She crammed her gloves in her reticule and grabbed the portfolio. "Let's go." She flung open the door and almost ran from the building.

On the way home Beau felt excitement still pumping through his veins. He found himself grinning, then he burst into laughter. "You should have seen Frank's face. His expression was worth a hundred dollars. I thought he was going to break his neck getting out of there." He laughed again.

"Careful," Amanda said.

"Of what?"

"Do you feel wide awake, energized, and a little giddy?"

"Exactly. How did you know?"

She smiled. "I feel the same way. It's the thrill of flirting with danger or pulling off a ruse. You'll have to be careful, you might grow addicted to detecting. I think you might have a talent for it."

"Not me. I'd be gray-haired in six months. Do you really think Frank was behind the kidnapping?"

"I think it's too early to draw conclusions. He's not the only suspect in the family."

"Surely you don't think that Aunt Katie or my mother or my sisters could be involved in such an operation. And Morris tried to stop the kidnappers."

"But he didn't stop them, did he? Perhaps he wanted them to escape. He knew that we'd be watching. Perhaps he acted as he did to throw suspicion off himself. I'm not ready to eliminate any suspects yet. I haven't even completed my accounting of them. I still have to draw up a list of your uncle's enemies—or enemies of the family. That's something you might undertake while I study this information from Frank's ledger. I suspect that your Aunt Katie would be the person to ask."

"Even if she's a suspect herself?" Trying to imagine Aunt Katie as the ringleader of the grave robbers, he smiled and shook his head. "I just can't picture her being the one."

"I can't picture it either. It seems unlikely, but not impossible. In any case, suspects are the best people to ask about enemies. They're eager to throw attention away from themselves."

"Then I should talk to Frank about Uncle Angus's enemies as well?"

"Absolutely. But don't say or do anything to give him a hint that we're investigating him."

"My lips are sealed." He winked at Amanda and squeezed her hand, and damned if she didn't get all fidgety again.

He couldn't quite figure her out. One minute she was kissing him passionately, the next she was all business. The way she was acting didn't make a lick of sense.

Acting. Maybe that was it. Maybe she was acting.

But which thing was she acting about? Did she care anything about him or not? He couldn't believe that she could kiss him the way she did and not feel something. Or did she?

Oh, hell, it was enough to drive a man crazy.

No woman he'd ever met had kept him tied in knots the way Amanda did. But then, he'd never met a woman like Amanda. The more he was around her, the more he was determined to have her. It was time she settled down from detecting, and he could certainly use a woman with her brains to help him run the Blessing businesses—especially if Frank turned out to be a bad apple.

Who was he trying to fool? Right now he wasn't a danged bit interested in her brains.

They left the buggy by the stables for Harve to take care of and went into the big house. They didn't encounter a soul on the way to the study. Once safely behind closed doors, Amanda took off her hat and settled behind the desk with the batch of papers she'd copied. At once she began to scrutinize the pages.

"Need any help?" Beau asked.

"Hmmm?" she said distractedly.

"Need any help?"

"Not yet, thank you."

"May I get you anything?"

She glanced up and smiled. "A glass of lemonade would be wonderful."

When she smiled at him like that, he would have brought her a washtub full of lemonade, even if he'd had to squeeze every lemon in Austin himself. "Be right back."

He ran into Aunt Katie in the hall. "Amanda wants a glass of lemonade," he told her.

"Well, I wouldn't mind one myself. Come on and I'll help you fetch it. We had a jug left from the picnic. Plenty of food, too. 'Spect we'll have it for supper. No need in lettin' good food go to waste, I say. Where did you two get off to? You missed the excitement."

"What excitement?"

"Ellie knocked a wasp's nest down with a long stick. It was near the picnic table. All the kids had already run off to play after they finished the ice cream, so they escaped, but that bunch of wasps was sure mad, let me tell you. Your mama, Estelle, and Judith were running and screaming like wild women, and Morris was flailing his arms around like an idiot trying to swat them. Frank and me had sense enough to stand still, and I had Ellie tight against my skirts.

"Maud got stung twice on her arm, and Estelle got stung on her upper lip. It's all swole up, and she looks like she's been in a fight. Judith was lucky, but one of those mad little devils popped Morris on his ear, and another one got the end of his nose." Aunt Katie let out a cackle.

"If that ain't a sight! He had a whale of a honker to begin with, and it's three times as big now."

"Are they going to be all right?" Beau asked.

Aunt Katie waved a dismissing gesture. "Oh, they'll be fine when the swelling goes down and they get over their pique. Estelle threatened to switch Ellie good, but I wouldn't let her. She didn't do anything hurtful on purpose. She was just being a young 'un. You chip some ice, and I'll get the glasses."

Beau opened the icebox and started chipping at the block with the ice pick. He filled the three glasses that Aunt Katie set out, and she poured the lemonade.

"Aunt Katie, did Uncle Angus have any enemies?"

"Does a skunk stink when he lifts his tail?"

He chuckled. "Let me come at that another way. Could you help me make a list of his enemies?"

"I could. It would be a long one. What's the purpose?"

"It's for—for the Pinkerton agent. For the investigation. Let me take this glass to Amanda in the study, and we'll get started. I'll meet you in the parlor."

"Why don't we all go in the study and do it?" Aunt Katie said, looking at him pointedly over her glasses.

He knew that she figured Amanda was the Pinkerton agent, but until Amanda told him otherwise, Beau wasn't about to confirm his aunt's suspicions. "Oh, I wouldn't want to disturb her with this. She's busy writing some letters."

"Uh-huh," Aunt Katie said. He could tell that she didn't believe a word of it.

⌒ Fifteen ⌒

Katie Blessing sat in the parlor waiting for Beau to join her and feeling all the miseries of her eighty-four years in her joints and in her heart. She picked up a silver-framed photograph of Angus and her. A traveling photographer had taken it in the years before Austin had a full-time man with a studio on Congress Avenue.

Gray had not stolen all the color from her hair then, and the lines in her face and in Angus's were not so deep. She studied her brother's mouth, a straight slash, lips clamped together. Even then Angus was a stern man.

Angus had always been stern. Worse than stern. Angus had had a mean streak. Even she, who had always, begrudgingly, loved Angus more than any living soul had loved him, except maybe her mama, knew him for what he was. He was cunning and gifted with turning a dollar, but there wasn't a drop of warmth or softness in him. Their older brother Beaumont had gotten all of that. Everybody loved Beaumont, even old sourpuss Angus. He was charming and handsome and just plain nice—a lot like his grandson—but he had a bit of the Blessing stubbornness about him too.

"Angus," Katie said to the photograph, "we didn't do

well by Beaumont's grandchildren. You were a harsh man, hell-bent on having your way, and I didn't stop you. I don't know if I could have done anything more than I did, but there should have been a way. Poor Maud was never a match for you, but I could have tried harder. You kept on at young Beau until you ran him off, and you manipulated the girls into unhappy marriages. Now here we sit, in your stew pot.

"You controlled the money, and you had the authority, and you never let any of us forget it. Do you know how many times in all those years I wished I was a man? Hundreds. Thousands. You blamed warthog! You ruined my life, took my dowry for your stake, and when you died, you even didn't leave me a penny to call my own. That tore it for sure! I hope you burn in hell, you old fart!"

She plunked the picture back on the table just as Beau entered the room.

"Were you talking to somebody, Aunt Katie?"

"Just the old cuss there." She motioned toward the picture. "You want to know who his enemies were? I'll tell you who. Everybody who ever met him. Put me at the top of the list, then add every soul in the family—Maud, your sisters, Frank, Morris, Estelle's girls."

"And me."

"And you. And everybody who worked for him. And that woman he took up with—Fanny what's-her-name."

"Fanny Campbell?"

"That's the one. And all the people he did business with, I reckon. They might have respected his way with making a dollar—and he did have a keen talent for that—but not one of them came to his funeral. I suspect they were too occupied with celebrating."

"I can believe it. Wasn't there anything good about the man? As a kid, I couldn't see it, but I'd like to think he had a few redeeming qualities."

Katie thought for a moment. "Well, he was never sick a day in his life until the day he keeled over dead, so I guess you could say he had a good constitution. He never let his family go hungry, and he tithed to the church—though if you ask me, I figure God would have rather seen a few smiles and some loving words and deeds than all that cash. I think Angus's only joy in life was making folks miserable."

"Aunt Katie, do you really think he enjoyed being such a bastard?"

"I don't know, son. I honestly don't know. I've studied on it for many an hour and wept many a tear. I do know there was no turning him. Lord knows, though my efforts weren't worth a tinker's damn, I tried it enough times and prayed enough prayers."

"Why did you stay with him all those years?"

She shrugged. "After—well, I reckon it was because I didn't have anywhere else to go. Besides, I promised my mother on her deathbed that I'd look after Angus. She knew he was hard to love."

"I used to wish that Mama had gone anywhere but to Texas and to Uncle Angus's house."

"With the war and all, she didn't have much choice, Beau. Being a woman alone is bad enough, but having three children to feed and no way to make a living . . . Well, Maud did the best she could. She didn't know how harsh Angus was. I will say this in his behalf—he saw to it that you and the girls had an education and all the mate-

rial things. Your mama and I tried to provide the love."
She patted his knee.

He hugged her against him. "And you did a good job of
it, Aunt Katie."

She smoothed back an unruly lock from his forehead.
"You hit a rocky spot or two growing up, but you've
turned into a fine man, Beaumont Blessing Chandler."
She sighed. "It's the girls I worry about. Your mama wor-
ries too, but she wouldn't admit it for all the tea in China.
Maud's a proud woman—too proud, I sometimes think—
and she's taught the girls her prideful ways."

Maud Chandler lay in bed with soda paste and a cold
compress on her arm, Another cold compress was draped
across her brow. Pain and anguish tightened her throat
and gathered burning tears in her eyes. But it wasn't the
wasp stings on her arm that set the feelings upon her. It
was worry. She was worried about her girls.

Especially Judith.

She was loath to admit it, even silently, for fear God
would strike her dead or send some awful plague, but she
hated Morris Essig. Hated him.

There. She'd confessed it.

No one else had heard him but Maud, but after he'd
been stung, he had cursed Judith something fierce. He'd
grabbed her arm and cursed and threatened to beat her if
she laughed at him again. He'd left marks on her arm.
Maud had seen them.

It wasn't the first time Morris had marked Judith. Maud
had turned a blind eye to the truth for ages, fearing scandal should whispers about it get out. But Morris had
beaten her daughter almost senseless last year. The man

was a devil. Oh, Judith put up a good front and denied that her husband had touched her, but she didn't fool Maud— or Aunt Katie—for one minute with that story about a fall down the stairs.

It was a shame and a disgrace. Maud prayed constantly that the problem would right itself, but it hadn't. She wished she could do something to help Judith, but she was helpless. Aunt Katie tried to talk to Uncle Angus last year, after the worst incident. Maud had even spoken with her minister about the problem several months ago. Both men had brushed them off with similar responses. Man was head of the household, and woman was to be submissive to him. Judith was too independent and high-spirited; she needed a firm hand.

Judith high-spirited? Fiddlesticks! She was meek as a mouse—too meek to even consider leaving Morris, especially while Uncle Angus lived. Judith had always been terrified of the old toad. They all had been. And where would Judith have gone if she had left Morris? And how would she have provided for herself? Maud had been tempted to call on her son for help, but Beau was so hot-headed, she feared something dire would happen if he got involved.

Maud had very little money to call her own. Despite the shame divorce brought to a family, she would have braved the slurs and encouraged Judith to leave if she'd had the means to help her. She had prayed Angus would leave her a little something in his will, but the weasel hadn't left her a penny. Not a penny. And her hopes—

Well, that was water under the bridge now.

Her only hope now was her son. He was head of the family; he controlled the business and the money and the power—and Morris's livelihood. Please, God, let Beau understand and be willing to help. She was going to discuss this matter with Judith, and if her daughter would allow her, she'd approach Beau. First, of course, she had to get Judith to admit there was a problem.

"Swill!" Morris shouted. *"Verdammte Frau!"* He knocked the bed tray onto the floor. "Damned woman, you can't even make a decent bowl of soup. You're useless."

Judith bit the inside of her lip to keep from crying and schooled her features into the vacuous expression that irritated Morris even more. She wanted to tell him to go let his mistress fix his soup and listen to his ravings, but she said not a word. She valued her teeth. She simply got down on her knees, retrieved the broken pieces of china, and mopped up the food spills.

Her mouth may have been mute, but her mind shouted awful obscenities, and her imagination devised dozens of scenarios, all painful and insulting. She considered every option from beating him to death with his walking stick to packing her bags and leaving for Paris.

Unfortunately, murdering him would only land her in prison, and she hadn't the means to escape to Paris. Her meager savings wouldn't take her farther than an overnight trip to Waco.

Dear God, how she hated being a weak, dependent woman! There were times when she longed to be a man so desperately that she thought she would die of the ache. If she were a man, she would curse Morris Essig until his ears rang, beat him until he couldn't walk, then she would sell everything they owned, take a train to New Orleans or to Galveston, and sail for France.

She would spend those glorious days, free from Morris's insufferable presence, sculpting in her studio beside the Seine or visiting the marvelous museums of the city. At night she would dine with other artists in the lovely little cafés Madame Moreau had told—

"What are you doing down there?" Morris yelled.

An abrupt and painful yank of her hair brought a yelp from her lips and tears to her eyes. She grabbed her scalp and, begging for release, struggled from his hold.

"Get up and get out of here, *Sie Petze*! I can't bear the sight of you! Go to the big house and get me some decent food. And bring more ice for the packs."

Judith scrabbled away from his reach and pushed herself to her feet. "Which would you like first? Ice or food?" She tried to keep the disdain from her voice, but she failed miserably. Would she never learn?

"*Dummkopf!* The ice, then the food. And be quick about it. You're slower than any woman alive. Like a slug." He shouted more vulgarities in German and in English, but she was already used to being called a bitch and a whore and an idiot and a dozen other insulting names in both languages.

Clenching her teeth, Judith trudged to the kitchen. She picked up an ice pick, yanked open the box, and began chipping at the block. With every stroke of the sharp pick, she imagined that it was Morris's chest she stabbed.

Judith had endured his slaps and punches, his blistering tongue and wild threats for what seemed an eternity, and the punishment had grown steadily worse over the years. If she had to endure much more of him, she would lose her sanity—or what little of it she still clung to. She had been past endurance for months. She was desperate.

Desperate.

Her thoughts raced from one wild scheme to another. She would do anything to escape his abuse. *Anything.* It wasn't that she hadn't tried to do something before, but every plan she'd devised had failed. All her efforts had been fruitless, and her plight had become more hopeless with each vain attempt.

She was too ashamed to talk to her family about her circumstances. Beau had become almost a stranger. Her mother would be appalled and embarrassed, Estelle aghast.

Visits to the minister only brought admonitions to pray and learn to be a more humble and obedient wife. Perhaps her wickedness had brought this terrible penance on her, but hadn't she paid enough for her sins? Must she live in hell forever? She had tried every way she knew to be a good wife. Dear God, she had tried. She had jumped like a frightened flea to do Morris's every bidding. And she had read her Bible for hours and prayed until her knees were raw. None of it helped.

She felt like an animal in a trap, ready to chew her leg off to be free.

Judith stopped hacking at the block and looked down at the ice pick clutched in her fingers. How tempting was the thought of marching into his bedroom and driving the point into his black heart. A hollow, strangled laugh escaped from her throat. Impossible. Nothing she did ever turned out right. Morris was strong as an ox; he would easily wrest the weapon from her and beat her senseless.

Her shoulders slumped, and as she continued to stare at the ice pick, the familiar, overwhelming feeling of hopelessness sucked the spirit from her body and soul.

An easier escape would be to drive the point into her own heart. Or to leap from the craggy peak of Mt. Bonnell the way mythical lovers had done. Or to drink strychnine. Death would be a welcome release.

Only love for her family kept her from acting out her ungodly thoughts. Mama could never bear the shame, nor could Estelle. She couldn't bring that sort of disgrace on the girls. Louise and the others would be branded forever as having an aunt who killed herself—or committed murder. The scandal would be devastating for them.

Judith slumped against the icebox and wept.

"Oh, dear God, help me. Help me. I can't go on."

As the mantel clock struck twelve, Estelle sat in her chair, rocking and waiting. All the girls were asleep, even Ellie, but Estelle hadn't batted an eyelash. She waited for Frank. Alone and miserable, she sat downstairs in their lovely home in the dark, her sewing basket in her lap. She had been rocking and waiting for a very long time.

She knew where he was. She knew what he was doing.

Anguish clawed at her belly and whispered dreadful things in her ears. Humiliation burned in the depths of her soul.

Driven to relieve the overwhelming torment inside her, she reached into the basket, slipped the medicine bottle from the sock covering it, and uncorked the top. Her hands shook as she lifted the vial to her lips.

The bottle was empty.

Twice this evening she had emptied it. Or was it three times?

No matter. She had more. The larger bottle was upstairs in the chest, under her petticoats.

Estelle set the basket aside and tried to rise, but her limbs were unsteady, and she fell back into the seat. She started the chair rocking with the idea that the motion would propel her to her feet.

It only dumped her on the floor.

Frank found her crawling toward the stairs.

"Estelle! Are you hurt, dear?" He helped her up and kept his hands at her elbows to steady her.

"Fine. 'M fine." She licked her lips and tried to enunciate carefully. "Dropped off in my chair, and my foot went to sleep."

He sighed. "I can smell the gin."

She stiffened. "And *I* can smell the cheap perfume. You reek of it."

"It isn't cheap, Estelle." He hugged her close. "I've tried to explain a hundred times that my—other activities have nothing to do with you. I love you with all my heart. I have since the first time I laid eyes on you."

"I can't believe that you love me! If you did you wouldn't indulge in such awful, shameful—"

Frank kissed her into silence.

She melted against him. His kisses now had the same power to befuddle and inflame her that his first ones had. He cupped her breast and moaned against her mouth as his tongue thrust between her lips. Passion erupted between them like a lightning storm.

He lowered her to the stair steps and began to raise her skirts as he knelt between her legs. She reached for him, longing to have him inside her to quench the fire that burned there, but through the haze of gin and desire came an awareness of the girls.

"Not here," she whispered.

He groaned softly. She knew that his craving was as great as hers. He was a virile man, always had been, which had come as a surprise to her. Her own sensual nature had been a shock as well. Estelle might have been ashamed of her considerable ardor had not the slaking of it been so delightfully delicious.

"Come, my little rabbit," Frank whispered.

She giggled as he pulled her to her feet. Frank helped her up the stairs, stroking her breasts and murmuring sweet, wet love words against her ear as they headed for the privacy of their bedroom.

Estelle's apprehension was forgotten momentarily as her eager husband stripped her naked and worshipped her body in shockingly naughty and perfectly wonderful ways.

Her face burned in mortification, but it felt too good to have him stop. "Again," she whispered.

He chuckled and complied.

Her mother would have had a fit of vapors had she known the things they did. Staid Frank and very proper Estelle: they were as wanton as any of Guy Town's denizens.

Dear God, she loved him so. She couldn't give up this man, no matter what his awful vices. She couldn't.

⌐ Sixteen ⌐

Beau couldn't sleep. He prowled the house like a restless cougar. Aunt Katie had suggested warm milk, but he preferred something stronger. Thing was, the liquor was in the study, and Amanda had threatened him within an inch of his life if he disturbed her again. She was busy with the information she'd copied from Frank's ledger and had informed him that she found his looking over her shoulder and skulking around the room very distracting. She'd also told him that popping his head in every hour to check on her was annoying.

No, she didn't need to rest her eyes. No, she didn't want another glass of lemonade. Or a cookie. Or a piece of buttermilk pie. No, a walk wouldn't help her concentration. No, she wasn't sleepy. Yes, she knew what time it was. There was a clock on the mantel.

"Go away, Beau," she'd said, plainly exasperated.

He'd gone away. But it was after two o'clock in the morning. He didn't like to see her working such long hours. Hell, he didn't care who Frank owed money to. If his brother-in-law was in a tight spot, Beau would give him money. God knows, he had a piss-pot full of it now.

Fact was, he had more money than he'd ever find a

use for. His needs were simple. Maybe when it was all accounted for, he'd divide it up among the family members—except Morris.

He didn't like Morris Essig worth a damn, and every day he was around the son of a bitch, he liked him less. He couldn't quite put his finger on what it was about Morris that chapped his ass so bad—besides the obvious stuff. Something deeper about that bastard nagged at him. He hoped to hell that Morris did turn out to be the mastermind behind the kidnapping. Beau would love to have an excuse to send him packing.

Wonder if there was a way to give Judith a cut of Uncle Angus's money without Morris getting his hands on it?

Amanda might know. She was smart about things like that.

He looked at his fancy gold pocket watch again—or rather Uncle Angus's fancy gold pocket watch he'd taken to wearing—and saw that the hands were creeping closer to two-thirty.

Enough of this bullcrap! He sucked in a deep breath, strode to the study, and barged through the door.

What he saw squeezed the resolve from his lungs.

Amanda's head was slumped across her arm on the desk; she still clutched a pen in her fingers. Her lids were closed, her lips slightly parted. She was sound asleep.

His heart melted like a dollop of lard on a hot griddle. Feelings born of a deep, sweet ache filled every part of him. Strong feelings. Odd feelings. Feelings that made him swell up until he was ten feet tall and powerful as a team of logging oxen.

He was tempted to lift her onto the sofa and cover her, but he knew she'd be more comfortable in bed.

She looked so peaceful and sweet that he hated to rouse her for the walk upstairs.

Hell, he'd carry her. He'd done it once before. He lifted her in his arms. She seemed a mite heavier than last time. 'Course last time she was wearing boy's clothes, not long skirts with a bustle and a bunch of other stuff that weighed nearly as much as a washpot full of rain water.

By the time he stumbled over her skirt halfway up the stairs, he was winded and had broken a fair sweat. Come to think of it, last time he carried her up these stairs, he'd damned near strangled a gut. He was going to have to stop drinking hard liquor and start swigging milk. One good thing he could say about busting rocks and shoveling coal—he'd been strong as a bull back then. Since he'd become a saloon keeper, he was going soft.

Her arms went around his neck, and she nuzzled under his chin. That energized him for a few more steps, but by the time he got to the head of the stairs, he was past caring about nuzzling or anything except getting rid of this load. His arms were numb; his back burned; his knees wobbled like a new colt's. Damn, she was heavy.

What had seemed romantic a few minutes ago now sounded plumb crazy. For the first time, he fully understood the meaning of dead weight: much more of this and he'd be dead.

Using his knee and a chair in the hall, he shifted her weight around to get a better grip before her butt sagged clear to the floor.

Then he saw the doorknob of her closed door.

Why the hell had she closed her door? He hooked his foot around the chair leg and dragged it slowly toward the door, trying his dangedest not to make a noise and wake up his mother—though, listening to the log-sawing coming from her room, he figured if she could sleep through her own snoring, a little furniture-scraping wouldn't rouse her.

Using the chair again to prop his foot and balancing Amanda on his thigh, he managed to turn the knob and swing open the door. He wiped his dripping brow on the shoulder of his shirt and lugged her to the bed. Fighting the urge to dump her like a sack of potatoes, he eased her onto the covers and himself to his knees.

His forehead dropped to the mattress, and he sucked in great gulps of air while he waited for his heart to slow some. Damn. He was getting old.

He was still sweating, and he figured his face was about the color of a boiled crawfish as he struggled to his feet. He was still winded but no longer worried that his heart was going to explode.

Beau gently slipped off Amanda's shoes and set them aside. He looked at her dress and frowned. Sleeping in all that garb would be miserable. Hell, it must weigh fifty pounds.

He shook his head, sucked in another deep breath, and reached for the buttons at her throat.

A hand clamped around his wrist. "You do, and you're dead."

He looked down. Her eyes were wide open.

"How long have you been awake?"

"Since the first 'son of a bitch' you muttered on the stairs when you stumbled over my skirt. I think you ripped it. You have a very colorful vocabulary. I think I might have learned a new word or two."

He could tell that she was trying to keep from laughing,

but he wasn't in a humorous mood. "You mean I lugged you up all those stairs and you were awake?"

She pressed her fingers against her lips, but a laugh escaped anyhow.

"Damn." Like a pine tree toppled by a cross-cut saw, he fell into bed beside her.

"Beau," she said, pushing at him. "Get up. Get out of my bed this minute."

"I can't," he said. "I'm too tuckered out. The only way I'm leaving is if you carry me."

"I can't carry you!"

"Then I'll sleep here. Don't worry about your honor. God knows, right now I couldn't lift a hand to swat a mosquito."

Amanda.

Beau snuggled closer and wrapped his arms around the soft body next to him. Her scent enveloped him. He breathed deeply of her tantalizing fragrance, snuggled closer still, and squeezed—

"Uncle Beau," a voice whispered loudly.

He opened his eyes to find his arms around a pillow and Ellie staring at him intently.

"Are you awake?" she whispered again.

"I am now," he mumbled. "What are you doing here?"

"I'm your coffee girl, remember? I brought your coffee. Did you find the mouse?"

"What mouse?"

"The one that scared Miss Amanda last night. She said she was sleeping in your bed and you was sleeping in hers because she saw a mouse in her room last night. It ran from behind the curtain and across the room, and it scared her something awful, and you told her you'd catch it and put it out. Did you find it? I wanna see."

He closed one eye and frowned, trying to make sense out of Ellie's story.

"Uhhh, no. It got away."

"Oh, pooh. That's what Bonnie says when her hair won't curl right. She says, 'Oh, pooh.' Mama said she didn't want to hear her say that again. Where did the mouse go?"

"I don't know. Outside I guess. Where's Amanda?"

"She's downstairs in the study, the one that used to be Uncle Angus's study but now it's yours on account of you 'herited every blessed dime of the old gizzard's money. I didn't know dimes could be blessed. Does Pastor Samuels do it? Bless 'em, I mean. I don't have any dimes, but I've got some pennies in my bank. And one nickel. Will he bless them?"

"I don't know, Ellie. Where's my coffee?"

"It's right here, but I think it's not hot anymore." She stuck her finger in the cup. "Yep. Cold as a wedge. That's what Aunt Katie says. Cold as a wedge. What's a wedge, Uncle Beau?"

"I don't know. Why don't you have Lucy help you bring up another cup of coffee for me while I shave and clean up?"

"In here or in your room?"

"In my room."

"Okay." She smiled and skipped out.

His muscles and joints protesting like an old man's, Beau threw aside the quilt, dragged himself up, and sat on the side of bed. He was still fully dressed—he wiggled his toes—except for his shoes. They sat neatly on the floor beside the washstand.

He felt like a damned fool.

It was a shame that he had gained entrance to a beautiful lady's bed and was too weak to do more than go to sleep. He vowed to begin strengthening his body that very day. Next time the situation arose, he planned to be up to the occasion. This morning he could do with a nice Turkish bath. Unfortunately, he had to go to the office.

While Beau spent the day downtown becoming better acquainted with the ins and outs of the family business, Amanda spent most of her time deciphering the figures she'd arranged the night before. She was happy to have the excuse of "tending to some business accounts" to escape Maud Chandler. Not that she had anything against Beau's mother. Actually, she was growing rather fond of her, but Mrs. Chandler was anxious to begin wedding plans.

Amanda had easily broken Frank's code—not that there was anything clandestine about it, merely a personal method of noting payments to the grocer, the butcher, the milliner, the tobacco shop, and such. There were the usual disbursements to servants, charities, and quite a number to dressmakers—logical she supposed with seven females to clothe. Only a few of the entries still eluded her. The cryptic B.P., of course, and monthly payments for "P. St. rms."

Pecan Street rooms? Pine Street rooms? Did Frank indeed have a mistress? Did she reside on Pecan or Pine or some other P. Street?

A shame that she hadn't had more time in Frank's office. She'd bet a silver dollar that those envelopes of receipts would tell her a lot. She needed a peek at them.

If Frank went to another of his meetings that night, she and Beau would visit the office again.

"Where did he go?" Amanda asked. She sat in the buggy parked on Bois d'Arc Street, one block north of Pecan and parallel to it.

Beau climbed in beside her. "To the Benevolent Society Hall on Pecan. At least he turned in at the sign. I didn't want to follow him upstairs."

"Hmmm," Amanda said. "They certainly have frequent meetings." Being more experienced at such things, she'd wanted to follow Frank herself, but that would have required a disguise, and there wasn't time to change between dinner and his departure. She and Beau had already announced they were attending a lecture on Egyptian artifacts that evening, so she couldn't plead another headache.

"You think his lady friend might have rooms upstairs as well?"

"I suppose it's possible. I think Pete needs to check out the premises tomorrow while you and Frank attend the horse auction."

"Who's Pete?"

"My red-haired lad. Or perhaps young Thomas would be better. He has lank brown hair and looks the part of a country boy."

Beau drove the buggy a few blocks east and parked it near the lecture hall. He and Amanda walked the short distance back to the Blessing building. By the time Beau unlocked the front door, dusk had settled to darkness and the street lamps were on.

"Won't having lights on inside invite suspicion?" Beau asked.

"From whom? You keep forgetting this is *your* building. You have every right to be here. True, we need to be in and out of Frank's office quickly. We'll take the material to your desk to read."

While Beau held a lamp, she made quick work of the locks. She left the ledger in place and took the envelopes, closing the drawer and the door behind them.

In his office, Beau turned up the gaslights while Amanda slid the contents from the first envelope. In the corner was written "H-1," and under it, "84–86."

"What are those?" he asked.

"Bills and receipts." She slipped a rubber sheath on her finger and went through the stack carefully but quickly, mindful of maintaining the proper order. "They're all for household expenses since the year before last. Nothing unusual here." She replaced the papers and picked up another envelope.

"That's a fat one," Beau commented.

"Clothing and accessories. Not surprising."

"Exactly what are you looking for?"

"Anything to explain B.P. or P. Street rooms or anything else out of the ordinary."

Only the rapid riffle of paper disturbed the quiet as she continued searching the stack. Though she worked swiftly, her trained eyes scanned every leaf. As she worked her way through a sheaf of dressmaker bills and receipts, a vague nagging furrowed her brow.

"What?" Beau said. "Found something?"

"I don't know. Something here is not quite right." She

went through the stack again, more slowly this time. Several receipts struck her as odd.

"Did you find what you were looking for?" Beau asked.

"Not exactly, but this is strange. And this."

Beau looked over her shoulder at the papers she pointed out. "Bills from a dressmaker. What's odd about that? God knows poor Frank must have more than his share of those."

"But look at the sizes and the colors of the clothing Mrs. Jurney provided."

"So?"

Amanda shook her head. Trust a man not to notice such things. This was exactly the reason Mr. Allan Pinkerton liked having female agents on certain cases. "These dresses sound very wrong for either Estelle or the twins. Can you imagine any of them wearing red satin? The girls are too young and Estelle is too fair and too retiring to wear such a bright color and fabric."

"His mistress, do you think?"

"It certainly looks suspicious." She made a notation of the bills in question, including the date and the dressmaker's address. She also found a bill for petticoats in a size much larger than the willowy Estelle or her girls would wear. There were a number of such items of apparel. She made notes of them all. She supposed they might be Maud Chandler's, but why would Frank be paying her bills?

In another envelope, among charitable contributions, she found the receipt for P. St. rms., or more fully, Pecan Street rooms.

"Look here," Amanda said, showing Beau several receipts. "These are made out to the Austin Benevolent Society. Why would Frank pay for the organization's rental space from his personal funds?"

"Beats me. Maybe this is his contribution. After all, the receipts are in with the charity stuff."

"Something about it strikes me as odd. Did you notice how Frank acted when you mentioned joining him at the society meeting one night?"

Beau grinned. "You mean when he looked like he'd been goosed with a broomstick?"

Amanda struggled not to laugh at Beau's colorful description. "Yes," she replied drolly. "That one."

"I just figured he wasn't interested in keeping company with the likes of me. I was always an embarrassment to some of the family, and I suspect Frank topped that list. He's kind of prissy. Did you find anything else about B.P.?"

"Nothing. And that's very strange, given how precise Frank is about record-keeping." She tapped her pen against her chin as she began to map out strategy. "I definitely think Thomas should stop by the Austin Benevolent Society tomorrow and nose around a bit. And I want to speak to Mrs. Jurney, the dressmaker."

"I'll go with you."

"No. I'd much prefer that you stick with Frank. Keep him occupied while I investigate."

⌁ Seventeen ⌁

At half past nine on Tuesday morning, Amanda, in the guise of Thomas the country lad, clambered up the stairs to the Austin Benevolent Society on Pecan Street. Her destination was a mere three and a half blocks from Frank and Estelle's home and the Blessing mansion. Under her arm she'd tucked a package wrapped in brown paper and tied with twine, backing up her cover story that she was delivering it to that address. In truth, there was something inside, a rather nice edition of *The Prince and the Pauper* that she'd stashed in her trunk.

The society's rooms were above Mrs. Simpson's Millinery Shop, an establishment she recognized from Frank's receipts. She'd also noticed a nice selection of straws displayed in the window. Indeed, a blue one there rather caught her fancy, and she intended to return later and try it on.

Exactly who, Amanda wondered, had purchased the hats Frank had paid for? Frank? Estelle? Or Frank's lady friend? The latter, she suspected, from the descriptions. Given her coloring and style, she doubted that Estelle would be caught dead in a red hat, especially a large one.

Hats this season were smaller, with high crowns, not wide-brimmed, brow-shadowing creations of the sort popular a few years before.

Amanda found two doors on the second floor landing. One led to a lawyer's office, and by peering through the glass-topped door, she could see a clerk bent over a stack of books. The other door had a small brass sign with AUSTIN BENEVOLENT SOCIETY neatly engraved on its surface.

She knocked, then waited.

After a minute or two, she knocked again.

She glanced over her shoulder, but the clerk hadn't looked up. She studied the lock briefly. It was incredibly simple. People in this town needed better locks. She retrieved the implement folder from her jacket pocket, selected a skeleton key and a thin metal pick, and with a few simple jiggles and turns, the door swung open.

After another quick glance over her shoulder, she eased inside and closed the door. The window coverings were drawn, and she could barely see. Rather than use lights, she risked opening the heavy drapes a bit.

What she saw in the harsh sunlight surprised her.

The area seemed to be an apartment rather than a hall and looked more like a bordello than the meeting place for citizens dedicated to civic concerns. Everything was in shades of red—wallpaper, rug, drapes, everything. The sitting room where she stood contained a red velvet settee and two plump chairs in a garish red stripe pattern. Tasseled pillows and tasseled lamp shades were everywhere, and gaudy pictures hung on the walls. She felt as if she'd fallen into a pot of strawberry jam.

Amanda, her mouth agape, wandered into the bed-room, which was also red and even more bedecked with tassels and bows and lace ruffles. She went immediately to the wardrobe and opened it.

A red satin dress hung there. Other ostentatious cre-ations trimmed lavishly with large roses and tasteless bows hung beside it. She found several tawdry dressing gowns, incredibly sheer and with a plethora of ruffles, satin rosettes, and black lace.

She held the red dress against her and looked into the gilded cheval mirror. It was at least three inches too long and many more inches too wide. The lady who wore these clothes was ... well, Rubenesque, to be polite. Why on earth would Frank prefer a cow of a woman with such dreadful taste when he had Estelle? And dear Lord, judg-ing by the shoes she saw, the woman had an unbelievable foot on her.

Continuing her search through every nook and cranny, Amanda found all sorts of women's clothing, both inner and outer garments, hats, shoes, bags, cosmetics, and per-fumes. She even discovered a black wig on a head stand and several fashion books, but she didn't find a single scrap of paper that gave a clue to the woman's identity. Not a receipt nor a letter nor a photograph. She hesitated to tarry longer, fearing the woman would return and find her nosing about.

Confident she'd found all there was to find, Amanda hurried to the door and, after checking to see if the coast was clear, exited and locked up.

Strange. Very strange.

She knocked on the glass at the door of the law office.

The noisy rattle finally caught the jug-eared clerk's attention. He glanced up, then motioned her inside.

" 'Scuse me, mister," Amanda said as Tom. "I got this here package to deliver across the way, and they ain't nobody answering the door. Reckon when they're a-comin' back?"

"I wouldn't have any idea," the young man said. "I never see anyone there. I think they have their meetings at night. Tuesdays, I believe—or is it Thursday? I'm always gone by six, so I don't see them. I think my employer is a member of the society, but he isn't here."

"Your employer?" Amanda was surprised at the information.

"Yes, Mr. John Hardin Bullock. He's an attorney, but as I said, he's not here. He and Mrs. Bullock are in Biloxi for her sister's wedding. I don't expect them back until the end of the week, or maybe the first of next week."

Amanda touched the bill of her cap. "Much obliged to ya." She turned away, puzzled.

As she went down the stairs, her frown deepened. This was getting more strange by the minute. Convinced at first that she'd found evidence of Frank's mistress and a love nest, now she wondered. Did Frank and the attorney share a mistress? It seemed unlikely. But she'd run across many highly unusual things in her years as an investigator. What some could only imagine in their most bizarre and perverse fantasies, other people actually did. Very little about human nature surprised her anymore.

With the package still tucked under her arm, she opened the door to the millinery shop. A bell sounded above the door as she went inside.

A woman came to the front, a little bird of a woman with spectacles and gray hair. She couldn't have been more than five feet tall. "Yes, son?"

Amanda doffed her cap. "You Mrs. Simpson?"

"I am."

Her answer quelled any notion that the shop's proprietor might be the owner of the red satin dress upstairs. Amanda looked down at her toes and acted shy.

"Them's some right pretty hats you got. My ma'd dearly love to have one of 'em for Sunday-go-to-meetin'."

"Are you interested in buying a hat for your mother? Most of them are very expensive, but I might have one or two—"

"Oh, no, ma'am," Amanda said quickly. "I was just tryin' to deliver this here package to the society upstairs, but ain't nobody there. Feller across the landin' didn't know nothin' about them, and I's hopin' maybe you did."

"I rent the space to them, but I believe they're only there for meetings in the evenings. Perhaps you could deliver the package to the secretary-treasurer of the group, Mr. Frank Banks. Here, I'll write the address of his office. It's not far."

"Oh, thank you, ma'am. I'd be much obliged." While the milliner wrote, Amanda sidled closer and said, "Exactly what is a Be-nev-o-lent Society?"

"You know, I'm not really sure. I think they assist the city government and local charities in some way. Mr. Banks is a very upstanding gentleman and concerned about those less fortunate."

"Nice feller, is he?"

"Oh, yes. A nice man, a very nice man. Why he often buys hats from me for his mother and his wife."

His *mother*? Amanda was under the impression that Frank's mother was deceased. Perhaps they were for Mrs. Chandler. More likely they were for the mysterious lady who owned the clothes upstairs.

"They had that place up there long?" she asked casually.

Mrs. Simpson pursed her lips and looked impatient. "Six years or so, as I recall—not that it's any of your concern. Run along now, boy. I have to get back to my trims."

The bell jingled as Amanda left. *Six* years? As she walked back to the hotel to change out of her costume, Amanda mulled over the things she'd seen in the apartment. Something was wrong there. Very wrong.

Shortly before noon, the bell jingled above the door as Amanda entered Mrs. Simpson's Millinery Shop again. This time Amanda was attired in a simple but fashionable rose-colored dress with a matching bonnet. All her clothes were of excellent quality, a result of spending the first years of her life without a decent dress.

The outfit Amanda wore that day had been made for her in Chicago the month before. The hat had been purchased at one of that city's finest milliners, a detail Mrs. Simpson appreciated by the admiring gleam in her eye.

"Good day, ma'am," the tiny woman said. "May I show you something?"

"Yes." Amanda smiled. "The blue straw in the window is charming. I'd like to try it on."

While Mrs. Simpson fluttered around and fetched the hat, Amanda sat down at the mirrored table and removed her own bonnet.

Mrs. Simpson helped her with the placement of the

hat, then stood back, clasped her hands, and waited with an expectant smile as Amanda turned her head this way and that.

"I rather like it," Amanda said, using a hand mirror to see the back.

"It's beautiful on you," the proprietor said. "Matches your lovely eyes perfectly."

"I think I'll take it."

"Wonderful! May I show you something else?"

"Oh, my, yes. I have a terrible weakness for pretty hats. You know, I need something to go with a special red dress. I believe Estelle—Mrs. Frank Banks—said I might find something here."

Mrs. Simpson could barely contain her excitement over her new customer. "Is Mrs. Banks a friend of yours?"

"Her brother is my fiancé. Beaumont Blessing Chandler." Smiling, Amanda lifted her nose a tad. "I suppose that after we're married, we'll be living in Austin—now that he's inherited his uncle Angus's estate."

Amanda could see the gleam in Mrs. Simpson's eyes turn into dollar signs. "May I say that we're delighted to have a lovely new edition to our city? Red, you say? As I recall, I made a red hat for Mr. Banks's mother. She's rather fond of red, I understand."

"Ah, yes, the elder Mrs. Banks is an interesting woman, don't you think?"

"Well, I've never actually met her. Mr. Banks describes what his mother wants, and after the hats are made, he sends them to her—in Palestine, I believe he said."

"Frank is such a sweetheart," Amanda said gaily. "Oh, may I see that navy with the cherries?"

After priming the pump a bit more, she soon had Mrs. Simpson spilling everything she knew. Unfortunately, that wasn't much: only that Frank had bought several hats from her, mostly for his mother, whose taste ran a bit to the . . . well, extremely colorful and well decorated. She recognized several of the hats in the apartment upstairs as those Mrs. Simpson described.

Amanda left with two new hats and more questions.

After a quick lunch with the ladies of the family—Beau and Frank hadn't returned from the horse auction— Amanda excused herself, saying she had a bit of shopping to do. Actually, she planned to take advantage of Beau's absence to speak with Fanny Campbell.

Unfortunately, the ladies decided to join her—except for Aunt Katie, who looked as if she thought the incident amusing. Judith tried to beg off as well, but nothing would do Maud but for her younger daughter to come along.

"How long since you've had so much as a new hair comb or a pair of gloves?" Maud asked Judith. "You must come, dearest. It will do you a world of good. You've been cooped up with Morris for days now. It's enough to make anybody glum. We'll have a lovely excursion. We'll even stop by Mr. J. Prade's for a dish of ice cream. And, Amanda, we can begin shopping for your trousseau. Oh, I can hardly wait. I do so love weddings!"

They spent the entire afternoon shopping. Amanda would have been irritated at the loss of investigative time except for the color that came into Judith's cheeks and the first smile she'd seen on her face in days.

She wondered if Morris had been up to his old tricks despite her warnings. It had been her experience that such scoundrels rarely changed their behavior easily. And while Amanda hadn't seen any additional bruises on Judith, she knew from bitter experience that many injuries were deliberately inflicted on areas that didn't show: the back, the buttocks, the limbs.

Or on the soul.

Bastard!

On the way home from their expedition, Amanda slid her arm through Judith's and said gaily, "I think the new shawl you bought at Newman's was absolutely lovely. I think you should wear lively colors more often—don't you agree, Estelle?"

"I do. Judith has always worn yellow well."

Judith dropped her gaze. "Morris prefers more— somber colors." She sighed. "He'll probably make me take the shawl back."

Over my dead body! Amanda thought. "Perhaps not," she said. "We'll convince him that it's perfect for you. Tell him that I said you *must* keep it. By the way, how is his foot?"

"Better. Much better. Getting back to work is the best medicine for him. And I'm eager to get back to work as well. Have you forgotten you promised to sit for me? I'd like to get started tomorrow."

Fiddlesticks! Amanda thought. She needed to get on with her investigation, but Judith looked so stricken when she hesitated that she didn't have the heart to make excuses.

"Tomorrow will be wonderful."

* * *

Amanda didn't get a moment alone with Beau until after dinner. On the pretense of going to another lecture, they left the house and parked the buggy in a dark alley where they could see Frank if he entered the apartment on Pecan. While they waited, she filled him in on her discoveries.

"Did Frank mention he was going to a meeting tonight?" Amanda asked.

"Not that I heard. We may be on a wild goose chase. I got the idea from a couple of things Frank said today that he was concerned about Estelle, about leaving her home with the children so much. Sounded like she'd been complaining. He may stay home tonight." Beau shook his head. "I can't believe Frank has a mistress. Frank? Prissy Frank? If he wasn't married to my sister, the whole thing would be funny. As it is, I may break his danged neck."

"You know," Amanda said, "I've been giving this a lot of thought. Something's wrong about the whole situation, but I can't quite put my finger on it. Wait. Is that Frank?"

Beau craned his neck. "Looks like his walk. It's too dark . . . Yep. That's him all right, and he's heading for the stairs."

He started to climb out of the buggy, but Amanda grasped his arm. "Let's just watch for a bit. Did you notice that the windows upstairs are dark? They're covered by heavy drapes to be sure, but there isn't even a slit of light. Look. There are lights now. See the outlines?"

"That's peculiar. Has his lady friend just been sitting up there in the dark?"

"Beau, I'm not sure there is a lady friend. Let's move

the buggy back a way and watch for a while. See what happens."

When the horse and buggy were moved farther down the alley, they crept back to the corner and, staying in the shadows beside the mercantile building, kept their eyes on the space above the millinery shop.

A half hour passed.

Beau slapped at his neck. "Something just bit me. Sure hope it wasn't a mosquito. If we have to stay out here very long, they'll carry us off."

"I think it's too early for mosquitoes." She smiled. "Waiting and watching are a big part of detective work. It's not for the impatient."

"You're right again. I'm not cut out for detecting."

"Tell me about the horses you bought today." Not that she was particularly interested in horse auctions, but she thought it might help relieve his boredom.

While he talked, she watched.

Another half hour passed. The town was quiet; few people were stirring about. An occasional buggy or horse went by, and three men who were working late left buildings nearby, locking doors behind them.

"Damnation, what's he doing up there?" Beau said. "I've a good mind to—"

"Shhh. Here comes somebody."

A figure, dressed in red and wearing a jaunty hat with a cluster of plumes and a large bow, emerged from the passageway as they watched. They both flattened themselves against the building and went dead still as the large woman strolled by, coming within a few feet of them and leaving a cloud of perfume wafting behind her.

Although the street light was dim, Amanda could see

that she had dark hair and heavily rouged cheeks and lips. She watched the sway of her bustle as she walked—

"Is *that* her? Frank's mistress?"

"No," Amanda said as she suddenly realized what had been bothering her all day. "That's Frank."

⌐ Eighteen ⌐

"Frank?" Beau said, his mouth agape. "Can't be. No way."

"It is. Trust me. I recognized him."

"By God, I'll kill that prissy son of a bitch!" He started to stride from the alley, but Amanda grabbed him.

"Stay here! And keep your voice down." Amanda thought for a moment that she might have to hog-tie Beau and throw him into the buggy to keep him still.

"It was bad enough when I thought he was stepping out on my sister with another woman, I can't believe that damned pervert is interested in another *man*! But how can he be a blamed sodomite? He's got a wife and *six* kids, for godsakes."

When Beau lurched after Frank again, she held on to his arm. "He may not be a sodomite."

"How can you say that? He had on a danged dress and face paint! Looked like a blamed calico queen! Excuse my language, Amanda, but I'm madder'n old Billy Rip."

"I've heard worse. I understand that you're upset, but I mean to confront Frank while he's in his finery and vulnerable. It won't do for you to sock him in the nose. And as I said, he may not be—attracted to men. I've heard of one or two cases where a man had a perfectly normal family life with a wife and children, but he liked to occasionally dress as a woman. I believe there was a governor of New York—"

"For godsakes, *why*?"

"Why was there a governor of New York?" she said, feigning innocence.

"Dadgum it, Amanda! I don't care about the blasted governor of New York! I don't even care more'n a penny's worth about Frank Banks. I do care about my sister—and her girls. Why would Frank dress up like a woman if he didn't want to . . . you know."

"Well, in the cases I heard about—including the governor—it seems that the gentlemen in question simply enjoyed wearing women's clothing occasionally. They found it emotionally gratifying in some way."

"Emotionally gratifying, my aunt Jenny's ass! Excuse my language again. I'm gonna break both his legs."

Beau struck off down the street with Amanda hanging on to his arm and trying to dig in her heels to hold him back. He kept going, dragging her along and leaving furrows in the dirt where she tried to gain purchase.

Totally exasperated, she smacked his shoulder with her handbag. "Dammit, stop!" She smacked him again.

He stopped. She wasn't sure if it was because of her words or her deeds. "What have you got in that thing?" he asked. "Feels like a sack of doorknobs. And did I hear you say 'dammit'?"

"You did. And I'll say worse if you don't stop this instant and get control of yourself. You'll ruin everything if you go off half-cocked."

"What will I ruin?"

"Had you forgotten that I'm here to investigate your uncle's kidnapping?"

"Oh, that," Beau said. "Forget it. It's probably somebody who's long gone by now or a petty criminal who pulled back into his rabbit hole when things didn't pan out."

"I cannot simply forget to do my job, unless we sever our contract. And I don't think the person is either gone or a criminal. I've been making inquiries and giving this case a great deal of thought, and I believe the perpetrator is someone close to the family. It *could* be Frank."

"I hope to hell it is. Give me a good excuse to—"

"Beaumont Blessing Chandler! I am totally exasperated with you!"

He suddenly grinned. "You sound like my mother when I used to get in trouble."

"Which I suspect was often. Now are you going to let me handle my job or not? If you're not, I might as well go home and pack right now, for I'm no more use here. Make up your mind once and for all."

He sucked in a deep breath, then let it out slowly. "I want you to stay on the case."

"Fine. But you must promise to keep your temper under control and let me take the lead when we confront Frank. Agreed?"

He sucked in another deep breath. "Agreed. Let's go look for him."

"We don't have to look. I saw him go into the hotel restaurant on the next block."

"I didn't see him."

She smiled, feeling a bit smug. "That's why I'm the detective."

* * *

Since it was well after the dinner hour, only a few tables were occupied in the restaurant. Amanda scanned the half dozen or so people there and spotted her quarry drinking a cup of tea in a dimly lit corner, partially hidden by a potted palm.

"Give me a few moments' head start," Amanda whispered. "And stay out of sight." She withdrew her arm from Beau's and strolled across the room. She was sure Frank saw her coming for he averted his face slightly, tucked his chin, and held the cup to his lips with both hands.

Let him squirm, she thought.

Frank still didn't look up as she approached.

She slipped into the chair next to him, leaned over, and whispered, "Love your hat."

He choked on his tea.

"I'll bet you got it at Mrs. Simpson's. I bought two there myself today. I understand that you keep a little place upstairs."

"I beg your pardon?" he said in a falsetto.

She had to admire his grit in trying to bluff it out. "Nice try, but I'm not fooled by your masquerade, Frank."

"I have no idea what you're talking about, young woman. Excuse me, please. I'm leaving."

Just as Frank started to rise, Beau swept aside the palm fronds. "Going somewhere, Nancy-boy?" Beau grinned. "I wish you wouldn't. I just got here. You'll hurt my feelings running off. By the way, that's some hat."

"Isn't it?" Amanda said. "I've already complimented him on it."

Frank squirmed.

"Nice dress," Beau said. "I was always partial to red myself."

Frank looked as if he might pass out at any minute. "What do you want?" he asked, glancing from one to the other of them.

Beau gestured to Amanda to take the lead.

"We understand that you're in serious debt," she said sternly. "Is that why you hatched the kidnapping scheme?"

Frank gasped, then paled beneath the rouge. "Dear heavens, surely you don't think I—No, no. I would never do such a thing. Never!" He glanced back and forth between them again, and his attention landed on Amanda. His eyes narrowed. "Exactly who are you?"

She almost laughed. Here was the perfect opportunity to deliver her friend Webb McQuillan's infamous line: "I am the instrument of your doom." She wanted desperately to say it, but she didn't. Instead, she said, "I'm asking the questions here."

Frank looked to Beau.

Beau shrugged. "She's asking the questions. Better answer. She gets downright unpleasant if she's crossed. I understand that she's a good shot, too."

"A good shot?" Frank's voice went up an octave and his eyes grew as big as the teacup he clutched.

Beau nodded.

Amanda bit her lip to keep from laughing. "I am, but I don't think that's appropriate here. Do you deny being behind the kidnapping of Angus Blessing?"

"Of course I deny it!"

"He denies it," Beau said. "But reckon if I did it, I'd deny it too."

"Do you deny that you're in serious debt?" Amanda asked.

"How did—?" Frank slumped in his chair. "I can't deny that. I'm being blackmailed, and the payments have drained me dry."

"Blackmailed?" Amanda asked.

"Yes. Someone found out about this"—Frank fluttered his hand over his bodice—"and threatened me with exposure."

"Exposure?" Beau scowled. "You wouldn't have been in this fix if you hadn't exposed yourself sashaying around—"

Amanda kicked him under the table.

"Who's blackmailing you?" she asked, understanding at once that B.P. stood for "blackmail payments."

"I—I'm not sure. But it's dreadful. Dreadful. We—I live in constant fear."

Amanda hadn't missed the brief slip of the tongue. "You started to say 'we.' Is there someone else who shares your—taste for dressing? Like, say, an attorney with an office nearby?"

For a moment she was sure Frank might faint. His mouth opened and closed like a catfish out of water. "I—I—"

Beau's chair made a racket as he jumped to his feet. "Hell and damnation! I knew it! You *are* a danged sod—"

"Sit down!" Amanda ground out. "Now. And keep your voice down unless you want this conversation in the *Statesman* tomorrow."

He sat, but he looked as if he could have torn off both Frank's arms and beaten him with them. "Does my sister know that you have a boyfriend and that you wear . . . *dresses*?"

"I do *not* have a boyfriend. I'm not attracted to men—that way." Frank glanced to Amanda. "I'm not. I love Estelle. I love her deeply." He hung his head. "She knows . . . about my activities. I didn't want to keep secrets from her, but perhaps I should have. She doesn't understand any of it. I tried to explain to her that it's a harmless pastime—"

"Like stamp collecting," Beau said sarcastically.

Amanda kicked him again.

"Am I fired now?" Frank asked quietly.

The silence after his question was excruciating. Frank looked wretched and rather pitiable. The rouge he'd applied so deftly now looked clownish, the black wig and the red dress harsh; he resembled an aging bawd trying to recapture her youth.

"I suppose that depends on what Estelle wants," Beau said. "I need to think about this some more." He stood and offered Amanda his arm. "Shall we go?"

Beau pulled the buggy to a stop beside the river. The moon cast a shimmering spot of light on the dark water. The constant song of tree frogs filled the space under the canopy of oaks and echoed over the slow-moving Colorado. It was a peaceful place, and he needed a peaceful place right then. He wanted to breathe some fresh air, clear his head.

He and Amanda hadn't exchanged a word since they left the restaurant. That business with Frank had thrown him hard. He didn't know what to think or what to do. Hell, he was never cut out to be head of a family. He was too irresponsible. Isn't that what Uncle Angus always said? "Irresponsible young pup. You'll come to no good." Now, here he was, thrust into a position to make decisions that could alter the course of a person's life.

Several peoples' lives.

A hell of a spot to be in.

Suddenly Amanda kissed him on the cheek. "I'm very proud of you."

"You are? Why?"

"For not poking Frank in the nose. For realizing that this is a serious matter that will take some thought before anything can be resolved."

"Well, I guess I have learned over the years that a pat on the back won't cure saddle sores. But I'm worried about how this might hurt my sister and my nieces. I think it's already taken a toll on Estelle. Have you noticed that she's acted a little tipsy a time or two?"

Amanda nodded. "And I've wondered if that isn't the 'medicine' Ellie mentioned."

"God, what a mess." He put his arm around Amanda and pulled her against his side as he leaned back and looked up at the stars. "One of the few things I enjoyed about cowboying was lying out at night and looking up at the stars. Millions and millions of them up there. When you do that, sometimes your troubles don't seem quite as big. Do you know what I mean?"

"Yes. I've done that too. It helps to put things in perspective."

They were quiet for a moment, looking at the sky together, then he asked, "Do you think Frank was in on the kidnapping?"

"No, I don't. I thought he was telling the truth. Basically Frank is an honest man."

Beau gave a snort. "An honest man who sneaks around having tea parties in his dress. I wonder if Mama has any inkling of what's going on. Doubt if she'd let on, even if she did. Mama wouldn't admit there was a problem if her skirt tail was on fire, but seems like the family's got a bushel of them.

"Morris is an ass, and I think Judith is miserable. Frank is a Nancy-boy. Estelle is secretly hitting the bottle. God, what next? Oh, the devil with the whole blamed mess! It makes my head hurt to think about it."

"Give yourself some time, but the problem isn't going away," Amanda told him. "I've found that the best way to deal with situations like this is to be patient and talk openly and honestly. Getting angry and acting rash doesn't help matters, and no matter how hard we try, we can't bend people to fit our idea of what they ought to be."

"Lord, you're right about that. Look at Uncle Angus and me. All we did was butt heads." He put a finger under her chin, tilted her face upward, and touched his lips to hers. "How did you get to be so wise?"

He didn't wait for an answer. He kissed her again. Slowly. Sweetly. Longingly. At that moment he thought she might be an angel sent to earth just for him. Except that no angel should stir him the way she did. No, she was strong and sure and steady, but she wasn't an angel. She was flesh and blood and all woman.

He deepened the kiss while his hand cupped her breast and stroked it. She trembled at his touch, and he damned near went insane. At first she responded with an urgency that matched his, then she abruptly pushed him away.

"I think we need to go before—I think we need to go." She was breathing hard and her voice caught.

He lifted her face again. Moonlight glittered in her eyes like stars. "Amanda, I think I'm falling in love with you."

"Oh, you can't!" she cried. "You can't!"

"Why can't I?"

"Because—because I'm a *Pinkerton* agent!"

⌒ Nineteen ⌒

"Lift your chin and turn your head a little to the right," Judith said.

"Like this?"

"Perfect. You have such marvelous bone structure. Beau is going to cherish this bust."

"I hope so." As Amanda sat posing on the bench in Judith's studio, she couldn't help but think of Beau's words the night before. Was he truly falling in love with her? If he was, this was a serious complication. Getting personally involved with clients was highly unprofessional.

Especially when she felt the same way.

Oh, dear.

"Smile," Judith said. "You look so sad this morning, and you're so beautiful when you smile."

"As are you," Amanda told her, studying the wan face above the sketchbook. "But I've noticed that you rarely smile."

Judith glanced back down to her drawing and said nothing. Amanda didn't press the point, but in a moment when Judith reached for another piece of charcoal, her cuff rode up to reveal fresh bruises on her arm. Fury shot through Amanda when she saw them.

"That *bastard*!"

Judith startled, and her eyes widened. "I beg your pardon?"

Amanda sprang to her feet, strode to where Judith sat, and pulled back a sleeve. "Morris did that, didn't he? And I'll bet that isn't the worst of it. I've noticed you walking gingerly this morning."

Looking panicked, Judith withdrew her arm. "I—I think we'd better stop our session for now."

Kneeling before the nervous woman, Amanda took Judith's hands in hers. "I know that you're frightened, and I know that perhaps it's none of my business, but I understand what it's like to live with a man like Morris. I know the terrible torment of being beaten and cursed and feeling helpless and trapped. No woman should have to endure such treatment! Ever!"

Judith began weeping, and Amanda drew her into her arms. "I'm so ashamed," the young woman said. The words began tumbling out along with the pain that had been bottled up for so long.

The more Judith described the assaults she'd been enduring, the more angry Amanda became—and the more resolved to put an end to this abuse. She allowed Judith to get it all out, patting her, consoling her, lending her a handkerchief.

When Judith cried, "How long must I pay for my sins?" Amanda stiffened as a barrage of old memories struck her. She drew back, lifted the weeping woman's chin, and looked at her eye to eye.

"I don't want to ever hear you say such nonsense again! Morris Essig is the sinner here, not you. And you don't have to put up with such handling for one single minute longer."

"But there's nothing I can do. If I try to defy him, he beats me worse. I'm afraid that he might kill me—though sometimes I believe that I would welcome the peace of death."

"Don't talk that way, Judith. I'm going to put a stop to this immediately."

"I welcome your concern, Amanda, but he's my husband. I have no rights, no means of support, nowhere to go. It's hopeless. There's nothing you can do either."

Amanda stood, squared her shoulders, and smiled. "*Never* underestimate me, my dear."

Still in a high dudgeon and with her hat slightly askew, Amanda threw open the door and strode into Beau's office in the Blessing building. Beau and Frank were in deep conversation, but at that moment she didn't care a fig if she interrupted or not.

Beau looked up and smiled. "Amanda, come in. What brings you here?"

She slammed the door behind her. "Morris Essig is a bastard! What are you going to do about it?"

"Cut his heart out and feed it to the coyotes."

"I'm in no mood for humor."

"What has Morris done?"

"Cursed Judith, demeaned her, burned her new shawl to a cinder. Then he shook her and slammed her against a wall so hard that she can barely walk this morning."

Beau jumped to his feet. "That *bastard*!"

"My reaction exactly. But last night's abuse wasn't the worst of it. He beats her all the time, with a belt, with a cane, with his hands. She didn't have an accident in her studio last week. It was Morris's fist that caused the injury to her face. And she told me that last year he beat her so badly that the doctor had to be called."

"Oh, my God," Frank said. "She told us it was a fall down the stairs."

"And you believed it? Everybody believed she was so clumsy that she fell down stairs and ran into doors and had accidents with chisels all the time? Dear God, she's married to a monster, and her family didn't even try to help her? Did Estelle know the truth?" she asked Frank. "Did you?"

"I'm sure she didn't," Frank said. "Or at least she didn't know how bad things were. I . . . suspected there were problems, but I have no influence with Morris. I know the man's a monster, but he had Angus's ear, and I . . ." He hung his head.

"I've heard enough of this," Beau said. "I'm going to the brewery and toss that—"

"Wait," Amanda said, putting a hand on Beau's arm but keeping her gaze on Frank. "How do you know Morris is a monster?"

Frank looked up at her, misery etched in his face.

"He's the one who's been blackmailing you, isn't he?"

He nodded briefly and dropped his head again. "Somehow he found out about—my activities, and he threatened to tell Angus if I didn't pay. I paid. Dear Lord, I paid in so many ways. He's bled me dry, and now he's making terrible threats about exposing everything. I could stand it, but Estelle and the children would be devastated. I don't know what to do."

"By God, I do," Beau stormed. "And if you were any

kind of man, you would too." He yanked open a desk drawer and pulled out a six-shooter. "I'm going to blow that sorry son of a bitch to kingdom come!"

Amanda rolled her eyes. "Sit down, Beau. Killing him will only get you thrown in jail. We have to be smart about this. We need to make a plan."

Amanda, Beau, and Frank marched into Morris's office. Beau, who wore a rather nice pair of Colts strapped to his hips, seated Amanda and motioned for Morris to sit as well. Frank stood to one side looking very uncomfortable, resolute, but decidedly uncomfortable.

"Are you sure you won't join me in the *bierstube* for refreshments?" Morris asked.

"Nope," Beau answered. "This isn't a social call. It has come to my attention, Morris, that you're a sorry, low-down son of a bitch."

Morris jumped to his feet. "See here—!"

"Sit down, Morris!" Beau slickly tucked his coat behind his pair of guns and rested his hands on the pearl handles. Morris sat. "As I was saying, I just found out that you've been beating hell out of my sister, blackmailing Frank here, and for all I know, you've been stomping baby ducks for fun. All this is about to end."

The veins on Morris's neck stood out in bold purple relief, and his eyes blazed with fury. Jumping to his feet again, he said, "I'll—"

In a lightning-quick move, Beau cleared leather and stuck the barrel of one of the widow-makers under Morris's nose. "You'll nothing. Shut up. Sit."

He sat.

"Now, since I don't cotton to a man that mistreats my

sister, I voted to blow your damned head off. Frank was in favor of slicing off your balls, and Amanda, with her feminine sensitivity, thought you ought to leave on the afternoon train. So we decided that if you don't leave on the afternoon train out of Texas, we're gonna slice off your balls and then blow your head off."

"You wouldn't dare!" Morris said. "I'll go to the authorities."

"Then you'll be the one in trouble," Amanda said.

"For what? A husband has the right to chastise his own wife."

Struggling to remain calm, Amanda smiled. "Ah, but he doesn't have the right to blackmail someone. That's a crime."

Morris sneered at Frank. "That sodomite would never press charges against me."

Amanda could have kissed Frank as he drew himself up to his full height. "Oh, but I would," he said. "And if there threatens to be a scandal, Beau has promised to move my family and me to St. Louis or New York City or London if necessary. I'm not afraid of you anymore, Morris. And I'm *not* a sodomite, dammit!"

"Angus Blessing isn't around any longer," Amanda said. "Beau is in charge now. *He* has the money and the power. You no longer have a job, and if you try to fight, you'll go to prison. I'll make it my mission in life."

"And who would listen to a silly woman?"

"A great many people," she said evenly. "I'm a respected detective with the Pinkerton Agency, and I have the full force of that company behind me."

Morris seemed to shrink before their eyes.

Beau said, "We'll accompany you to the bank and the

house. I'll allow you to take a fair amount of cash with you, after you repay the money you bilked Frank out of, and you can take what you can carry in two suitcases. When you leave Austin today, I don't want to ever see or hear of you again."

Morris sputtered a bit more, but it was only for show. He knew when he was licked.

While Beau and Frank escorted Morris to a judicious meeting with the attorney before they went to the bank, Amanda took a hired cab home. She wanted to speak with Judith privately before they brought Morris home to pack.

Oh, dear, she thought on the way back to the Blessing mansion, *what if this isn't what Judith wants?* She had run across women who insisted on staying with men who mistreated them terribly.

She needn't have worried. When she found Judith in her studio and told her what had transpired, she burst into simultaneous laughter and tears.

Judith fell into Amanda's arms. "Oh, thank God. Thank God. My prayers have at last been answered. I could sing! I could dance!" She grasped Amanda's hands and whirled in a circle, laughing and crying. Then she hugged Amanda again. "I don't know how to begin to thank you. To be rid of that ogre! To be free! Oh, what a burden has been lifted from my shoulders. You're an angel, Amanda."

Amanda laughed. "Far from it. I'm a devil when I get angry. And you should have seen your brother. He was magnificent."

Judith drew Amanda to a settee. "Tell me again what Beau said to Morris."

Amanda repeated the entire episode in Morris's office,

leaving out her admitting to being a Pinkerton detective and any reference to Frank's indiscretions.

When she got to the part about slicing off his balls, Judith covered her mouth and giggled. "I can't imagine Frank suggesting that."

"Actually, he didn't, but Beau carried it off better than Edwin Booth. It was all I could do to keep from bursting into hilarity."

Judith laughed and hugged Amanda again. Then suddenly she stiffened and drew back, her face troubled. "What if something goes wrong? What if Morris changes his mind? I am, after all, still his wife. He could—"

"Shhhh. Don't worry a minute about it. That's why they went to the lawyer's office. They intend to have Morris sign incriminating documents. I can't give you the details without revealing someone else's secrets, but I can tell you that you'll be able to secure a divorce if you so choose."

"Oh, I'll choose all right. I don't care about the stigma being a divorced woman carries, not one iota. And rather than be an embarrassment to my family, I'll leave town. I'll go to—" Judith stopped abruptly and looked away.

"To where?"

She sighed. "I was going to say that I would go to Paris. I've dreamed of living there so often. Moving to Paris and living among other artists was a fantasy that kept me going when things were at their worst, but it's still only a dream. I don't have the means to live in France—or anywhere other than here."

"Oh, yes, you do. With Morris gone, I know that Beau plans to settle some money on you, a great deal of it. You can go anywhere your heart desires."

Judith beamed. Deep dimples in her cheeks and a bright gleam in her eyes transformed her features into beauty. "Truly?"

"Truly."

Amanda could almost see fetters fall away and Judith's soul soar. "I'm so happy things have turned out well for you. I'm only sorry you had to endure such terrible treatment for so long."

"It's over now. Finally over. I only wish—Amanda, the other person's secrets you spoke of, were you talking about Frank?"

"You know?"

"About his strange obsession? Yes, I know. Estelle confided in me. It haunts her. I tried to tell her that if I had a husband who loved me as much as Frank has always loved her, I wouldn't care if he wore a corset to church. But Estelle isn't like me. She's more like Mama and more concerned with what people might say than I am. Frank doesn't seem to be able to stop, no matter how much Estelle begs. She lives in terrible fear that the ladies in her circle might find out. Recently she's taken to hiding a medicine bottle full of gin in her sewing basket. I worry."

"It's a terrible dilemma."

Judith nodded. "You know, I've been giving the matter some thought. I wasn't able to solve my own problems, but I've come up with an idea for Frank and Estelle that might work."

⌒ Twenty ⌒

At dinner that night, when the whole brood had congregated at the table and before the soup was served, Beau stood and tapped his glass with a spoon.

"I have an announcement to make," he said. Though Frank had prepared Estelle for the news, and Judith had told Mama and Aunt Katie, Beau hadn't had an opportunity to address the entire clan.

He took a deep breath, then said quietly, "Uncle Angus is dead, and I'm head of the family now." His statement of the obvious was more for himself than for the rest of them. Saying it out loud committed him to the responsibility, and surprisingly, it didn't bother him as much as he thought it would. In fact, it made him feel pretty good.

"I suspect that I'll make a few mistakes," he told them, "but I hope I'll be better at admitting them than Uncle Angus was. Be that as it may, we're going to do things a little differently than he did. First, we're going to be as honest and open as we can be. Now you may have noticed that Morris is missing from the table."

Every eye went to his empty chair beside Judith.

"Did he die?" Naomi asked.

"Naomi!" Estelle said.

207

"But, Mama," Naomi said, "Uncle Beau said we should be open and honest, and I honestly wondered."

"No," Beau said, fighting a grin, "he didn't die. But he came close." He cleared his throat to keep from laughing when he thought of the skunk's reaction to that six-shooter under his nose—and his guns hadn't even been loaded. Amanda had insisted he keep the bullets in his pocket, lest he lose his temper and shoot the bastard after all.

"Morris didn't die, but he's gone from our family for good. He wasn't a nice man, he did some very bad things, and we kicked him out of the family. He won't be back."

"Good," Helen said. "I never liked Uncle Morris. He was an old sourpuss, and he pinched me once. Hard."

"Me too," Ellie piped up. "And he yelled. Loud. That's very rude."

"Uncle Beau," Ellie said, a worried look on her face.

"Yes, Ellie?"

"If I do bad things, will you throw me away?"

"Nope," Beau replied, smiling. "I wouldn't throw you away even if you did awful, awful things. You're blood kin. And before any of you kids wonder, I'm not planning on throwing out your daddy or Amanda either. Only Morris. And while we don't intend to take out an ad in the *Statesman* to announce his departure, we're not going to make up stories about it either. People don't have anything to gossip about if you tell the truth. And the truth is, Morris was not a nice man, and we asked him to leave our family."

"Are you sad about that, Aunt Judith?" Louise asked.

"No, dear, I'm not sad at all. Your uncle Beau is right,

Morris wasn't a nice man. I'm very happy that he's gone."

Louise smiled. "So am I," she whispered.

"Me, too," Aunt Katie chimed in. "Good riddance, I say. Never did give a tinker's damn for that German."

"Aunt Katie!" Maud said.

"Oh, Maud, come down off your high horse. You didn't have much use for him either. Admit that you're glad to see his tail feathers."

Maud glanced around at everybody, then caught Judith's eye. Her words could barely be heard, but she said, "Good riddance."

"Thank you for that, Mama."

Aunt Katie let out a cackle, and everyone began to smile and chatter. Dinner was a delightful affair. Everyone seemed considerably more at ease.

With her social smile firmly in place, Estelle stared down at her pork roast and spiced apples. She knew she couldn't take another bite.

She was happy for Judith, truly she was. Lord knows Morris Essig was a terrible man who treated her sister unspeakably, but now with Judith's problems solved, her own seemed to loom twice as large.

It was all well and good for Beau to blithely spout his pronouncements about being open and honest and avoiding wagging tongues by not hiding things. They didn't know the devastating secret that could tear the family apart.

Judith was happy to be rid of Morris. Estelle's own situation wasn't as simple. She didn't want to be rid of Frank; she loved him dearly. Her girls adored their father. But if her daughters and her mother—or even her brother—had any inkling that Frank cavorted around town in satin dresses and flowered hats, they would be mortified. They wouldn't be so ready to tell the world that Frank engaged in heinous perversions that were an abomination before God and would make the entire family a laughingstock if the truth were known.

Open and honest indeed!

She had begged Frank, *begged* him on her knees to give up this terrible behavior before someone caught him. He had tried, or at least he had seemed to try, but it hadn't lasted long. It was like a sickness with him. Soon she would notice signs that he'd been up to his old stunts— the strong scent of the perfume he preferred, or rouge stains on his clothes.

Estelle didn't know how much longer she could endure living in mortal fear that someone in her mission society would catch him parading around in skirts. Her stomach stayed tied in knots, and she rarely got a decent night's sleep anymore.

"Estelle," her mother said, "you've hardly eaten a bite. Aren't you feeling well?"

She forced a smile. "I'm feeling fine, Mama. Actually, I'm saving room for dessert. I understand that Mrs. Kilgore made blackberry cobbler."

"She did," Barbara, one of the twins, said. "Bonnie and I are serving dessert tonight, and I'll make sure you get an extra big portion."

Estelle nearly gagged.

Judith saw through her sister's ruse. She knew that Estelle was miserable, and her own happiness dimmed because of it. She hoped that she would be able to do something to help Estelle. Maybe her plan would work. Estelle wasn't nearly as adventurous as she or Beau was, but perhaps she might be flexible enough to try something that might save her marriage—and save face at the same time.

Pushing aside her concerns, she vowed that she was going to enjoy this first night of freedom. She didn't want anything to blunt the happiness she felt.

A little niggle of guilt crept into her awareness. She felt it start to grow. Shame began to spread through her, followed by dark and heavy dread. Quickly, she tamped it down. Tomorrow she would deal with her sins. She would savor tonight.

After dinner Judith, Amanda, and Beau strolled through the side garden where Aunt Katie's carefully tended roses were beginning to open.

Beau lit a slim cigar and blew the smoke upward as he shook out the match. "Judith, Amanda said you wanted to talk to me about something. Are you having second thoughts about our running Morris out of town?"

"No. Nothing like that. I'm happy that he's gone. I feel better than I have in years." She tiptoed to kiss his cheek. "Thanks, big brother. I wanted to talk to you privately about something else—two things actually. First, I have an idea for a way to help Frank and Estelle. It might not work, but it's worth a try."

"I'm listening."

"Well, you know how much Frank likes to sing—or maybe you don't since you've been away so long. He sings beautifully—you heard him in church. And he's very fond of Gilbert and Sullivan, as I am. We'd even discussed forming a Gilbert and Sullivan society here at one time. I read someplace that there are casts of plays and such where there are all-male companies."

"Oh, yes," Amanda said. "There are many such productions."

"Well," Judith continued, "what if Frank formed an all-male Gilbert and Sullivan society whose object was to perform?"

Amanda smiled as she caught Judith's train of thought. "The society could practice and present an entire operetta or even a few selections for various audiences in the city."

"Exactly." Judith beamed.

Beau nodded. "Frank could play female parts, and he would have a perfectly legitimate reason for wearing a dress. He ought to be in hog heaven doing that. And Estelle wouldn't be throwing a conniption fit about him being decked out in skirts. In fact, knowing Estelle, she'd like the attention when he brought the house down."

"Do you think they'll be agreeable?" Judith asked.

"I think it's worth a try," Beau said. "Let's talk to them about it tomorrow morning while the girls are in school. I'll get Mama to keep Ellie occupied for a few hours while we talk."

"Better yet," Amanda said, "I'll take Ellie on an excursion while you two talk with Estelle and Frank. I think this is something too intimate to include me. Estelle is going to be embarrassed enough without a near stranger being privy to her secrets."

Beau brought her fingers to his lips and kissed them. "Another pearl of wisdom." To Judith he said, "Is it any wonder I love her?"

His sister smiled. "None at all. Amanda, I'm going to adore having you as a sister-in-law. See you in the morning." With a jaunty wave, Judith struck out for her cottage.

"I wonder what the other thing was that she wanted to talk about," Amanda said.

"What other thing?"

"She said that she wanted to talk to you about two things tonight."

He shrugged. "She must have forgotten. I'll ask her tomorrow." He took another couple of puffs from his cigar, then stubbed it out on his boot heel and tossed it away. "I hope this idea of hers about Frank pans out. He and I talked a good while this morning before you showed up. From what he tells me, he's really tried to change, but he can't. I don't know if I believe him or not. Sounds like a bunch of hogwash to me."

"I don't understand what happens to him either, but I think Frank's sincere. And I think he would be willing to try anything to ease Estelle's mind. She's the person you have to convince. It might be best if you let Judith talk to Estelle before the four of you get together. She might feel overwhelmed otherwise."

"Good idea. And I can tell Frank about Judith's solution, see what he thinks."

A breeze kicked up, bringing a freshening to the air. Amanda lifted her face to the wind. "Smells like rain."

"I caught a flash of lightning toward the northwest a bit ago. I 'spect we'll see a thunderstorm before morning." He sat down on a garden bench and pulled Amanda down beside him. "Have you thought any more about what I said last night?"

She started to feign innocence or act coy or play just plain dumb, but she didn't. She knew exactly what he was talking about. But she didn't want to tell him that her mind had been filled with it since he'd said those unsettling words. "Yes, I've thought about it, and—"

He put a finger across her lips. "Don't tell me again that I can't be falling in love with you. If you did, you'd be right. I'm not falling in love with you."

A sudden swell of sorrow swept over her, a terrible aching sorrow. She should've been cheered by his words, but she wasn't. She was devastated.

"I'm not falling," he said. "I've already fallen. Amanda, I love you with all my heart."

Joy burst through the sorrow and broke with a radiant smile. "You do?"

"I do."

He kissed her then—kissed her with such feeling that she was grateful to be sitting. And as unwise as it was, she kissed him back. His lips were warm and wonderful, and when they parted slightly, she parted hers as well. When his tongue slipped into her mouth, she startled at the thrill that raced through her, and opened wider for his entry.

His arms drew her closer, and his hands moved firmly along the curve of her back. Her arms went around him as well, and she could feel his muscles bunch under her touch.

As he continued kissing her, his hand went between them to tug at the buttons of her collar. And though there were a dozen or more, he slipped them easily and quickly from their moorings until her throat was laid bare to him.

His hand gently stroked the exposed flesh, and she

moaned against his lips. His mouth left hers and moved lower.

"Amanda, my love," he murmured against her throat. His tongue did maddening things to the hollow there while his fingers explored her collarbone, then slipped downward to the swell of her breast.

She shivered.

"Cold?" he asked.

"Yes. No. I don't know."

His hand slipped even lower inside her bodice, and she squirmed. "I, uh—I—"

"Yes, love?"

"I forget."

He chuckled and kissed her lips again, more passionately this time, and his hand cupped her bare breast. She felt a terrible wonderful ache low in her body, chill bumps racing over her skin, and wetness pummeling her.

Wetness?

She pushed away. "Beau! It's raining."

"Is it? I hadn't noticed." He reached for her mouth again.

"Beau, we're getting drenched! We have to get inside."

Thunder rolled and the drops increased in frequency. Beau grabbed her hand, and they dashed for the house. They made it to the cover of the porch barely ahead of a torrential downpour.

She scraped back her wet hair and flung water from her fingertips. "Look at me! I'm soaked."

"You're beautiful."

Glancing up, she could see the color of his beautiful green eyes illuminated by the gaslight. They shone like emerald chips, and raindrops caught on his long thick lashes and on his mustache glittered like diamonds. She touched the scar running along his jaw, and he moved to nibble at her finger.

She smiled. How was it possible that this face, unknown to her such a short time ago, had become so dear? How had a man so quickly captured her heart? How had she allowed it to happen?

He began buttoning up her dress, and feelings of sweet, sweet tenderness filled her totally. When he had finished, he bent and touched his lips to hers briefly. "Let's get you inside and dried off before you catch cold."

"And you too?"

He smiled. "And me too."

They went inside and found Aunt Katie waiting in the hallway. "I was wondering if you two had sense enough to come in out of the rain. Get out of those wet clothes, the both of you. I'll make some hot chocolate. Nothing takes a chill off like a good cup of hot chocolate. And while you're a-drinkin' it, I want the real low-down on what happened to that bastard Morris Essig."

They laughed and ran upstairs.

⌒ Twenty-one ⌒

As it turned out, Aunt Katie accompanied Amanda and Ellie on their excursion. Maud had a meeting with one of her ladies' groups, and Aunt Katie declared that she was tired of being cooped up in that big house and needed a breath of air and an opportunity to stretch her legs.

Ellie was delighted to be on a grown-up outing with Amanda. She jabbered the entire block from the house to the streetcar line and was thrilled with the conveyance and the mules that drew the car along its tracks.

"I've never ridden a streetcar before," Ellie told the conductor when they boarded, "not since I was little."

"That so, young lady," the conductor said, smiling amid his great quantity of whiskers.

Ellie could barely sit still as they rode to the end of the Pecan Street line, then back again to Congress Avenue. Along the way they looked out the windows at the activity along the street and watched people get off and on the car, including one man with a rooster under his arm. Ellie put her hands over her mouth and giggled at that, but she was especially taken with the woman sitting across from them, who carried a basket full of kittens.

Aunt Katie seemed to enjoy their adventure too, and

when Amanda helped her down from the car when they exited on the avenue, there seemed to be a new spring in her step.

"Oh, Miss Amanda, look! A monkey!"

Amanda grabbed Ellie just as she was about to dart off. "I see it, but you mustn't run ahead. Stay beside me and hold on to my hand."

They stopped to listen to the organ grinder. The monkey, which was tethered by a small chain, performed all sorts of tricks while his master entreated the passersby to come to the medicine show that evening in the big tent next to Waller Creek.

"Can we go to the medicine show, Miss Amanda? Please. Please. I wouldn't wiggle a bit. I promise."

Amanda smiled. "You'll have to ask your mother about that. Aunt Katie, do you feel up to walking to the department store on the next block?"

" 'Course I do. And I wouldn't mind seeing that medicine show myself, Ellie. We'll talk your mama and daddy into taking us, how about that?"

"Oh, goody! Can Naomi come too? And Helen and Louise. They'll want to see it for sure. And maybe Bonnie and Barbara, but you never can tell about them."

"We'll ask everybody," Aunt Katie told her.

Ellie was thrilled at the prospect, and she danced along beside Amanda to the store and the toy section inside. When told she could select one toy for herself, Ellie immediately selected a doll with a porcelain face and dark hair.

"She's beau-ti-ful," Ellie crooned, then she smiled shyly. "She looks like you, Miss Amanda. And that's what I'm going to name her. Amanda."

Amanda's heart swelled to twice its size. How dear this child had become to her. Again, as seemed to have happened several times in the past few days, a poignant moment had made her long for roots again, for a family to call her own. She would miss these dear children and curt Aunt Katie and the rest.

"Why, thank you, Ellie. I'm honored," she said, smiling. "Now, let's select things for your sisters."

After a great deal of looking and pondering and discussion among the three of them, they settled on a similar doll for Naomi, marionettes for Louise and Helen, and music boxes for Barbara and Bonnie. Amanda made arrangements for all the packages to be delivered, except for Ellie's new doll, which the little girl insisted on carrying with her.

"I'm ready for an ice cream soda," Amanda announced. "How about you?"

"Oh, yes!" Ellie danced around like an excited puppy. "Strawberry."

"Sounds right tasty to me too," Aunt Katie said.

After a visit to the ice cream parlor, they watched the workers at the Capitol site for a while, then stopped by a bookstore to browse the shelves and glance through the latest publications. Ellie was an angel, content to play with her doll while Aunt Katie and Amanda each bought a book.

They arrived home just in time for lunch. Maud, Judith, and Beau were waiting for them in the parlor. Amanda was anxious to know the outcome of the talks with Estelle and Frank, but with the others present, she didn't have an opportunity to ask.

Ellie showed everyone her new doll and gave an excited, if slightly garbled, account of their morning, then dashed off to ask her parents about going to the medicine show.

A few minutes later, as Amanda spooned her corn chowder, she glanced at Beau and furrowed her brow. She was hoping for some sign from him to relieve her mind. He smiled and winked. She glanced at Judith, who also smiled.

Amanda took the smiles to mean that things looked favorable between Estelle and Frank. Although she knew she was being as nosy as Aunt Katie, she could hardly wait until the meal was done to hear the details. Threads of the table conversation flitted in and out of her head: Maud's recitation of somebody's illness, Aunt Katie's embroidered account of the man with the rooster on the streetcar, other trivia that she didn't even try to follow.

After the meal was finally over and Maud and Aunt Katie had moved to the parlor, Amanda practically dragged Beau and Judith into the study. The moment the door closed behind them, she said, "Did it work?"

Judith laughed. "It worked. Sort of."

"What do you mean 'sort of'?"

"Frank thought it was a grand idea," Beau said.

"Estelle wasn't so sure," Judith added, "and she was embarrassed that Beau knew about the situation, but she's willing to try it. She's asking some concessions of Frank, and I think they're reasonable."

"Such as?"

"That he get rid of the rooms in Austin and confine his dressing up to visits out of town or to the Gilbert and Sullivan society activities. Frank agreed."

Beau said, "She doesn't want to discuss his behavior anymore or know anything about what he does out of town. Frank agreed to that, too. She agreed to pour out the gin. I don't think everything is perfect between them yet, but I think it's a start."

"Wonderful!" Amanda said.

"Yep," Beau said. "I think this family is on the road to getting its problems straightened out. The only thing still hanging is finding out who kidnapped Uncle Angus. Judith, do you suppose Morris could have had anything to do with it?"

Judith's smile died. She paled. "No. I'm sure he didn't."

"I don't know," Beau said. "Seems like he was stirring the kettle in a lot of the family troubles."

Judith looked stricken and sank into a chair as if her limbs would no longer hold her up. She dropped her face into her hands, and a muffled cry escaped her.

"Judith," Beau said, looking alarmed, "are you okay?"

He started toward his sister, but Amanda grasped his arm. She shook her head. He frowned, clearly puzzled.

Another terrible cry came from Judith. "Oh, I'm so sorry. So sorry. Forgive me."

Amanda knelt beside her. "For what?"

Judith looked up, tears streaking her cheeks, her face a mask of misery. "I did it. I planned the kidnapping. I hired those men from the stable."

"*You?*" Beau said. "Good Lord, why?"

"Paris?" Amanda asked softly.

Still weeping, Judith nodded.

"Paris? What the dickens are you talking about?" Beau asked.

"She's talking about her desperation to escape Morris's abuse."

"I had to get away from him. I had to. I longed to move to Paris, to be among other artists and away from *him*, but I had no money of my own and no means to get any. Morris controlled every penny and wouldn't even let me sell my sculpture. Even if Uncle Angus had left me something—which he didn't—Morris would have controlled that, too. Oh, Beau, please understand how very desperate I was." She began sobbing again.

He pulled his sister in his arms. "Oh, honey, don't make yourself sick over this. Hell, if it was you, I don't care. Forget about it."

"I think your plan was extremely clever," Amanda said, laughing. "I applaud your creativity."

Red-eyed, Judith pulled back from Beau's embrace. "You do?"

"Hell, yes," Beau said, fishing out his handkerchief. He started laughing, too. "I think it's a hoot that you were using the old codger for something worthwhile. Here, blow your nose."

She honked a good one and dried her tears. "You're not going to throw me away?" she asked, trying to smile.

"Nope. You're my sister, and I love you. Do you still want to live in Paris?"

Her eyes lit up. "More than anything."

"Then start packing."

"Do you mean it? Do you really mean it?"

"Yep. I'll see to it you have everything you need."

Judith threw her arms around Beau and hugged him. "Oh, Beau, you're the best brother in the whole world. You're better than a fairy godmother."

He laughed.

Amanda laughed, too. She wanted to hug him herself. He was such a good man, such a loving man. He would make a wonderful husband and father for—

Her heart tripped. *For somebody,* she was going to say. For somebody, but not for her. With Judith's admission, the case was closed. Her work was over. It was time for her to move on.

After Judith left, Amanda said as much to Beau.

"Leave? But you can't leave!"

She tried to smile, but she couldn't quite manage it. "I must. The case is solved."

Beau began pacing. "But what am I going to tell everybody when you just up and leave? Mama about has our entire wedding planned. And the girls. Ellie will probably cry for days. She's crazy about you, you know." He strode to her and grasped her shoulders. "And what about me? I'm crazy about you, too."

"Beau," she began, but her voice broke and she had to clear her throat and start over. "Beau, our engagement was always a sham. Have you forgotten? We can either tell them the truth about my identity, or we can concoct a story to explain my departure, whichever you prefer, but depart I must. Staying longer would only make my leaving more difficult."

"But, Amanda, I love—"

She put her fingers to his lips to keep the words at bay. Her heart was almost breaking when she forced a smile and said, "I'm honored by your declaration, truly I am, but I don't see any possibility of a future for us."

His grip on her shoulders tightened. "Dammit! Why not?"

"Let go of me! *Now*."

Instantly, he dropped his hands. "I'm sorry, Amanda. I didn't mean to squeeze you so hard. Lord a-mighty, I wouldn't hurt you for the world. You know that, don't you, darlin'?"

"I'm not afraid of you, but you have too quick a temper, Beau. Your short fuse and brashness may be your undoing one of these days. In any case, I'll be leaving in the morning. Tell your family what you will."

Beau felt like a sinner in a cyclone. He'd made a mess of things with Amanda. She was the only woman he'd ever truly loved, and he'd fouled up his chances with her. Hell, he knew he had a quick temper, but he'd never hurt her. He wasn't the same kind of son of a bitch that Morris was. Beau had never struck a woman in his life—in anger or any other way. Dammit, if she knew that, why was she leaving?

He paced the study some more, trying to think of a plan to keep her in Austin. All that came to mind was to convince her that he loved her and would spend the rest of his life trying to make her happy. He'd see to it she never wanted for a thing.

Flinging open the door, he started down the hall and ran smack into Aunt Katie. "Whoa," he said, steadying her.

"Where you going in such an all-fired hurry?"

"I have to talk to Amanda."

"She's gone."

The blood drained from his face. "*Gone?*"

"Yep. Said she had some errands to run. She'll be back directly. You look plumb whey-faced. What's got into you, boy?"

"I thought you meant she was gone for good."

"For good? Why'd you think that?"

"Because she said she was leaving. I have something to tell everybody. Where's Mama?"

"After Judith confessed to the kidnapping, Maud took to her bed." Aunt Katie chuckled. "All this honesty round here nowadays is gettin' to be too much for your mama. Me, I think it's about time we all started totin' level."

"Judith told you?"

"She did. Blurted out the whole mess to Maud and me. I thought it was right clever of her, but Maud like to have swooned on the Turkey rug—though I'll say this for your mama, she held her counsel till Judith left. I think Judith meant to tell Frank and Estelle, too."

"That's good. How did Mama take the news about Judith moving to Paris?"

"Paris? She didn't tell that part of it. Prob'ly figured Maud would fall out in a faint for sure. Was that what you were gonna tell everybody?"

Beau raked a hand through his hair. "No. I was going to tell them about Amanda."

"About her being the Pinkerton man? Shoot, I reasoned that out a long time ago. Don't 'spect anybody else has caught on to it yet. She leaving soon?"

"Tomorrow morning, she says."

"You look like somebody tore you down even with the ground. You not happy about her leaving?"

"No, ma'am, I'm not happy about it at all."

"You love her, son?"

"Yes, ma'am, I do."

"You tell her?"

"Yes, ma'am, I did. But she's leaving anyhow. Mama's

really going to be sick when she finds out there's not going to be a wedding."

"Did you ask Amanda to marry you?"

"Well, not in so many words, but I figured—"

"You *figured*! Ain't that just like a man? Don't *figure*. Ask her plain out. See what she says. From the way I caught her looking at you a time or two, I'll bet my last nickel that she cares more about you than she's letting on."

He kissed her wrinkled forehead. "Aunt Katie, how did you get to be so wise?"

"Don't know about wise, but in eighty-four years, a body's bound to learn something."

Beau grinned, and walked away grinning. He had a chance after all. Aunt Katie was right. Amanda cared for him. Oh, maybe she didn't love him like he loved her, but she cared. She couldn't have kissed him the way she had if she hadn't felt something special for him. He meant to corner her the minute she got home and propose—and kiss the dickens out of her, too.

☙ Twenty-two ❧

For the second time that day, Amanda boarded the streetcar. This time she rode to a stop near the Chicago House where her disguises were stored. She sat ramrod stiff, staring straight ahead, ordering herself not to cry. These good people would have been shocked if she'd broken down and wept the way she wanted to.

One of the cardinal rules of good detective work was *never* to get emotionally involved in cases. It clouded the judgment and invariably caused complications. She hadn't paid attention, and now she was paying the consequences. She had no one to blame except herself.

Stepping off at the intersection, Amanda briskly walked the short distance to the rented room. Once safely inside, she allowed herself to let go of the tears that stung her eyes and clogged her throat. She threw herself across the bed and wept.

She wept until she had no more tears in her. They hadn't washed away her pain. It persisted.

Rolling over onto her side, she stared at the pattern of sunlight cast through the lace curtains and onto the opposite wall. How familiar this room seemed: lace curtains, chipped washbowl, the lingering smell of lye soap and strangers. During the past several years, she'd spent countless hours in dreary hotel rooms like this one—alone and lonely.

She wanted to stay. She wanted desperately to stay, but she was afraid. And the fear ran deep.

Now she had freedom and self-respect. She had an excellent job with the regard of her company and cohorts. She was dependent on no man's whims. She'd fought too hard for too long to give up all she'd earned for someone she'd known only briefly. Oh, Beau made her body behave strangely and caused her heart to sing, but the heart was a fickle thing. Lust was fleeting. Logic would serve her better. She'd made her choices long ago; she must ignore temptation's whispers.

She sat up, took several fortifying breaths, and rose. She washed her face, straightened her garments, and began to gather her belongings.

Once packed, she checked out of the hotel, hired a cab, and had the driver stop by the telegraph office. Her business there was brief: to scribble a ten-word telegram to her supervisor and pay for it. Her next stop was the train station, where she bought a ticket and made arrangements to leave the bag she carried until her departure the following morning.

Not feeling ready yet to return to the Blessing mansion, she asked the driver to drop her off at the ice cream parlor. Men preferred to drown their sorrows in strong liquor; even Estelle had tried that method. Amanda had always found that ice cream did wonders for a flagging spirit.

She ate three dishes of vanilla.

All it did was make her bilious.

Walking. That always cleared her head.

She walked all the way down Congress Avenue to the toll bridge at the river. Her head was still a muddle, and her feet hurt.

Finding herself on the edge of Guy Town, she considered stopping by to see Fanny Campbell at the Pink Feather Saloon, but since the sun was riding low, she abandoned the notion as foolish. Instead she caught the north-south streetcar and rode it to where the line intersected that of the east-west car.

Dinner time approached, and she could no longer avoid the inevitable. She went home. No, not home. She went to the Blessing mansion and the family table for the last time.

Beau had paced the entry hall and peered out the window scores of times before he finally saw Amanda opening the front gate. He was waiting for her before she got to the steps. Dear God, she looked sweeter than stolen honey coming toward him, so damned beautiful that she could make a man plow through a stump.

He smiled and tried to act natural. "I was about to send the posse after you. Ellie and Aunt Katie have talked the family into going to the medicine show, so we wanted to have dinner a little early."

"Sorry. I hope you didn't wait for me."

"No, we're just now gathering." He offered her his arm.

"I'm really not hungry. Perhaps I'll skip dinner."

His heart about dropped to his boot tops, but he didn't let on. "On your last night here? Not on your life. You can at least have a bowl of soup with us. And I've had Harve out in the back yard cranking out your favorite dessert. Vanilla ice cream."

She didn't act as thrilled over the ice cream as he thought she would, but he didn't let it bother him. He grabbed her hand, tucked her arm through his, and took off for the dining room before she could object again.

"Look who finally made it home," Beau said to the family.

"Oh, Miss Amanda," Ellie said, beaming, "we're going to the medicine show as soon as we eat dinner."

There was an excited buzz around the table as Beau seated her. Besides the anticipation of the medicine show, the girls' presents had been delivered. They were all delighted with her choices and everyone thanked Amanda exuberantly.

In keeping with Beau's new honesty policy, Amanda considered telling the family her true identity and that she was leaving, but everyone was in such good spirits that she didn't want to spoil the revelry. After she was gone, Beau would find the right words and the right time to explain.

Dinner was finally over, though Amanda ate little, and Ellie ran to Amanda's chair. "I can hardly wait to see the medicine show, can you?"

Amanda smoothed back a blond wisp tangled in Ellie's eyelashes and smiled. "I don't think I'm going with you tonight, dear. I'm very tired."

"Oh, but you have to. Please, please, please."

"Everybody's going," Helen said. "Daddy says we won't be out late. We have school tomorrow."

"Do come," Judith said. "Even I'm going."

With the whole bunch urging, she finally agreed.

Harve and Frank each drove a carriage, and somehow Amanda ended up in the buggy alone with Beau. She'd tried to get one of the girls to ride along with them, but Beau had outmaneuvered her.

They did have a pleasant time of it. The organ grinder and the monkey were outside the tent greeting patrons as they entered. The show featured a magician and a couple who sang and danced. They weren't among the best entertainers Amanda had ever seen, but they weren't bad either. The children were enthralled. Frank even bought two bottles of tonic that promised to cure everything from bunions to baldness.

"It couldn't hurt," Frank said, winking as he smoothed his sparsely covered pate.

As they drove home, Beau said, "You're very quiet this evening."

"I don't have much to say. I should have stayed home and packed. I'm leaving in the morning."

"Is there anything I can say to make you stay?"

"No."

He pulled the buggy over to the side of the street and stopped. Taking both her hands in his, he kissed first one palm, then the other. "I forgot something. I hope it will make a difference. Amanda, I love you, and I want you to stay in Austin and become my wife. Will you marry me?"

His smile was so open, so hopeful, it broke her heart to give him her answer. "I'm honored, Beau. Truly I am. But, no. I can't marry you, won't marry you. I'm sorry." Her words were barely a whisper and every one of them almost choked her.

"But why? For godsake, *why* won't you marry me?"

She hung her head. "I don't think I could make you understand."

He lifted her chin. "Try."

"I've told you a little bit about my life growing up. My father was a preacher, but he had the devil's own temper. I know exactly how Judith felt, because I endured all that she endured, maybe worse. I was cursed, beaten, spat on. I swore then if I got away from that man, I would never let any man dominate me again."

"My God, Amanda, do you think I would treat you like that?"

"Perhaps not, but you have a temper, Beau. Even if you were as docile as a lamb, it wouldn't matter. No man will ever have lawful dominion over me. I refuse to be shackled and powerless. You can't imagine how much I value my freedom."

"Oh, I think I can. I was in prison, remember? I used to dream of freedom, dreamed of it every night I was in that hellhole."

"Would you go back to prison again?"

"Not still breathing."

"That's how I feel," she said quietly. "Marriage would be a prison to me. Please take me home."

"Amanda—"

"Please."

He snapped the reins and headed home.

Amanda packed her trunk, leaving out only the things she would need the following morning. She tied the ribbons at the neck of her nightgown, turned down the light, and climbed into bed.

Bone-weary and soul-weary, she longed for sleep, but

it didn't come quickly. Her thoughts were filled with Beau. How tempted she'd been to accept his proposal. She'd grown to love his family and, yes, him.

But love wasn't enough. She recalled another time when a man had muddled her reason and laid siege to her emotions. He wasn't like Beau, not anything like him—except for his quick temper. And his charm. A leading man with one of the acting troupes she'd joined, Douglas had pledged his undying love too. She'd been young and naive and believed in fairy-tale endings then.

Douglas was every woman's fantasy. He was handsome, suave, talented. Their engagement had been wonderful. He'd treated her like a princess—until the first time she defied him. They'd been having a lovely private dinner when things got ugly. Douglas, who had promised to love her and protect her with his life, lost his temper and slapped her.

She would never forget his expression when she grabbed the mutton knife, held it to his privates, and threatened to unman him if he touched her again. That was the end of both the engagement and her tour with that company. She'd vowed that night she would never allow herself to be in such a vulnerable position again. She'd joined the Pinkerton Agency soon after.

Perhaps Beau would never do such a thing as Douglas had, but she couldn't bear it if he did. Her heart would be shattered beyond repair. If she left now, it would be only damaged.

She also knew something else. There would never be another Beau in her life. She would never let another man past her defenses.

Her biggest regret was that she would leave this house

never having made love with him. She would have cherished the memory, one that would keep her warm on nights ahead when a spell of loneliness might carry a melancholy chill.

Her theater friends would have been shocked to hear that the worldly Amanda had never taken a man to her bed.

She hadn't. Not one.

She'd never really wanted any man enough—until Beau. He was the special one she'd never forget.

Fitful, she turned under the covers and punched her pillow.

She closed her eyes and waited for sleep.

It didn't come.

Her whole body quivered like a banjo string. Her head felt as if someone had struck a tuning fork and held it to her temple.

She turned again. Then again.

An ache started to unfurl low in her belly, then lower still. She moved her legs restlessly. The ache increased.

A sudden memory came of Beau kissing her bare throat, cupping her breast. She could almost feel his fingers on her skin and the wetness of his tongue—

What madness tortured her? She yanked the covers over her head and turned again.

The memories crept back.

Hot, she flung aside the quilt.

She was still hot.

Her problem wasn't the weather or the temperature of the room. Her heat grew from desire. Just because she'd never had a man didn't mean that she was unaware of the process, of the passions and reactions of the body. No one could live in close quarters with a group of actresses and remain ignorant. She recognized the source of her yearning, though she never dreamed it could be so . . . consuming.

Once before she died, just once, she wanted to experience sensual pleasures with a man. And she wanted that man to be Beau.

Slowly, she pushed open the door to his room. "Beau?" she whispered into the darkness.

"Yes," came the reply from near the window.

"I can't see anything."

The scratch of a match, then a flare cast a glow where he stood. He lit the two candles that sat on the table beside him. "What are you doing here?

"I couldn't sleep," she said, leaning back against the door. He wore only a shirt and trousers, and the shirt was unbuttoned and hanging loose outside his pants.

"I couldn't either." He tipped a brandy glass and drained it.

Candlelight caught the contours of his bare chest, glistened like oil on his skin and tipped the fine hair there with gold. Her mouth went dry. The ache increased.

Without a word, she turned the key in the lock behind her and walked toward him, leisurely but unwavering in her destination. He waited, silent, eyes following her every step.

When she stood before him, she lifted her hand to his chest, laid it flat against his bare skin, and stroked slowly upward to his collarbone, then downward to his abdomen. His muscles tensed under her ministrations, and her breasts swelled with both excitement and a sense of power. He watched her intently, but his arms stayed at his side and he said not a word.

So that there could be no question about her intentions, she stepped back and untied the sash of her robe. She wore nothing beneath it.

⌒ Twenty-three ⌒

When her robe fell to the floor and puddled around her feet, Amanda heard the sharp intake of air between Beau's teeth. She glanced up into his eyes, but his gaze didn't meet hers. His attention was riveted lower, scrutinizing her naked body. She could see his Adam's apple move as he swallowed, and the pulse throbbing at the side of his neck. Her own pulse seemed deafening.

Neither spoke, neither moved.

After an eon, he said in a hoarse voice, "Is this some kind of test?"

She smiled. "Not that I'm aware of. I wanted to stay with you tonight. Don't you want me?" she asked quietly.

"Not want you? Woman, are you crazy?" He gathered her into his arms and kissed her with an urgency that sent her soaring. "Dear Lord, Amanda, I've never seen anything in my life more beautiful, never touched anything more precious. You're everything I've ever dreamed—and more."

He kissed her again, a hot, hungry kiss designed to sear her soul. Her hunger matched his. His tongue thrust deeply into her mouth, and she clutched the cloth of his shirt in her fists and stripped it away.

Never had she felt anything more erotic than the sensation of her bare breasts against his skin. The hair there acted as silken strands of stimulation, titillating, enticing. She rubbed against him, heightening the pleasure and drawing a groan from him that reverberated in her throat.

He tasted of brandy and smelled of bay rum heated by desire, all of it intoxicating. She couldn't get close enough or drive her tongue deep enough. His big hands stroked down her back and over her buttocks to lift her upward until their mouths were even. Her legs went naturally around his waist, and he went wild.

"Oh, Amanda, my love." He lifted her higher until he could bury his face between her breasts. He murmured love words and praise for her body between trailing kisses over and around the swells. When he took one nipple in his mouth and sucked, *she* went wild.

"You like that?" he asked.

She nodded. She was hot, burning, slick with wanting, consumed with indecent sensation. She never imagined lovemaking could be like this. "Please, please," she cried, begging for something, anything. She arched and offered the other breast, and he sucked from it as well. She wasn't satisfied. Her frantic hunger only grew. "I'm so hot. I'm burning."

"Me too, darlin'. Me too."

Beau laid her on the bed and stretched out beside her, continuing to caress and taste and touch and do maddening things with his tongue. The low ache grew unbearable, and she moved her hips restlessly. His hand stroked upward between her legs, and his palm cupped the sensitive flesh there. She strained against the pressure, instinctively ground against his hand.

A finger slipped inside her, and she gasped.

"You're wet," he whispered, "and so tight."

His thumb brushed a responsive spot, and she almost came off the bed. He brushed it again.

"Oh, dear. Oh, dear. Stop. I can't stand that. It's too much." He chuckled, but he immediately moved his hand, and she came totally undone. "I lied," she said. "It felt wonderful. I've never felt anything so wonderful. What were you doing?"

"Loving you."

"Do it again."

"Why don't I do something even better?"

"Is there anything better?"

"Oh, yes."

While one hand stroked her breasts, he shifted until his mouth was against her inner thigh. He nudged her legs farther apart and trailed his tongue upward toward the juncture.

"Beau! What are you doing? You can't—"

Words left her as his tongue thrust, and she was filled with the most glorious, obscene pleasure she had ever experienced. He did it again and again, and she couldn't get her breath to protest. She could only lie there awash in mounting ecstasy until it reached a peak of such intense sensation that she cried out. Spasms began to wrack her body, and she thought she was dying for sure.

"Oh, Beau, Beau, what's happening to me?"

"You've touched heaven. Want to go again?"

"I don't know if I can stand it. I've never felt anything like that in my life."

He laughed. "You've never been loved by me before." He stood and stripped off his remaining clothes.

Her eyes widened when she saw the size of him. She'd been raised on a farm. She knew about the aroused male member and understood its function, but she'd always assumed that a man was considerably smaller than a stallion—proportionally speaking, of course. But he was huge. And fully erect.

"It will never fit," she said nervously.

He laughed again. "We'll make it fit."

He knelt between her legs, lifted her hips, and began doing some more deliciously depraved things with his teeth and tongue. She was soon thrashing around and moaning and so absorbed in pleasure that she forgot her concerns.

Until he tried to enter.

Initially things went all right, then he hit a barrier and stopped.

"I told you it wouldn't fit."

"Amanda, are you a virgin?"

She nodded. "Pure as the driven snow."

"Shit!"

"What? I understand that men are usually delighted to find their women in that state."

"I've never had a virgin before. It's going to hurt, and I'd rather die than hurt you. Dammit! I'm going to stop."

Sudden tenderness filled her, and she held him fast. She touched his cheek. "It won't hurt. Go ahead."

He hesitated for a heartbeat, then thrust.

She gasped. She was mistaken. It hurt. Dear heavens, she was torn in two. She didn't move. She couldn't. She felt as if a tree trunk was shoved inside her.

"Oh, love," he whispered. "I'm sorry. I'm sorry. That's the last time I'll ever hurt you. I swear."

He didn't move for the longest time except to kiss her and stroke her and murmur sweet words, until she relaxed and the pain lessened. He moved slowly inside her, thrusting gently until he stiffened, and she could feel pulsations deep inside her.

After a few moments, he withdrew and sat up. When she started to rise as well, he said, "Stay here."

She watched as he dipped a rag into the washbasin and brought it, along with a towel to the bed. When he started to clean her, she tried to protest, embarrassed by the intimacy without the heat of passion.

"Shhh," he said. "I want to do this. There'll be blood. Why didn't you tell me you were a virgin?"

"It never came up in the conversation. It's not the sort of thing one announces at the dinner table, especially in front of children."

He laughed. "You're very responsive for a virgin."

"How do you know? You said you'd never . . . done this with a virgin."

"You've got me there."

When he had cleaned her and him and soothed her tender area with a cool compress, she started to rise again. "Stay here with me," he said. He stretched out beside her, pulled her close, and tugged the covers over them. He kissed her forehead. "I'm very pleased I was your first. It's a gift you can only give once, and I'll cherish it forever."

Smiling, drowsy, she rolled onto her stomach, seeking her familiar position of comfort for sleep. Shadows danced over the bed and the walls as the candles burned lower, reminding her that soon their night would be over.

Making lazy eights, his hand traveled along her back

from the swell of her buttocks to her neck. She purred like a kitten.

"Feel good?" he asked.

"Mmmm. Very."

His hand stopped abruptly, and he sat up. "Amanda?"

"Hmmm?"

"What's this on your back?"

"Scars."

"Dear God, what caused them?"

"My father wielding a razor strop."

"Oh, sweetheart." He kissed every faint line crisscrossing her back. "I'm so sorry. I wish I'd been there to stop him. You must have gone through hell."

"I did. That's why I left."

He brushed his cheek against her shoulder blades, and kissed the spots once more. So tender and so thorough was his treatment that she could almost imagine the scars fading and disappearing from her skin.

She drifted off with his hand still softly stroking her back.

Sometime before dawn she awakened him with more kisses, and they made love again. This time he was so sweet and so gentle with her that tears stung her eyes and escaped down her cheeks.

"Oh, darlin'," he said. "Have I hurt you again?"

"No," she whispered. "It was glorious." And it had been. A perfect memory for a melancholy night.

"I love you so," he said, pulling her against him and nuzzling the cap of her shoulder.

Amanda lay awake until long after she heard Beau's breathing change to signal he was asleep. She lay savoring his warmth, the comforting feeling of his muscular body, the scent that would linger with her forever. She stored up every memory of the moment and of the love-making they'd shared.

When the sky hinted of the first lightening of daybreak, she stole carefully from his bed, leaving a pillow in her place. His arm immediately gathered it close. She wrapped her robe around her and tiptoed from the room.

She dressed quickly and packed the last few things in her trunk. By the time Harve tapped on her door at six, she was ready to have him take her belongings downstairs.

Aunt Katie, wearing a lilac robe and with her gray hair still in its night braid, stood at the foot of the stairs waiting for her. "You'll have coffee before you go. And a bite of breakfast. I'll wake Beau."

"No," Amanda said. "Let him sleep. It's best."

"He loves you, you know."

Amanda nodded. "He told me."

"Did he ask you to marry him?"

She nodded again. "I can't. I don't plan to marry."

"Believe me, child, you'll have a cold and lonely bed."

"Perhaps so. I'm sorry I can't say good-bye to every-one. Will you say it for me?"

"I will."

Amanda kissed the wrinkled cheek that had become so dear to her. "You're a treasure, Katie Blessing."

The smell of coffee twitched Beau's nose. He opened his eyes to find Ellie, elbows propped on the mattress and chin in hands, staring at him.

She grinned. "Good morning, Uncle Beau. I brought your coffee."

He looked down at the pillow he clutched, then felt around frantically on the bed. "Amanda? Amanda?" He sat straight up. "Where's Amanda?"

"Harve took her to the depot a long, long time ago."

"He can't have. Amanda!" He started to jump out of bed, then realized he was naked. Gathering the covers around him like a Roman toga, he struggled to his feet and went tearing from the room. "Amanda!" he shouted.

Aunt Katie stuck her head out her door. "What are you caterwauling about?"

"Where's Amanda?"

"Gone."

"What do you mean, gone?"

"Harve took her to the depot at daylight, and I imagine she's on her way to Houston by now. That's where she said she was going. Houston."

Beau started stomping around in his toga, cursing and shouting.

Maud's door flew open. "Beaumont Blessing Chandler! Such language! And with a child in the house."

"Those are very ugly words, Uncle Beau. I said 'dammit' once and Mama washed out my mouth with soap. It tasted awful. Gramma, are you going to wash out Uncle Beau's mouth? Can I watch?"

"I apologize for my language, Ellie," he said as he strode by her. "I have to get dressed."

Beau yanked on a pair of pants, stomped on his boots, crammed a hat on his head, and grabbed a shirt as he ran out the door. By the time he reached the stable, he had his shirt buttoned and was tucking it into his pants. He threw a saddle on the first horse he came to and rode like hell to the depot.

* * *

The ticket master pulled out his pocket watch and looked at it. "Yep. Train's been gone near 'bout half an hour. On time this morning too."

"Dad blast it!" Beau slammed his hat on the platform and kicked it. "How could she . . . After last night . . . Dad blast it!"

He climbed on the horse and rode home a lot more slowly than he'd ridden in.

But he sure wasn't riding home a beaten man. If Amanda thought he'd give her up without a whimper, especially after last night, she didn't know a blasted thing about him. When she'd surprised him last night in his room, he'd been trying to figure out a plan to keep her around. Now he'd just have to figure faster.

If he'd had any notion that she meant to light out in such an all-fired hurry, he'd have tied her to the bed. But playing "what if" didn't do a blamed bit of good.

Now there wasn't but one thing for him to do. He nudged the horse to a faster pace, breaking the speed limit considerably and coming within a hair of trampling a loose pig rooting through the ditch debris.

He hit the house running and took the stairs two at a time. Aunt Katie met him in the hall and followed him to his room.

"I take it you didn't catch up to her," she said.

"Nope, but I plan to. I'm leaving for Houston on the next train." He stripped off his shirt as he went and threw the wad on the floor.

Aunt Katie picked it up and hung it on the bedpost. "You've got plenty of time. The next train won't pull out until two o'clock this afternoon. Clean up and come have breakfast with your mama and me. Judith and Estelle will be over directly. You have some explaining to do about Amanda, and I don't intend to do it for you."

"Yes, ma'am," he said, winking at her from his reflection in the shaving stand mirror.

After he shaved and dressed, Beau joined the women of the family at the table. The girls had left for school, and Ellie was occupied helping Mrs. Kilgore in the kitchen. He'd sooner have a beating than to tell everybody the truth, but you couldn't get lard without boiling a hog.

He bucked up, went in, and told them.

"A Pinkerton agent?" his mother said. "Oh, dear. I was so counting on a wedding. And I'd grown rather fond of Amanda, too."

"We all had," Judith said, "including you, Beau, if I'm not mistaken."

"You're not mistaken. I'm in love with her, and I'm leaving this afternoon to follow her to Houston. I don't know when I'll be back, so I'm leaving Frank in charge of things. I intend to dog Amanda's tracks until she agrees to marry me. I don't care if it takes forever."

Estelle smiled. "I wish you good luck."

"Thanks, I'm going to need it. That woman is as stubborn as a herd of mules."

⌒ Twenty-four ⌒

Amanda discovered that riding a train was the worst place in the world to be if one didn't want to think. When reading a novel or writing reports couldn't keep the mind occupied, there was nothing to do but to sway to the clack of the rails, stare out the window, and think.

And she thought of Beau.

Over and over for miles and miles and miles.

She breathed a sigh of gratitude when the conductor announced that the next stop was Houston. About four o'clock in the afternoon, after what seemed like an interminable trip, the train pulled into the station. Steam still billowed from the big engine when she alit. Very familiar with the station and the town, she quickly collected her baggage, had it loaded aboard a cab, and was on her way to her usual hotel.

A telegram awaited her when she checked in. From the district office, she was sure. She delayed reading it until she was alone in her room. When she scanned the contents, she groaned. Knowing that the only way to keep her mind off Beau was to get back to work instead of taking a few days leave, as she normally did after a case, she'd requested an immediate assignment.

This was her new post: as a spotter on a train.

Although the message was cryptic to avoid alerting anyone via a loose-lipped telegraph operator, she realized that "Uncle Henry" telling her to be "vigilant on her rail excursion to Corsicana" meant that she was to act as spotter on the Houston to Corsicana run. It was among her least favorite jobs, but the agency liked to use her because of her gift with disguises.

Spotters were undercover agents who rode the trains to detect excessive "knocking-down" by railroad employees, especially conductors. Many passengers, instead of purchasing tickets from an agent at the station, if indeed their small town had a ticket agent, simply paid their fares to the conductor. A goodly number of conductors encouraged the practice by charging a lower fare to these passengers who put the money directly in their hands, and which they put directly into their pockets. Fares of others, who paid full rate, frequently landed in the con's pocket as well—or at least a sizable portion did.

Knocking-down was a common practice, and most of the time railroads simply looked the other way and ignored the problem. Obviously Mr. Henry, the conductor she was to spot plying his larceny, had become excessively greedy. If the man was guilty, she vowed to get the goods on him quickly so that she could move on to a more challenging assignment.

After resting a bit, she changed for dinner, picked up a newspaper on her way out, and walked to a nearby restaurant that was one of her favorites. Its shrimp creole rivaled any in New Orleans, and the seafood was delivered fresh from Galveston daily. While women on the street alone were a rarity at night, she wasn't the least bit concerned for her safety and walked with her head high. She was, after all, armed as usual and in a surly enough mood to use her weapons if provoked.

In truth, misery squeezed her ribs like a corset drawn too tight. She was already lonely beyond measure. But she simply couldn't give in to those feelings. They would pass. With time, all things passed. Or at least, like her scars, they grew fainter.

Perhaps seeing an evening's entertainment at the Pillot Opera House would raise her spirits, she thought as she passed an advertising poster. Yes, absolutely. Attending the new comedy was exactly what she needed.

It was after midnight when the train pulled into Houston. Beau's butt was sore, and his mood was black. He didn't have any idea how to begin looking for Amanda. No, that wasn't true. She'd need a place to stay, just like he needed one. The problem was finding which hotel she'd gone to.

He paid a sleepy-looking cab driver ten bucks to drive him around to a dozen hotels trying to find her. By three o'clock in the morning he hadn't had any luck, and he was dead on his feet. He decided to check into the last one he stopped at, get a few hours' sleep, then continue his search in the morning when the people likely to have seen her would be working the day shift.

His sleep was fitful, and he woke early. When he'd dressed, he went downstairs to the hotel's café for breakfast.

Finding a table by the window, he sat down and ordered a big meal. He'd just cut into his steak and eggs when he glanced out the window. Across the street, in front of another hotel, a butt-ugly woman with buck teeth and a mop of red hair lifted her skirts and stepped into a cab. The driver pitched her valise in after her, then took the reins.

Beau frowned. That woman reminded him of somebody, but for the life of him, he couldn't think who. Then it suddenly popped into his head.

The ransom. The redheaded boy.

Pete.

My God, it was Amanda!

He jumped up and ran out the front door, yelling after the cab. The driver didn't stop, so he took out running after it.

"Amanda! Wait." He waved his napkin, yelled some more, and kept running.

"Amanda!"

He couldn't catch them—hell, were they going to a damned fire?—but he kept them in sight. They were headed to the train station. So was he. Winded, but determined, and running as fast as his legs would go.

Beau made it just in time to see her toss her valise aboard a train and climb on. The wheels were already moving. His lungs were about to burst, but he poured it on and kept going.

The train was picking up speed. Oh, shit!

He grabbed for the hand rail of the last car and barely caught it.

By some miracle, he swung himself up on the platform and collapsed, sucking wind, seeing spots, and sure his heart was going to explode any minute.

He didn't have any idea how long he lay there, but he couldn't have moved if he'd landed on a bed of red ants.

* * *

"Ticket, miss?"

Amanda gave the conductor a toothy grin. "Don't have one. I near 'bout didn't make the train. Had to run for it. Overslept, ya know. Can't I buy a fare from you?"

"Yes, ma'am. How far you traveling?"

"Oh, I'm just going as far as Spring," she said, naming a small town a short distance out. "Gonna spend a few days with Meemaw. She's ailing. How much I owe you, mister?"

"That'll be two dollars even."

She knew the fare he named was fifty cents too much, but she didn't comment as she handed over the money. Nor did she comment when he failed to give her a receipt. And she simply smiled vacuously when he greeted a pair of men across the aisle and took two dollars cash from each of them for a ride to Huntsville. Quite a bargain since Huntsville was more than three times the distance that Spring was. They didn't receive a receipt either.

She made a quick notation in her notebook, then grabbed her valise and stood. She tapped the conductor on the shoulder.

" 'Scuse me, Mr.—Mr.—"

"Henry."

" 'Scuse me, Henry. Where's the necessary?"

"Mr. Henry. And it's that way." He pointed and turned back to taking tickets and knocking down a pretty penny in cash while he was at it.

She hadn't made two steps when a big hand clamped down on her shoulder. "Amanda, where the hell are you going?"

Beau! What was he doing here?

She turned, a sappy grin pasted on her face. "Well, howdy there, Mr. Chandler. I'm a-goin' to Meemaw's house in Spring. She's down in her back and got nobody to hoe her garden or tend the chickens."

He looked at her as if she'd lost her senses. "Hoe her—?"

"Yes, sir. Where you headed?"

"Ticket, mister?" the conductor said.

"I don't have a ticket," he said, never taking his eyes off Amanda. He pulled a gold eagle from his pocket and flipped it to Mr. Henry. "I'm going to Spring. Keep the change."

Amanda noticed the ten-dollar piece go into the deep left pocket of the conductor's coat along with her two dollars and the four from the Huntsville pair. Only an occasional cash fare had gone into his right pocket.

Mr. Henry touched the brim of his hat and squeezed past them as they stood in the aisle.

"Amanda, we need to talk," Beau said.

She grabbed his hand and yanked him down onto an empty bench. "Hold your voice down," she whispered, keeping Henry in sight out of the corner of her eye. "I'm on a job, and you'll make a mess of it. Please don't draw attention to me. I have to go."

"Not without doing some explaining to me first."

"There's nothing to explain. I told you that I wouldn't marry you, and I told you that I was leaving Austin. I never led you to believe anything different, and I haven't changed my mind."

"But I thought after the night we spent—"

"It was a wonderful night, but it didn't alter anything. I meant what I said."

She started to rise and leave, but he blocked her way. "Oh, no, you don't. You're not getting off that easy. They probably have a warrant out for my arrest in Houston. The least you can do is let me get in a few words."

"Your arrest?"

"I skipped out of the hotel and left without paying for my breakfast."

"Good heavens, why?"

"Because I was running after you. I danged near didn't make it."

"Well, I'm very sorry, but I'm in the middle of an assignment, and right now I have to go to the necessary. If you're bound and determined, I'll talk to you later."

It was obvious that he didn't want to let her out of his sight, even on a moving train, but he finally relented. She brushed past Mr. Henry and hurried to the toilet at the back of the next car.

A few moments later, Thomas, the country boy, came out of the toilet carrying his belongings in two ragged bundles. Thomas was sprawled in a seat chomping on an apple when the conductor passed by.

"Ticket, boy?"

"Don't have no ticket, sir, but I got money." Amanda fished a tattered coin purse from her coat pocket, opened it, and made sure he saw the gold coins there. "How much I owe you to go to Huntsville?"

"This your first trip, son?"

"Yes, sir. I'm goin' there to live with my sister."

"That'll be five dollars."

"*Five* dollars? My sister said it was only four."

"That's if you buy a ticket at the station."

"Oh." Amanda handed over a half eagle, one as carefully marked as the greenbacks she'd given him earlier.

She didn't need any more information to know that the conductor was crooked as the Brazos, and she had to shake Beau. If she went back and talked to him, she was afraid he'd persuade her to do something stupid.

She returned to the cubicle in the rear and began changing quickly.

There was a banging on the door. "Amanda, you in there?"

She ignored him and dressed faster.

"Amanda!"

She flung open the door and stepped out as a wrinkled, gray-haired fat lady in a calico dress and a blue bonnet. She poked Beau in the belly with her cane. "Quit yer bellerin', boy. I ain't Amander."

"Sorry, ma'am." Beau turned and took out for the next car, nearly knocking Mr. Henry out of his way as he ran past him.

She marched up to the conductor. "How long to Westfield?"

"Not more than a minute, ma'am."

"Good. Here's my six bits. I'll be a-gettin' off there."

The coins went into his right pocket, and he scribbled her a receipt. First one she'd seen him write. She turned and hurried in the opposite direction from Beau.

Beau had been from one end of the train to the other three times. The only redhead he'd seen was a snot-nosed boy about four. She had to be aboard, somewhere. The train had stopped a while back, but nobody got off except a Mexican family and that old—

Damnation! Sonofabitch!

If brains were leather, he couldn't saddle a flea.

She'd gussied up like an old woman and slipped by him. If he'd had a hat, he'd have thrown it down and stomped on it. But he didn't have one. His was still hanging on the hat rack in that Houston café.

He located the conductor and grabbed his arm. "Listen, mister, I gotta get off this train."

"We'll be stopping at Spring in a few minutes."

"But I can't wait till then," Beau said. "I have to get off *now*."

"You're welcome to try it, but this train's not stopping till we get to Spring."

Cursing, Beau strode to the rear platform. They'd picked up a good head of steam and were clacking along at a pretty good speed. He considered jumping, but if he did, he'd probably break both legs. Then how would he get back to Houston? He was out in the middle of nowhere, twenty miles to water and ten miles to Hell. No horse, no saddle, no hat.

He yanked the napkin out of his pocket, slammed it down and stomped on that. It didn't help his feelings much.

Shoulders slumped, he leaned on the railing and watched the tracks taking him farther and farther away from her. "Amanda, honey, you may have won this round, but I'm not licked yet."

⌒ Twenty-five ⌒

A month later, much to Amanda's chagrin, she sat on a train bound for Austin. Beaumont Chandler had hired the Pinkerton Detective Agency, and he'd requested Amanda Swann in particular.

Angus Blessing, it seemed, had come up missing again. The family had received another ransom note.

Amanda smelled a rat. She didn't believe the story for a single minute—hadn't believed it when she first heard it, didn't believe it then. This reeked of a ruse by Beau to entice her back to Austin.

At first she refused to take the assignment, but after a flurry of telegrams between herself and headquarters, her options dwindled. She got the impression that Beau had dangled a lucrative contract their way, and the agency had applied pressure on her. In the end, she folded.

But she wasn't happy about it.

Well, that wasn't exactly true. She was ambivalent. On one hand, she didn't want to see Beau again. On the other hand, she did. Desperately.

One thing was for sure. This time she aimed to stay in a hotel, lest she be tempted by that green-eyed devil who could charm the bark off a tree. Before she even checked in, she intended to go to the cemetery and see for herself that Uncle Angus was truly missing. No one knew the exact date and time of her arrival, so no one would be there to meet her and interfere with her plans.

The train hissed to a stop. She got off along with several other passengers, watching her feet as she stepped down. When she looked up, there stood Beau, grinning.

She tried not to smile, but his familiar expression was simply too infectious. She beamed in spite of herself.

He strode forward. "Amanda," he said, opening his arms to her.

She deftly sidestepped an embrace and offered a handshake instead. He laughed and took her hand. She never knew a handshake could be so intimate, so— erotic. And she hated the way laughter crinkled his eyes and set incredible lights dancing in their depths and poignant memories stirring in her head. Her insides went all mushy.

"How did you know I'd be on this train?" she asked.

"I didn't. I've met every one that's arrived for the past week."

His statement shouldn't have made her feel quite so— proud. But it did. She fought back a smile and schooled her features into a businesslike expression. "I understand that you're missing something. Again." Her tone clearly implied that she didn't believe his subterfuge for a single moment.

He nodded. "A second ransom note came this morning. I don't know if word of the earlier kidnapping got out and now somebody else is trying it or what, but things are in an uproar at home. Mama is having the vapors. Estelle is terrified that there will be a scandal yet, and Aunt Katie is convinced that it's all Morris's doings. Judith filed for divorce and left for Paris last week."

For the first time a niggle of doubt crept in. "I want to go to the cemetery first," she said. "I'm not convinced that Uncle Angus really has been kidnapped again."

"Of course," Beau said. "I'll take you there right now, and you can examine the site yourself."

"Just let me see to my luggage."

"No need to worry about that. Harve is taking care of it. Your trunk is already loaded and on its way to the house."

"But, Beau—"

"I know, I know. You're going to say that you prefer to stay in a hotel," he said, taking her arm and guiding her to the waiting buggy. "But Aunt Katie and Mama threatened me within an inch of my life if I didn't bring you home to stay. Mrs. Kilgore will be cooking a special dinner, and the girls will be beside themselves with excitement. Ellie asks a dozen times a day when you'll be coming. Now we can't disappoint them, can we?"

She sighed. Arguing was a lost cause. Besides, she did want to see his family. She'd missed them.

Amanda stared down into the gaping hole. "He really is gone."

"Of course he's gone. Did you think I was lying about it? Amanda, I'm wounded."

She merely rolled her eyes. "Has it rained since the grave was reopened?"

Beau nodded. "Twice. Once just yesterday. I'm afraid any clues are obliterated by now. It's been over a week, you know." His tone stopped just short of censure for her tardy arrival on the case.

"Did the groundskeeper—?"

"He didn't see or hear a thing, but you know how deaf he is. The first the family knew of it was when a ransom note appeared. Early last Tuesday morning, Harve spotted it tied to the front door knocker. He and I came out here right away, and this is what we found. A hole. Seems almost like somebody's idea of a bad joke, doesn't it?"

"Did you notice anything unusual?"

Beau shook his head and leaned on the new marble tombstone inscribed with his uncle's name and date of birth. "Saw a hole and a pile of dirt. Oh, there were lots of footprints around, but you know I'm not much of a detective, and Harve can't see as good as he used to. Shame about the rain."

He said all the right words, but Amanda wondered if he was sorry about the rain at all. The obliteration of any clues she might have discovered meant that her job would be harder and take longer.

"Mama is really in a state about this. She cried buckets when Judith left, and when Uncle Angus came up missing the next morning . . . Well, we had to put her to bed for three days."

"That's a shame. I'm anxious to see the ransom notes."

"Then let's go home. If you don't mind, I'm going to get this grave filled in until Uncle Angus turns up. There's supposed to be a funeral here tomorrow, and somebody's bound to notice. I'd hate for old Edwin P. Brown to come nosing around for news again."

"Good idea."

Amanda was nervous on the way home, sure that any minute Beau would begin avowing his love and pressuring her to marry him. Neither subject arose. Instead, he related news about the family, anecdotes concerning his nieces or Aunt Katie.

"Aunt Katie has been stepping out with a younger man," he told her. "They went to a box supper last Wednesday evening."

Amanda laughed. "Good for her. Who is he?"

"Howard Conn. He'll be eighty in September. Aunt Katie says he's not spry enough to keep up with her, which may be the truth. And Frank has already organized the Gilbert and Sullivan Society. Guess who joined? The choir director and the preacher from our church—Estelle is ecstatic about that—plus about a dozen other men including a lawyer, a judge, and a state legislator from Dallas. They're having a grand time." Beau snapped the reins. "We'd better hurry or we'll be late for dinner and everybody will have my hide."

At they drove by, she noticed that the first floor of the Capitol was completed, and the blocks were going up for the second. Otherwise, the town seemed the same. Had it been only a month since she'd left? In some ways it seemed like a lifetime.

"Come in this house, child," Aunt Katie said, holding her arms open wide.

The moment Amanda stepped in the door, she was surrounded by people, children as well as adults, all greeting her excitedly. Ellie and Naomi each latched onto one of her hands and didn't let go until they sat down at the table for dinner.

Dear Lord, how she'd missed them. And how easily she slipped back into being a part of the family.

"Oh, I do miss Judith," Maud Chandler said, "but

Madame Moreau, who was Judith's teacher, and her husband were going to visit relatives in Paris and the opportunity to travel with them was timely, so she went. I worry."

"No need to worry, Mama," Estelle said. "The Moreaus will be there for six weeks," she told Amanda, "and Judith will decide during that period whether or not she wants to live in France permanently."

"I hope she does," Bonnie said, sighing. "Paris is so romantic, and I've always wanted to visit."

"Romantic? Ugh." Helen made a face.

"Aunt Judith said that Bonnie and I can spend next summer with her if she stays," Barbara said.

"I want to go to Paris, too," Ellie said.

"Oh, you'd probably get seasick," Naomi told her.

"I would *not*. What's seasick?"

"That's when—"

"Naomi!" Estelle frowned at her youngest two.

Amanda hid her smile behind a napkin. How different this dinner was than most of the ones she'd endured alone in the past month.

As soon as dessert was over, Frank glanced at his pocket watch and rose. "If you ladies and gentleman would excuse me, I have to leave for my society meeting. Rehearsal starts promptly in half an hour."

"Don't be late, dear," Estelle said.

Frank bent to kiss her cheek. "I should be home by ten." To Amanda he said, "We've formed a gentleman's Gilbert and Sullivan Society recently. We're planning to present an entire operetta, complete with sets, next year, but we're preparing something less difficult now. In

June, we're performing a variety of selections from *H.M.S. Pinafore*, *The Pirates of Penzance*, and *Patience*."

"Sounds exciting," Amanda said. "I've always been fond of Gilbert and Sullivan's work. Your productions might rival the Savoy's."

Frank laughed. "I doubt that, but it's entertaining."

Estelle shooed her brood home, and Aunt Katie and Maud moved to the parlor. Amanda and Beau went into his study to look at the ransom notes.

Although these weren't quite as grubby as the notes from the original kidnapping, there were definite similarities. They were printed in block letters, and the spelling was atrocious. The demand was for forty thousand dollars this time—due the following night. The cash, wrapped in oilcloth, was to be left beneath the south end of the Congress Avenue toll bridge. At midnight.

Amanda studied the papers carefully, then said, "Do you suppose that Taft and Boozer have returned to town? They strike me as dumb enough to try the scheme again on their own."

"I hadn't thought of that," Beau said. "I suppose it's possible. I guess we'll find out when the thieves come to collect the ransom. Frank got the money together for me today."

"You know, there's something I've wondered about, and I didn't have an opportunity to ask her before I left, but how did Judith locate Taft and Boozer? They're considerably outside her social circle."

"She got their names from Fanny Campbell."

"Fanny Campbell?" Amanda said. "I can't imagine Judith consorting with her either."

Beau laughed. "I think she heard Fanny's name from

Aunt Katie. Even Mama knew about Uncle Angus's lady friend. Judith figured that a person of Fanny's reputation would know men who were more concerned with money than morals. She was right."

"Do you think Fanny knew about the kidnapping?"

"I don't think so. Judith made up some story to tell her about why she wanted to locate some fellows for a bit of larceny."

"Hmmm. I think I should have a talk with Mrs. Campbell tomorrow."

"Amanda, I don't want you going anywhere near—"

She glared at him. "Who is the detective here?"

He grinned. "You are, darlin'."

"Don't forget that."

"I'm not likely to."

"I'll telephone her in the morning and have her meet me at the Chicago House."

Amanda rose to answer the knock at the hotel door. She'd engaged a suite this time, and she'd ordered tea delivered about the time Fanny was to visit.

The Fanny Campbell she invited in was only slightly more subdued in dress than a carnival clown, though obviously she'd taken great pains to deck herself out in her finest. This time she wore purple—from shoes to plume, purple. Except for the red gloves and red rushing at her throat, she reminded Amanda of a giant eggplant.

"Ah, good morning, Mrs. Campbell," Amanda said. "Don't you look lush this morning. Come in. Come in. Our tea just arrived. Won't you have a seat? I stopped for some little cakes at the bakery, and they smell so heavenly, I could hardly wait until you arrived."

" 'Morning, Mrs. Swann." Fanny Campbell and her sizable bosom strode into the room. "I could use a little pick-me-up. I don't usually roll out till about this time, and I missed my breakfast."

"Well, aren't you a dear to make this special effort to see me. Have a seat, and I'll pour. Sugar?"

"Yep. And lots of cream. I though you'd left town."

Amanda smiled and handed her a cup and plate. "I did. Business, you know. But I'm back." She offered the tray of napoleons.

"Glad to hear it. That feller of yours sure missed you. He dropped by to see me a time or two."

Amanda's brows went up. "Really?"

Fanny let out a howl of laughter. "Not for *that*. He signed over the Pink Feather and the boardinghouse to me. He's a square shooter for sure, but I 'spect you had a hand in it going off so slick. Now, what can I do for you, sugar?"

Deciding to take Fanny into her confidence, Amanda told her that she was with the Pinkertons and why she'd come to town originally.

Fanny's eyes grew big as the tale unfolded. "You mean them half-wits Taft and Boozer *kidnapped* Angus? I should'a figured something was up when they kept pinching all that ice. And I heard some strange tales about goings-on in the cemetery late at night, but I didn't pay much mind to it. Kidnapped. Well, I'll be. Was that what she—" She grabbed another napoleon and stuffed it into her mouth.

"Don't worry. I know that Judith hired them. That's not a problem. We've worked everything out there. The problem is, Angus has come up missing again."

"The devil you say!"

Amanda nodded. "Have you heard about Taft and Boozer being back in town? I thought maybe they decided to try it again on their own."

"Haven't heard a word about them being back, though you'd most likely smell 'em if they'd turned up." She laughed so hard her wattle shook.

"I imagine not much goes on in this town that you don't know about, Mrs. Campbell."

"Not much, honey, not much. Between me and my girls, we hear it all sooner or later."

"Would you keep an eye and an ear out for any information about who might have kidnapped Mr. Blessing? Ask around and find out if anybody has seen Taft and Boozer in town."

"Bet your boots, sugar. If them two's back, I'll know it by tomorrow. I'll tell my girls to keep their ears open for anything strange, too—though I'll not say a word about Angus's corpse being snatched. Some of them gals ain't too bright—if you know what I mean."

"Wonderful! Have another cup of tea. Tell me, Mrs. Campbell, where do you get your hats? I know of a lovely little place over on Pecan. Mrs. Simpson's. Have you tried it?"

⌁ Twenty-six ⌁

About ten-thirty, a pair of riders pulled up in a stand of scrub oaks on the south side of the river. After securing their horses, they made their way through the darkness to the foot of the toll bridge and picked a surveillance spot under a shadowy cedar clump.

Beau, dressed in trail clothes and Harve's old work hat, spread out a roll he'd brought along. Amanda, in her Pete persona, complete with crooked teeth and red wig, sat cross-legged on the quilt. Beau got down beside her and started pulling things out of his pockets.

"What's that?" she whispered.

"Victuals, according to Aunt Katie. In case we get hungry."

"We're not here for a picnic."

He grinned. "You're just lucky I talked her out of coming along."

"Shhhh."

"Right," he whispered. "Chicken?" He offered her a drumstick.

She shook her head. He ate it.

"Fried pie?"

"What kind?"

"Peach, I think."

"Okay." She sighed and stuck her ivory teeth in her pocket. Mr. Allan Pinkerton would turn over in his grave if he could see her munching away instead of being alert to business.

After the pie, she wiped her fingers on her pants and took a drink of water from the jar she'd brought. She stretched out on her stomach to keep watch.

The night was still except for the constant shrill chirr of tree frogs and an occasional splash in the dark current. There were distant muffled sounds, but nothing close.

"How much longer, do you think?" Beau asked.

"It's not even eleven yet. Frank won't bring the money for another half hour. Be quiet. Don't talk."

They'd decided to have Frank deliver the money and be gone well before midnight. Waiting and listening, she lay mute as the minutes passed slowly.

A loud crunch, magnified tenfold by the silence and the expanse of water, startled her and set her heart to racing. Pushing to her knees, she glared at Beau. "What are you *doing*?"

"Eating an apple. Want one?"

"No!" She snatched the half-eaten apple from his hand and chucked it as far as she could. "Quiet!"

"Darlin'," he whispered, "you're the one yelling."

She fell prone and covered her head with her arms.

He stretched out alongside her. "Sorry." He rested his cheek against her shoulder for a moment, then began rubbing her back. "You're tense."

"Really? I can't imagine why."

"Take off this jacket, and I'll rub some of the kinks out."

She tried to protest, but it was simpler to give in than to argue about it. She shrugged out of the jacket.

Beau began massaging her shoulders and neck, which felt marvelous, then moved downward. "What's this?"

"Binding. To make me look like a boy."

"Isn't it uncomfortable?"

"Some."

The next thing she knew, Beau had yanked up her shirt and was unwrapping the binding. Short of whacking him with her sap, there was little she could do without making more noise than a cornhusk mattress.

Truth was, she felt a lot better with the binding off. And he was a master at massage. His strong, magical fingers kneaded her back and shoulders, worked out the kinks, and had her all but purring in no time.

Somehow in the process—she wasn't quite sure of the exact maneuvers—her shirt came off, and his lips replaced his fingers on her back. Then his tongue trailed up her spine, slowly, vertebra by vertebra.

She sighed.

Somehow, again she wasn't sure exactly how, she found herself on her back with his tongue making lazy wet circles over her breasts. She should have protested, but it felt so darned good that she didn't.

As long as she kept her pants on, she was safe.

"What are you *doing*?" she whispered.

"Taking off your boots. I'll rub your feet."

"Leave my boots alone."

"Too late, darlin'. Doesn't that feel good?"

She wiggled her toes. "Heavenly."

The next thing she knew, her pants were gone too.

"Your calves are all knotted up," Beau explained, kneading the muscles there.

A rumble came from the bridge, and she jerked up to a sitting position.

"It's just Frank bringing the money," Beau whispered against her ear.

His mouth lingered to blow gently, and his tongue teased until she wiggled. She didn't dare make a sound.

Frank came and went.

Beau's tongue continued to make forays into her ear, down her spine, under her breasts, into her navel. And while his tongue moved, his fingers stroked and she writhed, awash with exquisite sensation.

He kissed her, a long, greedy, mind-numbing kiss. And before she knew it, he'd nudged her thighs apart and slipped inside.

Amazing. He fit perfectly. Filled her with glorious warm hardness, stole her breath. Then he moved. And moved again. She began to move with him, then gasped. Sensations more wonderful than any she'd ever experienced rushed through her and taught her new movements that heightened the sensations even more.

"That's the way, sugar," Beau whispered. "That's the way." He rolled over onto his back and brought her with him until she sat astride.

She arched her back and sucked in a cry at the glorious feeling she encountered. Straining toward the source of her pleasure, her sensations increased when he guided her hips into a rocking motion.

His hands cupped her breasts and drew her downward until he could take a nipple in his mouth, and she nearly came undone, assaulted as she was by a barrage of gloriously decadent debauchery.

She reveled in sensation, lost herself in pure feeling, plunged into hedonism.

Her movements became more demanding, her focus more direct, her journey more urgent. Higher and higher, harder and harder. She wallowed in erotic sensation until the first spasm broke. She keened and convulsed, shot to the sky, and burst into a million shining stars raining light on her upturned face.

She felt Beau stiffen, then arch beneath her, grasping her hips as he throbbed inside her.

She dropped down, her head against his chest. "Beau. Oh, Beau, I—I—"

He kissed the top of her braids. "I know, sweetheart. I know."

He stroked her back with such gentle fingers that she almost wept.

Amanda's eyes popped open, and she bolted upright from the warm cocoon enfolding her. The sky was turning gray. Beau lay asleep on the quilt beside her. They were both stark naked.

She shook him and started yanking on her clothes. She shook him again. "Dammit, Beaumont Chandler, wake up! It's morning, and we've been sound asleep."

Beau shoved aside the corner of the quilt that had been covering them, stretched, and grinned. "Mornin', darlin'."

Amanda rolled her eyes and sat down to pull on her boots. "Oh, good Lord! Don't you realize what's happened? You've probably lost forty thousand dollars."

He only grinned wider. "It was worth every penny of it."

He reached for her, and she dodged. Pushing to her feet, she ran from their cover to the foot of the bridge. Early traffic made rumblings over the span, noises of hooves and wheels. Expecting the money to be gone, she was surprised to find the oilcloth-wrapped bundle where Frank had left it.

Tucking it under her arm, she hurried back to where Beau was pulling on his shirt. He looked surprised when she showed him the intact package. "Looks like they didn't show," he said.

Amanda snatched her wig from a cedar branch and crammed the curly mop on her head. "They probably showed all right, but we scared them away with all the apple-crunching and the—the other."

He kissed her nose, then held out her jacket. "You were pretty noisy there a time or two, especially when I—"

"You needn't go into the specifics."

He grinned. "I like it when you make noises. There's one little screech you make that drives me wild."

"I don't *screech*!"

She located her cap, slapped it against her leg to dust it, and plopped it on her head. She patted her pockets, then knelt and began patting around on the quilt.

Beau knelt beside her. "What are you doing?"

"I've lost my teeth."

He fished the false plate from his pocket and handed it to her. She grabbed it, stuck it over her own teeth, then set out for the horses.

"Hey, wait for me," Beau said, snatching up the quilt

and hurrying after her. He handed her the pack of money and bundled up the quilt as they walked to where the horses were tied. "Where are you going in such an all-fired hurry?"

"I have to get back to the hotel and dress, then think up an excuse to give your family for being gone all night."

"How about the truth?"

"Your mother would have us married by sundown."

"That's not such a bad idea."

She glared at him and walked faster.

Ellie met Amanda and Beau as they came in the back door. "Where were you?" she asked. "I brought you coffee and you weren't there."

"Sorry, dear," Amanda said. "We had some early errands to run."

"You're just in time for breakfast. Mrs. Kilgore made cinnamon buns. I told her they were your favorite. Did you know I have a loose tooth. Dis 'un," she said wiggling a front incisor. "Daddy said it may be ready to come out in a week or two, and I can put it under my pillow. Uncle Beau, you look funny in that hat."

He removed his hat and hung it on a peg. "This is Harve's hat. He loaned it to me."

"Don't you have a hat?"

"Nope. Not an everyday kind of hat. Seems like they keep getting lost, stolen, or stomped on. I'll have to get another one at Newman's."

Amanda joined the family at breakfast while Beau went upstairs to shave and wash up. Frank had gone to work, so only the girls and women were at the table.

"Any luck?" Aunt Katie asked.

Amanda shook her head, then dished up eggs, ham, and a bun from the sideboard. She joined the others, and by the time Beau came downstairs, the girls were leaving for school. He kissed them all as they left, even Ellie, who wasn't going anywhere but didn't want to be left out.

"I like your kisses," Ellie said, giving him a hug. "You smell good." She ran off to the kitchen.

Aunt Katie, Maud, and Estelle all turned expectant faces after he sat down with his plate.

"Well," Aunt Katie said, "out with it."

Beau shrugged. "Nobody showed up to claim the money."

"Why?" Estelle asked.

"I don't know. Something spooked them, I guess."

"What are we going to do now?" Maud asked.

"Nothing to do but wait."

"I'm going to speak with a contact I have and see if I can turn up something," Amanda told them.

Nothing turned up.

Nothing turned up the next day either. No word. No more notes. Nothing happened.

Well, nothing relating to the recovery of Angus Blessing's corpse. Beau spent his days and nights entertaining her. They played croquet and went for boat rides and saw the horse races at Hyde Park. They ate ice cream at Mr. J. Prade's and stopped for lemon drops at Lamm's and saw an excellent performance of *Zo-Zo, the Magic Queen* at the opera house.

And at night they made love. Amanda knew that allowing Beau into her bed was foolish, even destructive, but she couldn't seem to get enough of her newfound pleasure. She was as insatiable as any morphine addict.

Amanda was quite sure that Aunt Katie, given her insomnia, suspected that the late-night traffic in the hallways wasn't due to mice. But the old lady never said a word. She merely smiled knowingly and winked occasionally.

By Saturday Amanda had grown impatient with the case. The trail was growing cold. She had to do something to earn her salary.

She tried telephoning Fanny Campbell several times during the day but couldn't reach her. What would Mr. Allan Pinkerton have done in her situation?

She could almost hear him saying that an operative of "considerable intellectual power and knowledge of human nature" would have the insight necessary to crack any criminal. She was bright enough to know that the sort who would rob a grave and hold the departed for ransom was unlikely to be sitting around a parlor tatting pillow case edging.

If nothing was happening, she had to make something happen. And if she wanted to catch the thief, she had to go where a thief might hang out.

An idea struck her.

Knowing that Beau would certainly object to her plan, she waited until he left the house on an errand. She quickly changed her dress, donned a hat, and rolled a cape and a few other items into a bundle and tossed it out the window.

Downstairs she fluttered her fingers at Maud as she sailed by. "I'm off to meet a friend downtown. Don't wait

dinner for me. Tell Beau I may be late and not to worry."
She hurried out before Maud could respond.

Once outside, she retrieved the bundle and hurried to
the streetcar stop.

276   KRISTIN HANNAH

worried for me. Sometimes I can't let these things work
for future use by these...and could not
to you enjoyable to explain it clearly...and further to
the terms of the.

⌐ Twenty-seven ⌐

Not worry? Of course he worried. When Beau returned
and heard Maud's explanation of Amanda's departure,
the first thing he did was go tearing upstairs to her room.
Thank God, her trunk was still there. Her tooth powder
was on the washstand, and her nightgown was folded under her pillow.

Clutching her nightgown in both hands, he sat on the
side of her bed to catch his breath and calm himself. For a
minute he'd been scared to death that Amanda had found
out everything and had high-tailed it on the afternoon
train.

She'd probably just gone to have tea or a soda with one
of the ladies she'd met at Mama's mission society. Or she
might be shopping for a new hat or some of those lacy
thingamajigs women liked.

When Amanda didn't return for dinner, Beau began to
pace. He questioned his mother again, but Maud didn't
know any more than she'd already told him.

Aunt Katie drew him aside. "I got a feeling she might
be out detecting. I was getting a book from the study
when I saw a bundle of something drop past the window

and land by my rose bushes. Amanda went out and got it and carried it with her."

"Damnation! I knew she wasn't at a tea party," Beau said, striding for his hat. "I'm going to find her before she gets into trouble."

"Aren't you going to have dinner first?" Maud asked as he stalked by. "Mrs. Kilgore has made some wonderful veal in wine sauce. With plums. I got the recipe from Madeline Hix."

"Tell Mrs. Kilgore that she can . . . Tell her to put mine in the icebox. I'll eat later. What was Amanda wearing?"

"Well, let's see. I believe it was a blue silk dress. Yes, yes, it was blue. With white rushing and a lace inset here"—she gestured around the neck area—"and on the sleeves. And I remember the hat because it didn't quite seem to go with her dress. Amanda's always so well put together, you know. The hat was black with fuchsia plumes, rather large plumes, three of—"

Beau tore out the back door, leaving his mother still describing Amanda's hat. He threw a saddle on the roan and rode like hell to the Chicago House. It was getting dark, and with the head start she had, no telling where she was by then or what she was gussied up to look like.

At the hotel, he hurried upstairs to the suite she'd rented and banged on the door. He waited a minute and banged again. Still no answer. He'd didn't have a fancy set of keys and picks along—and wouldn't have known how to use them anyhow.

He got in the best and quickest way he knew. He kicked the damn door open.

She wasn't there.

But she had been. The black hat, minus the plumes, lay on the dresser. Beside it lay a pair of scissors and a wad of white lacy stuff that looked as if it had come from the neck of a dress. He searched the room, but hell, he didn't know if anything was missing.

Where the dickens had she gone?

He tried to picture what she might look like from the clues he'd found. That's when it dawned on him.

Oh, shit!

Spouting steam at every joint, he stomped out of the hotel cussing like a cook with his biscuits burning. He jumped on his horse and lit a shuck for Guy Town.

His first stop was the Pink Feather, where all the saloon gals wore pink feathers pinned in their hair.

The place was packed. He scanned the room, but he didn't see any sign of Amanda—of course, the light wasn't too good. He strode to the bar.

"What'll it be, mister?" the barkeep said.

"I want to talk to Fanny."

"And just who are you?"

"I'm Beau Chandler, Angus Blessing's nephew. Tell her I'm here."

A young blonde attached herself to his arm. "Won't I do?" she asked.

"Nope. Sorry."

"Tyann," the barkeep said, "go tell Fanny this gentleman wants to see her." To Beau he said, "How about a drink while you wait."

"Gimme a shot of your best Tennessee sippin' whiskey."

While the bartender poured, a pair of cowpokes bellied up to the bar.

"Gawd, did you see the tits on that redhead playing roulette?" the tall one said.

"Yeah, Slim," the other one answered, "but did you see her face? Ugliest woman I ever did see. She could eat corn through a picket fence."

"Hell, if I had a chanst to hunker up next to a body like she's got, I'll put a sack on her head and blow out the lamp. I'm gonna get me some of that. You jist see if I don't."

"Slim, you barely got money to pay for another beer. How you gonna 'ford that?"

"I won't have to pay nothin'. I'll catch her outside after closin' time. And shoot, it'll be so dark I won't be able to see her face no how."

Beau's eyes narrowed, and he scanned the room for the roulette wheel and the redhead. When he spotted her, sick fury flew over him. He swung around to the two cow-pokes and tapped the tall one on the shoulder. When Slim turned, Beau cold-cocked him and stalked away before the man hit the floor.

He made a straight course for the woman in the blue silk dress and with the fuchsia plumes pinned in her curly red mop. Coming up behind her, he said, "Evenin', Amanda."

When she whirled around, Beau could see that maybe Slim had a point. Her breasts were almost falling out of the low-cut dress—and they were beautiful. But her face—God, not even a mother could love a face like that. It was full of freckles and boils and her teeth were awful, worse than the ones Pete wore. Not only were these crooked and protruding, but they looked half rotten.

She didn't act a bit shocked to see him. She only gave him a stupid-looking smile, which exposed more rotten teeth, and latched on to his arm. "Evenin', Mr. Beau. You come to buy me that drink?"

"No. I've come to take you home." He tried to hitch up the front of her dress, but she batted his hand away.

"I'm not right ready to go yet."

"That's too damned bad. I'm not leaving you here alone." He picked her up, threw her over his shoulder, and strode from the saloon.

She hissed and kicked and wiggled like a wildcat, but he didn't break stride. She called him a dozen kinds of lowdown polecat and cussed a blue streak.

"Amanda! The ladies of the mission society would be shocked to hear your language." Though it was like trying to rope a snake, he managed to get her in the saddle with him, and he rode for home.

She called him every name in the book and then some. And she hadn't cooled down one iota by the time they reached Guadalupe Street. When he rode into the stable and dismounted, she was off like a shot.

"You mangy, lop-eared bastard! How dare you man-handle me, interfere with my work, insult my intelligence! How dare you throw me over your shoulder like a sack of potatoes and humiliate me! You're a sorry excuse for a man, and I'll never speak to you again as long as I live."

She whirled and strode to the house.

"Oh, hell, Amanda honey, listen to me—"

"I'm not listening!" she shouted. "I'll never listen to you again!"

She yanked open the back door and hurried toward the stairs. Beau was right on her tail, trying get her to listen to reason.

Maud grabbed his arm as they brushed past. "Beaumont, who is that—that awful woman?" she whispered.

"That's Amanda in her whore costume."

Maud made a strangling sound as he shook her off and raced up the stairs.

Amanda slammed her bedroom door in his face just as he got there. He heard the lock turn. He'd have busted it down, but he was in deep enough as it was.

Shoulders slumped, he walked halfway down the stairs and sat on a riser.

His mother peeked around the door and glanced up at him. "Beaumont—"

"Not now, Mama."

"Very well. I'll just go into the parlor and work on the monogrammed napkins. The veal was quite good, I—" She clamped her lips together and hurried away.

Aunt Katie clomped into the hall with her cane. "Have you split your britches with Amanda, boy?"

"Yes, ma'am."

Aunt Katie nodded and clomped into the parlor.

In a few minutes, Amanda's door opened. She came out, her face washed, her hair arranged, wearing a rose-colored dress and hat. She carried a valise. She started down the stairs.

Beau stood and blocked her way. "Amanda, talk to me."

"I have nothing to say. Anything personal that was between us is over. Please move."

He didn't budge.

She drew a four-shot pistol from her pocket and leveled it at his heart. "Move. I'm angry enough to shoot you."

He moved.

"Please have my trunk sent to the Chicago House in the morning." She stuck the gun in her pocket, walked to the parlor door, and stopped. "I must leave now," she said to Aunt Katie and Maud. "Thank you for your hospitality. Good night."

Her chin held high, Amanda went out the front door. It closed with a soft click.

It took Amanda the better part of two days to get control of her emotions. She was by turn angry and heartsick. She stormed and cursed and paced and wept. And she didn't sleep well at all.

On the second day, Aunt Katie knocked on her hotel door. Amanda hugged her and invited her into the suite.

"Now I don't like to meddle," the old woman said, "but seeing how you don't have anybody to talk to, I figured I might could offer an ear."

"Thanks, Aunt Katie—I mean, Miss Blessing."

"Aunt Katie will do."

"I appreciate your concern, but there's nothing to talk about. Any—tender feelings Beau and I might have had for one another are gone. I'll be happy to stay on the case if the family still wants me, but I don't want to have any more dealings with Beau."

"Honey, that boy is sick about what happened and about how you took things, but he was scared nearly out of his wits, and when that cowboy said what he did, well, he just acted to protect you without thinking."

"What cowboy?"

Aunt Katie repeated the conversation word for word. Amanda was shocked as much by Aunt Katie telling it as she was by the cowboy's comments.

"So you see," the old lady said, "it was just his protective instinct coming up on him. Males are that way, you know, least ways the ones worth having are. He might could've been a tad less . . ."

"Brutal?"

"Oh, no. I was going to say 'theatrical.' Beau wouldn't no more hurt you than he'd hurt me. I've never known him to raise a hand to a female. Won't you at least talk to him, child?"

Amanda shook her head. "I think it's best to end this now, and if the family would like for me to leave the case, I will."

"Nope. You stay on the case, and I'll let you know if we hear anymore. If you ask me, Angus's corpse isn't worth all the fuss."

Amanda talked to everybody she could think of— Fanny Campbell and Frank, Mr. Jenkins at the livery stable, Harve. None of them knew anything except Mr. Jenkins, who'd heard that Taft and Boozer were in jail in San Antonio.

A telegram to the police in San Antonio confirmed it. Taft Whisenant and Boozer Hemphill were in jail for horse theft, and had been for three weeks.

So much for that lead.

She walked the cemetery over a dozen times, talked to the groundskeeper, and tried to come up with another clue. It wasn't Morris, either. He was confirmed to be living in Milwaukee and working for a brewery there. She even tried to locate Doyle and the other fellow who had helped them rebury Angus the first time, but Harve told her Doyle had moved to Dallas and the other guy was visiting family in Louisiana.

By the time another week had passed, the trail was stone cold, and she was out of ideas. Staying in Austin was futile and every moment was agonizing. Everything there reminded her of Beau. She needed to move on, find a challenge, get busy.

She wrote out her final report, dressed in her best blue suit, and took the streetcar to the stop near the Blessing mansion.

As Amanda walked along the iron fence to the front gate, she noticed that the roses in the side garden were in full bloom and their fragrance scented the air around the house. She remembered the day she'd noticed their first buds, the day Beau had kissed her in the rain. She could almost hear the remnants of their laughter as they ran for cover.

Shaking off the memory, she took a fortifying breath, opened the gate, and went up the walk.

Harve let her in, told her everybody was out except Mr. Beau, and he was in the study.

"Tell him that I've come to hand in my final report, please." She waited until she was announced, then stiffened her spine and followed Harve to the familiar room.

She was shocked when Beau turned to her. He looked as if he'd aged ten years and lost twenty pounds. He smiled, but the smile didn't reach his eyes or spark the light in their depths. She desperately wanted to take him into her arms, soothe away his troubled expression, and bring that light back.

She didn't.

But when she saw the bust, she almost came undone.

Beau stood beside the bronze, his hand on the hair. It was her.

"Judith finished the clay model before she left," he told her. "She sent it to a friend of hers to have the metal cast. It came yesterday. I spent the night in here just looking at it. Beautiful, isn't it?" He turned away from her to look at the sculpture. His tone seemed formal, almost cool.

Amanda couldn't speak for a moment, fearing that she would break down completely. If he'd held out his arms to her, she would have fallen into them, pride be damned. But he didn't move, and her pride remained intact. Damn him!

"My final report," she managed to say. Thrusting the document to him, she turned and hurried from the room.

She ran into Aunt Katie in the hallway.

"Amanda. I just got home. I'm glad I didn't miss you. What brings you here? Have you found Angus?"

"No. I've just left my final report with Beau. I'm leaving Austin this afternoon. Aunt Katie, what's wrong with him? He looks wretched."

"And he acts wretched. He's changed, Amanda. Changed for the worse. He stays in terrible humor, and the girls are becoming afraid of him. I can't remember when I've heard him laugh. Give him another year, and he'll be as sour tempered as Angus."

"Is it because of me?"

"Of course it's because of you. And speaking of wretched, you don't look any too pert yourself. You've got bags under your eyes. When's the last time you had a decent night's sleep?"

"When I . . ." *When I last slept with Beau,* she finished silently.

Was the price of freedom too dear? What good was freedom if joy left her life?

She turned back to the study and had made only two steps when the door was yanked open, and Beau stood there.

"Amanda," he whispered. "Don't go." He held open his arms.

She ran into them.

He grabbed her and swung her around. They kissed and laughed and hugged. "Oh, darlin', I love you so. Please don't leave me behind. If you don't want to get married, that's all right. I'll go anywhere with you, do any—"

She kissed him quiet. "You don't have to go any-where. I want to stay here with you. I want a family and roots. And I want you."

He laughed and kissed her again, murmuring some-thing between kisses.

She stopped and drew back. "You did *what*?"

"I dug up Uncle Angus myself and moved him to a new spot. Forgive me, sweetheart."

"Where is he now?"

"We replanted him in his rightful place the night after you arrived."

"Do you mean that all this time I've been trying to find a lead, Uncle Angus has been in the cemetery?"

" 'Fraid so. Sugar, I was desperate. I love you so much. Forgive me?" A dimple flashed in his cheek. The light came back in his eyes.

She laughed. Dear Lord, she loved this crazy man.

"Perhaps I'll forgive you. In time. But you're going to have to grovel."

He roared with laughter.

☞ Epilogue ☜

Beau held his mouth and made a face like a cross-eyed goldfish. The toddler on his lap laughed and clapped. "You funny, Daddy. Do it again. Make a fiss."

He did it again—even though Amanda's secretary rolled her eyes. Not much, mind you, just a bit. He winked at her, and she looked down quickly at her typewriting machine. Miss Moffett was a bit of a prune, but Amanda said that she was an excellent assistant, so he supposed it wasn't up to him to complain. Amanda adored having her own detective agency, and as long as his wife was happy, he was happy.

"Down," Susan said, wiggling to get free.

Beau couldn't deny this child—or her mother—anything. He set her down, and she ran straight to Miss Moffett.

Susan cocked her dark head, flashed her dimples, and asked, "Doin'?"

"I'm typing a letter for your mother."

"Susan type? Peas?" She smiled again, her green eyes flashing.

Miss Moffett smiled. How could the woman resist? She put a fresh sheet of paper into the machine and hoisted Susan onto her lap. "See, this is what you do. Push these keys very firmly, but very carefully."

"Careful."

"Yes."

In a few moments, the door to Amanda's office opened, and she escorted her new client out. "Hello, darling," she said to Beau. "Sorry to keep you waiting." She pecked him on the cheek. "And what are you doing, Miss Susan?"

"Me type."

"I see that. You've typed your name. SUSAN. Ready for ice cream?"

"Ice cream! Straw-very!" Typing was forgotten as the child held up her arms.

Amanda hugged her and kissed her and handed the wiggly body over to Beau. "Miss Moffett, let me sign that, and you can go as soon as you lock up. And it looks like I'll be out of town for a few days."

Amanda gave her assistant final instructions, then tucked her arm in Beau's. "I have an exciting new case, and I have to go to Dallas to run down some leads. Mr. Grayson is trying to locate his sister. He hasn't seen her in thirty years, and they've inherited some property. I'm going to find her. Want to leave Susan with Maud and Aunt Katie for a few days and come along?"

He kissed her nose. "You bet. Ever think of trying to find your own sister?"

Sorrow crept over her face, and she nodded. "I did try. I looked for her a long time after I learned that she'd left home too, but I didn't have any luck. The trail was cold, and the few clues I found led me nowhere. Her face haunts me still. I can only pray that wherever she is,

Susan has made a good life for herself; that she's safe and happy."

Seeing the melancholy in Amanda's eyes hurt Beau to the core. He could cut out his tongue for mentioning her sister. He hated anything that brought his wife pain. Hugging her against his side, he said, "I'm sure she's fine. In fact, I'll bet she's doing great. She probably has a terrific husband and a beautiful little girl named Amanda." He kissed her nose again and smiled.

"Ice cream! Ice cream!" Susan said, patting Beau's face and wiggling impatiently.

Amanda laughed. "A girl after my own heart. Let's go to Mr. Prade's. I think we should all get a big dish of vanilla."

"Straw-very, Mama! Straw-very!"

Amanda lifted her eyebrow at Beau, and this time he laughed.

Maeniel placed the saddlebag on the bench beside Gavin and
stood, waiting expectantly. A few minutes later a very dressed
up Elfgifa stepped out of the door of the triclinium. She wore
the silk shift and the stiff gold and white brocade overgown
she'd worn to the pope's banquet. A string of pearls was
wound into her short golden hair.

She looked up at Maeniel, expectantly, and said, "Aren't
you going to give me a kiss?"

Both Gavin and Maeniel stared at her in complete bewil-
derment for a second. Then Gavin dissolved into roars of
laughter.

Maeniel glared at him.

"Did the letter . . ." Gavin said, choking with laughter,
"did the letter they sent you say anything about your future
wife's age?"

Maeniel turned and kicked him hard in the ankle.

Elfgifa's lower lip shot out.

"I knew something was wrong," Gavin said. "I knew
something had to be wrong," he moaned. "Now I know what
it is."

Elfgifa's lip protruded even further. "There's nothing
wrong with me," she said, stamping one little foot. "Everybody said I was very pretty. What's the matter with him?"

"Gavin," Maeniel said between his teeth. "Shut up. Yes,"

he said with forced cheerfulness to Elfgifa. "You are very pretty." Bending over, he dropped a soft, very gentle kiss on the child's forehead.

"Poor Maeniel," Gavin said, wiping his eyes. "You're going to go without for a very long time."

"Without what?" Elfgifa asked innocently.

This set Gavin off again. Faint sounds of incipient hysterics emanated from behind the curtains that shielded the triclinium. Maeniel knew every servant in the villa must be there listening.

"My lady," Maeniel said to Elfgifa. "If you don't mind, would you bring me a cup of wine and when I'm finished strangling my friend, here," he directed a quelling look at Gavin, "I'll join you and we'll talk over the future."

Elfgifa studied Maeniel darkly for a moment. "If he's your friend, why would you want to strangle him?"

Gavin was nigh paralyzed but he managed to jump off the bench and sidle well away from Maeniel.

"I always thought," Elfgifa went on, "that you strangled people you didn't like."

Gavin staggered against one of the columns supporting the porch roof. "It's going to be wonderful," he said, "waiting for this consummation."

"What's a consummation?" Elfgifa asked. "And why is he acting that way? Is it because you're going to strangle him? And if you are, can I watch?"

"Yes," Maeniel said between his teeth. "Only I may not strangle him, I may just drown him, slowly."

Suddenly Gavin stopped laughing and stared at the two women walking along the porch from the garden.

"Look," Elfgifa said to Regeane, clutching Maeniel's brown mantle. "This is the man who's come to marry you."

Regeane stopped dead in her tracks. The blood left her face in a rush, leaving her almost as pale and waxen as the lilies blooming beside the pool.

"Oh, good heavens," Lucilla whispered.

A volley of half-stifled giggles erupted from behind the curtains to the triclinium.

"What's going on here!" Lucilla demanded.

"This is the Lord Maeniel," Elfgifa said, excitedly. She still had hold of Maeniel's mantle. "You know, the mountain lord who's going to marry Regeane. The servants said to greet him properly and be nice to him. And since I'm going to be one of Regeane's ladies, I came out to talk and that red-haired man there," she gestured at Gavin, "started laughing. I don't know why. I don't think I'm funny." She pointed at Maeniel. "He said he was going to strangle him and promised I could watch."

"He won't," Lucilla said, "and if he did, you couldn't, and thank you for bringing me up to date, you terrible, terrible child."

Elfgifa's face clouded over, the lower lip protruded. "I'm not terrible. I'm very nice. Regeane says so. I told you where she went when she ran away. I set Hugo on fire and made him let her go—"

"Enough," Lucilla roared. "Besides, as a lady's maid—"

"I'm not going to be a lady's maid," Elfgifa piped up. "I'm going to be an attendant. Postumous says as the daughter of a thane I am too highborn to be a lady's maid. I'm—"

"I said, enough," Lucilla commanded in a voice like a boulder dropping to earth. The murderous look she directed at the closed curtains of the triclinium promised dire consequences for the authors of this particular mischief. "Having a little fun with the bridegroom, are we?" she asked in artificially dulcet tones.

Sounds of feet moving away quickly followed her words. Elfgifa stood her ground. She tugged twice at Maeniel's mantle and whispered. "Bend down." She looked anxiously at Gavin.

Maeniel obediently bent down. Elfgifa placed her lips near his ear. "Do you know what my father says about red-haired men?"

"No," Maeniel whispered back.

"He says Judas had red hair," Elfgifa whispered breathlessly. Maeniel's face convulsed with mirth.

Gavin, who had been standing openmouthed a second before, drew himself up in fury. "Now wait just a goddamn minute . . ."

Maeniel straightened up, his hand on Elfgifa's golden curls. "Gavin may have red hair," he said, "but I don't think he and the apostle are related."

"I certainly hope not," Elfgifa said, casting a second suspicious look at Gavin. "My father says—"

"That is quite enough," Lucilla said. "That father of yours has filled your head with every manner of nonsense. You will go inside and trouble us no more. At once." She clapped her hands.

The young girl who had answered the door reappeared, looking suitably abashed. She took Elfgifa by the hand as if to lead her away, but Maeniel sank to one knee beside Elfgifa and looked up at Regeane. To his relief, her waxen pallor had faded and color flooded her cheeks.

"You will be a good lord to Regeane, won't you?" Elfgifa asked. "My father told me that if a man is the head of the house, the woman is its heart. And a man without a heart is no more than a corpse." Elfgifa spoke quickly but clearly, as if to make sure Maeniel understood.

"Yes," he promised. "I will. I could never forsake my heart, little one. So go with an easy mind. I will welcome you to my home as one of my lady's attendants."

The girl sped Elfgifa away. And Regeane stood face to face with Maeniel. She saw a tall man. He was a little over six feet, thick bodied. His bare arms rippled with muscle, massive and powerful, that clothed his frame.

He wore trousers with cross-gartered leggings and over that a heavy white linen shirt, long enough to be a tunic. Over that a cuirass of chain mail. His brown mantle was secured to his shoulder with a golden brooch, a lion's head with large ruby eyes.

His face was the most striking of all, powerful, with a strong nose and cleft chin, and an air of seeming sternness. But the deep laugh lines around the mouth and crow's feet at the corners of his eyes indicated that this man smiled often and loved laughter. Overall, a kind face, sure and strong.

His hair was thick, dark, and coarse. It curled freely at his neck and forehead. It was roughly cropped, short. Long hair was a hindrance to a warrior and wouldn't fit properly under a helmet. It was clear he was a fighting man. He wore a long sword, very plain, utilitarian, suspended from a heavy ox-hide belt and baldric.

Fascinated, Maeniel stepped toward Regeane as if they were alone. She'd been in the kitchen garden with Lucilla, and was wearing a tabard of brown wool over her simple white gown. She was holding up the skirts of the tabard. In it were pouched a few late peaches from Lucilla's trees.

Her hair was drawn back in a loose fall from the top of her head, streaming down her back, the silver ends shining in the sun.

Maeniel took another step closer. Regeane's hands were locked in the tabard, and she thought absurdly as Maeniel's arm went around her waist, *I can't let go or the peaches will fall.*

His kiss was a chaste one, closed soft lips on her own, but there was such an immense naturalness in the strength of the arms around her and her presence in their embrace, that Regeane quivered all over. Afterward, she was never sure whether she trembled in fear or desire. She relaxed against a body so strong it seemed made of sun-warmed stone.

Her lips parted slightly and her mouth opened. But Maeniel didn't press his advantage. The kiss eased and he took a step back, releasing her both from his arms and his spell.

"Happy," he said, "are the words of the poet. 'She is,' " he quoted, " 'a fair gem from the realm of sun and wind, a cup of honey. A man might drown himself in such sweetness.' May I have a peach?"

"A what?" Regeane asked, bemused. She came back to

herself with a shake. She stretched the tabard out toward Maeniel. "They are touched by frost," she said.

"Like your hair, exquisite one," he answered as he selected one of the velvet-covered fruits. He ate it in a few bites, holding Regeane's eyes with his own. He tossed the pit into a flower bed.

"Rich, ripe, and rare," he said. "Like she who gave it to me." The juices gleamed on his lips.

Regeane permitted herself a little shake as she tried to regain her wits. Somewhere she knew the wolf was lying on her back in a bed of flowers, all four paws in the air, wiggling with delight. Regeane shot a thought at her dark companion, *You're thoroughly disgusting.* The wolf really didn't care.

Lucilla stared at them both in something like horror. Gavin stared too, his mouth open.

"Shut your mouth, Gavin, before your brains fall out," Maeniel said. "And fetch the presents we brought the lady."

Lucilla quickly removed the peaches from Regeane's tabard and brushed soft wisps of curling hair from around her face. "We didn't anticipate seeing you so soon," she said.

"Yes," Regeane said. "I expected to meet you at the feast tonight." She looked down at the brown tabard and the white dress. "I'm afraid I'm not properly attired. I'm sorry . . ."

"Don't apologize, please," Maeniel said. "It is I who should be contrite, coming unannounced."

"Ahem," Gavin said. He emptied the saddle bags on the marble table top.

Even Lucilla, who was used to wealth, gasped to see so much gold of every kind spill out of it. There were necklaces, rings, coins, pendants, torcs of twisted gold and silver, brooches of every kind. Gems, precious and semiprecious, glowed among the gold. Rubies, deep red, sapphires blue as the sky at twilight . . .